NOBODY KNOWS, NOBODY SEES

Also by Bob Sloan:

Bearskin to Holly Fork: Stories of Appalachia (2003)
Home Call: A Novel of Kentucky (2004)

Nobody Knows, Nobody Sees

Bob Sloan

WIND PUBLICATIONS

International Standard Book Number 189323956X
Library of Congress Control Number 2006922733

First edition

For my father,
Robert Sloan,
who gave me
the meaning of
the word
"home."

INTRODUCTION

This book is a sequel to my first novel, *Home Call*, but it's probably not necessary to read the first book to understand this one. I wrote *Nobody Knows, Nobody Sees* because I wondered what happened to the *Home Call* characters. There didn't seem to be any way to find out other than writing their story down.

Since the publication of *Home Call*, a number of people have asked if there would be a follow-up; if you're one of them, I hope this book satisfies your curiosity.

And in the event anyone's curious, there *will* be a third book about Hawkes County, Kentucky. That place exists only in my imagination, and perhaps in yours, but sometimes it seems as real as any other piece of geography. I'm going to spend some more time with Jesse and Margaret, Crow Markwell and the others who live there.

If you're interested in that third book, while you're waiting, if you care about Kentucky, learn all you can about the greatest threat ever to our Appalachian homeland: mountaintop removal coal "mining." It is a menace to all of us, those of us who see Kentucky mountains outside our doors, and those who live far away.

As always, thank you for your interest in and support of my writing.

Bob Sloan
Rowan County KY
May 29, 2006

CHAPTER ONE

Lying in a narrow iron bunk, Dave Brent studied cramped handwriting on three pages of cheap stationery. He frowned at the sentences wandering above and below pale blue lines. Their meandering was reckless as the path of drunk drivers Dave used to arrest on U.S. 60, back home in Hawkes County. He hoped his wife Patsy could decipher the words.

Their composition had taken an entire afternoon. While the letter could be called "finished," he thought he might add another paragraph or two before mailing the pages to his wife. The writing would fill dead hours before lights-out, and four pages traveled for the same postage as three.

Stamps were precious in prison.

There was money to send with the letter, too. A voucher, confirming a deposit of $820.00 into Dave's personal account, was part of his morning mail. Another envelope had contained a short message from Patsy, a note Dave knew had been as difficult to write as his own. She'd included an awkward crayoning from eight-year-old Amy. One wall of Dave's cell was crazy-quilted with similar artistic endeavors.

If he sent six hundred dollars back to Hawkes County he could still afford cigarettes and the occasional cold drink or candy bar from the prison store. He'd tell Patsy the money was generated by selling hand-made items to prison visitors in the inmate craft shop.

The lie would be transparent to anyone with knowledge of how things really worked in prison. Inmates were lucky to average as much as thirty cents an hour, selling hand-tooled leather, wood trinkets, other handicrafts through the gift shop outside the gates. The lie didn't matter. Patsy was unlikely to question her husband's honesty.

Their children needed the money too much to allow the luxury of doubt.

Dave hoped more words would come to him later, half-truths to keep alive his strained connection with his wife. Nothing in the letter would address the circumstances that required Dave to live in a cage at the LaGrange reformatory.

And nothing in the letter would give a hint of Dave's plans to leave Patsy.

It was a simple matter of arithmetic: Marnie was already twelve; Amy, their youngest, would graduate from high school a few years after Dave got out of prison. Once their children were adults there'd be no reason to stay with Patsy. Dave's father would probably be dead by then, wouldn't be shamed by any decisions his son made.

Outside the cell, keys chiming in the distance signaled three o'clock. An electric motor whined, and with a hard iron screech, the door to Dave's cell gaped open. "Exercise," barked a guard at the end of the corridor. "*Exercise, people.*"

Dave pushed the writing tablet under a thin pillow and rolled off the bunk. Most of the time the daily yard period seemed more trouble than it was worth. Occasionally, though, the six-by-eight cell where he spent twenty-three hours of every day seemed more confining than usual. Sometimes an opportunity to walk more than five steps in any direction made the annoyances that were part of getting outside bearable.

The preceding night had been long and nearly sleepless. For a few days, October had turned unseasonably warm, and guards allowed sweating cell block trustees to open windows. Around 2:00 a.m., awakened by a need to use the toilet, through the screened windows Dave heard the full-throated bay of running fox hounds.

When he lay down again, he'd focused his attention on the rhythms of a far-off race. An excited bitch ranged ahead of three slower dogs, her bellowing voice trumpeting the news of fresh scent. From time to time she sounded a series of impatient yips, begging the other dogs to hurry.

Despite the bitch's urgency, the hounds weren't likely to catch their quarry. Red foxes were too wise to be trapped, treed or cornered. Fox "hunting" was not a blood sport: the hunter's satisfaction lay in hearing the music of the hounds. There would be hours of excited pursuit before men called their blue ticks, red bones and Walkers away from the chase.

When a guard barked "Step *out*," Dave moved through the cell door into a narrow passageway. Facing straight ahead, peripherally he saw other inmates, rigid and unmoving, eyes fixed on grimy glass panes through which roofs of the prison complex could be seen. Sometimes the guards kept their charges waiting for a quarter of an hour, but the order "Face *right*," came after only a minute or two.

Dave had known a female led the pack of hounds, understood her messages to other dogs as easily as he comprehended words. As a free man he'd never missed an opportunity to go onto isolated hilltops with Crow Markwell, a retired Hawkes County deputy sheriff. They'd sit close to a fire and listen as the old man's dogs caroled over ridges and through wooded Hawkes County hollows. The old-timer taught Dave to understand the lyrics dogs sang in the manic joy of their chase.

The inmate just ahead moved forward, and Dave shuffled three paces toward the cellblock exit. A guard waited with a clip board, studying the faces passing in single file. "Brent, 2059778," Dave muttered as he stepped outside the block, and the man with the clip board put a mark by his name. Beyond the check-off point, Dave turned to another wall, and waited.

Another guard, a bored black man named Simpson, stood by the door leading to the yard stairs. One inmate was slow to turn, and Simpson shoved a club into the man's back. "You want to go outside, dick head?" Simpson hissed. "Then you put your face the right way *now*."

It was a small brutality, as such things were counted inside LaGrange, and Dave took only brief notice of the inmate's surprised grunt of pain. Hoping Simpson wasn't aggravated enough to pull a strip search or some other petty harassment, he kept his eyes toward the wall, focusing where a smeary stain marred the institutional green.

Dave let his thoughts drift back to the hounds of his long night.

After the canine cries had faded into post-midnight quiet, he'd ached with wanting to hear them again. He imagined the pack's owner climbing into a well-used pickup truck to move closer to the chase. Dave Brent would have traded a month of life to ride with him through the night, windows cranked down, listening for a glad, glorious aria from excited fox hounds.

He'd dozed off to dream of Crow Markwell, squatting beside a low fire on Big Perry Mountain. In the dream, Crow leaned over wavering oak embers to pour whiskey into Dave's cup. "Drink fast," the old man urged. "Them dogs ain't a'going to wait for us."

As Dave lifted the dream-cup of bourbon-laced coffee, he woke and cried out with knowing he was years away from sitting with Crow Markwell again. He was at least a thousand long days from feeling the cold wet muzzle of a friendly hound shoved eagerly into his hand, a thousand longer nights from freedom.

In the dimly lit, sweltering cell, Dave had sobbed out the unbearable ache of being locked away from everything that mattered, from family and life-long friends, from autumn hills heavy with dew, from the joyous sweet crooning of hounds.

He wasn't ashamed of his tears. Sooner or later everyone cried at LaGrange. Even professional criminals, for whom half a decade inside the walls was an expected, inevitable consequence of their irrational career path, sometimes cried after lights-out.

When all the inmates were in the hallway, the guard Simpson accepted the clip board, signed it, and unlocked the door to the stairs. "Step *down*," he chanted, and the line of men in state-issue denim filed into the stairwell.

The door at the foot of the long set of stairs opened onto the exercise yard, a block of asphalt fifty feet square. On all sides, sheer red brick walls rose four stories high. The only way Dave could know with real certainty he was outdoors was by craning his neck to stare straight up at a patch of blue sky framed by brick and steel.

There were worse dreams than the hounds. Sometimes he came half awake in the dark to a hallucinated ghost of perfume hanging in the musty cell, the odd scent of his lover. It was expensive, ordered from Europe, because it matched the smell of the hothouse flowers she was so proud of growing in her greenhouse.

Those nights his cell held a hint of her perfume, Dave would breathe so deeply his lungs ached with the effort, filling his nostrils and lungs with the flowery aroma. Always, when he came fully awake and the scent was gone, he cried out without caring who heard, without wanting to live.

Dave could never remember the name of her flowers, though she'd told him the word a dozen or more times. But he recalled their heady reek, blanketing the two of them when they made love on an old

4

sofa in her greenhouse. He remembered the scent between her breasts, in secret and illicit beds. Dave Brent had never felt more alive in his life than when he was with her.

Patsy didn't know anything about those times. Nor did she ask about hours spent away from the tight little house she and Dave shared with their children and his father.

His father. When would he see his poor, proud father again?

The guard Simpson leaned against the door and watched a group of younger inmates retrieve a basketball from a corner of the exercise yard. Soon a rough game, where no fouls were called, was underway below a netless hoop. Dave hiked the length of the brick wall opposite the basketball court, taking long strides, stretching cramped muscles.

Other inmates paced too, but there was no talking when they passed. Simpson would have tolerated conversation, but men from protective custody had little to say to one another. They were in Simpson's charge, in a special cellblock, because sending them into the general prison population would have been like signing their death warrants.

Some had murdered friends or relatives of other prisoners, others were known snitches who broke the convict code of never confiding in a guard. One of the other men in protective custody, like Dave, was a former deputy sheriff. Ex-cops didn't live long in the general population, and served their sentences in near-solitary confinement.

After three years at LaGrange, Dave was eligible for early release in four months. He kept in mind the advice of older cons, who told him the first parole board always said "No." Even model prisoners endured two or even three hearings before the board allowed the prison gates to swing open. Believing in early release, the old-timers counseled, was a step closer to madness.

They told him not even the attentions of the lawyer whose services *she* paid for would change that hard reality.

Walking aimlessly, Dave composed a story about the exercise yard. He'd append the tale at the end of his letter to Patsy, then seal it with the money order. Nothing of his gray, grim world would be in the story. He'd tell Patsy it had been a pleasant afternoon, sitting at a shaded picnic table with other inmates, drinking sodas, smoking hand-rolled cigarettes. He'd invent exotic prison gossip, report it as though LaGrange was hardly more than summer camp for naughty over-grown children.

"Jesus!" someone shouted, almost screamed. *"He's got a blade!"*

Dave stopped walking at once, put his back against the protection of the high wall and looked around, urgently scanning everything in his line of sight, desperately searching for the source of the shouts.

"Drop it, scum bag!"

The second voice was Simpson's. Shocked, Dave realized the guard was rushing in *his* direction. He raised both hands to show he wasn't holding any contraband. But Simpson's wide, alarmed eyes were fixed on a farther point, and Dave turned his head in time to see an inmate named Porter raise a homemade knife.

The shard of metal was dull-edged, hardly a blade at all, and an explosion of pain registered when Porter ripped it across Dave's throat. The heavier convict slammed into him, holding Dave against the wall while sawing the piece of steel back and forth.

Dave cried out instinctively, the effort emptying his lungs while Porter's relentless pressure on his chest kept him from filling them again. And what Porter was doing hurt. God but it *hurt.*

Then Simpson was on them in a club-swinging fury until a bloodied Porter dropped to his knees, holding his head and moaning.

Dave couldn't feel the solid wall at his back any more, he was falling, with no one to catch him before he collapsed onto pavement made blistering hot by the sun. Simpson ignored him and continued to beat Porter. Dave tried to sit up, but his body refused to obey commands from his confused mind. To his right another inmate stared, eyes bright with horror.

The door to the stairs crashed open and a mob of khaki uniforms spilled into the exercise yard, waving sticks the size of baseball bats, shouting orders at the prisoners to drop on their bellies with hands behind their heads. Even after stretching prone on the concrete the inmate on Dave's right continued to stare.

Dave read the terror on the man's face, and cold fear replaced the confusion from Porter's attack.

Raising a hand to his throat, Dave Brent felt life gush hot and sticky from a ragged tear below the jut of his Adam's apple. It was difficult to focus his vision, and he wondered what he'd done to antagonize Porter. Strong hands picked him up and settled him onto something softer than the concrete.

As the stretcher was elevated, Dave was ashamed, because it wasn't Patsy's placid, dull face that swam into memory, or his wife's name he whimpered as a stark blackness behind the stretcher bearers gathered closer. "Lorena. Oh God Lorena," he pleaded, as though the sweet syllables of the name might bring back the light which was fading so quickly.

Dave Brent wished he could die thinking of someone other than his adulterous lover.

He wished he could die someplace other than LaGrange Prison.

CHAPTER TWO

Sighting down a seven-inch pistol barrel, Jesse Surratt steadied the Ruger's brass front sight till it rested below the stiff and insincere smile spanning his own face. When he squeezed the revolver's trigger, his touch was gentle as a kitten's breath. Twenty-five yards away, a poster urging Hawkes County voters to elect him sheriff was ruined. Bark exploded as a hundred and fifty grain magnum slug smashed through cardboard, plowed into the tree underneath.

Jesse fired five more rounds, crouching in a two-handed stance learned in a crash course at the State Police Academy after the election. He shot methodically, realigning the heavy pistol between each round. Long before he emptied the gun, the center of the poster was only so much ragged, shredded paper.

After the sixth shot Jesse reached onto the front seat of the county cruiser and fumbled at an open box of ammunition. Counting out half a dozen more rounds, he leaned further inside the car for a fresh poster. The three-year-old pieces of cardboard showed him as the civilian he was before the election. Jesse's first term ended in less than a year. If he chanced running again, he'd get new posters printed, with a studio posed photograph of himself in uniform.

Lighting a cigarette, Jesse leaned against the squad car and wondered what Margaret would say about using old campaign placards for pistol practice. His wife liked playing amateur psychologist. Given the opportunity she could probably deliver a twenty minute monologue on the implications of her husband going off in the woods to shoot at his own face.

Jesse Surratt was not an ignorant man, and he briefly considered the possibility there *were* subconscious reasons he used election posters for targets. He didn't think so. At the Walmart off I-64, paper bull's eyes cost a dollar seventy-eight per package. Closets at the courthouse held dozens of the obsolete placards, free for the taking. They made fine targets.

While he smoked, Jesse reloaded his pistol. Hungry squirrels scampered over dry dead leaves carpeting the forest, taking advantage of the lull in his target practice. Under the trees, the ground was dusted with the acorn hull litter of their foraging.

Two months earlier, for eighteen consecutive mornings Jesse had driven to work in thick fog. Hawkes County old-timers said every August fog meant at least a tracking snow in the coming winter. Jesse wished the squirrels well in their struggle with approaching cold and gave them a few extra minutes to find food in the bright sunshine of an Appalachian Indian Summer.

While he smoked, Jesse looked at the fresh poster. He remembered how uncomfortable he'd been the day it was taken. He'd agreed to shave his beard off for the election, and his face was still stinging from the razor's scrape the day he posed in Ed Tomalin's studio.

Jesse had spent twenty-three years in the Navy before coming home to Hawkes County, and during his military career probably didn't skip shaving more than ten days. Still, he hated the daily ritual of hot water, lather, and blades that were never sharp enough. After retiring from the service, until the year he ran for sheriff, he'd left his beard alone.

He was pinning another poster in place when the radio in the squad car came to life. "Better come on in, Sheriff," Martha Compton, the day dispatcher, told him. "Something's come up. Something you need to know about."

Jesse considered refusing the summons back to his office. He was more comfortable in the woods than at the court house. Among the stands of tall oak and hickory no one would demand his help in resolving an argument, no obsequious county councilman could seek the sheriff's support for controversial decisions they all hoped voters would forget by election day.

More importantly, single-minded concentration on the revolver kept Jesse from wondering about Margaret. Lately his wife was making two or three calls a week back to Norfolk, where she'd lived during the period they'd been divorced. Jesse suspected his wife was about to leave him again. The possibility filled him with morbid dread.

If Jesse told the dispatcher he was busy, Martha wouldn't bother her boss again. He could stay in the woods until dark if he chose, wasting bullets and avoiding the frustrations of a troubled marriage. But during his tenure in office Jesse had developed a respect for the round-faced grandmother whose father had been sheriff thirty years earlier. If Martha Compton thought Jesse should be in the office, he needed to go.

"Be right there," he muttered into the microphone.

Securing his pistol in its holster, the sheriff grudgingly climbed into the car, tossed the box of bullets into the glove compartment and eased off the steep hill where he'd spent the afternoon. Passing a place where adolescents had within the week built a fire and left a pile of empty beer cans off the road, he reminded himself to mention the mess to the jailer.

A prisoner work crew could clean up the site in a couple of hours. Allowing long-term jail inmates to perform menial tasks for which the county had no spare employees turned out to be a popular innovation in Jesse's first term. It would be a useful thing to mention often, if he ran again.

Voters thought putting prisoners to work made their sentences harder. They didn't need to know prisoners vied for the privilege of picking up road trash. Earning twenty cents an hour picking up discarded beer cans was the only way many of them had of buying tobacco.

Jesse had driven deep into the National Forest surrounding the county seat, and it took nearly half an hour to reach Midland's small commercial district. On the high rolling ground behind the town, classes were in session at the college, and Jesse shared Main Street with a score or so of professors on their way home, Midland's version of a traffic jam.

In the courthouse, Martha Compton peered over her dispatcher's radio and nodded in the direction of Jesse's office. Through the open door he saw Tom Carruthers on a battered sofa by the desk, studying the Louisville paper. As the county's underpaid and overworked prosecutor, the young attorney was serving a difficult apprenticeship to the practice of law.

"He's been there a while." Martha looked away from Jesse, enormous sadness filling her dark eyes. "He didn't want me to bother you but I said to him there was no telling when you'd be back. He'd already waited half an hour when I called."

Certain he didn't want to know the answer, Jesse asked the obvious. "What's wrong?"

"Tom'll tell you." The elderly woman suppressed a fresh batch of tears.

Turning toward his office, Jesse steeled himself for bad news, wondered whose reckless child had managed to flip a car on one of the mountain roads snaking through Hawkes County. A county sheriff had to look at too many dead adolescents, and Jesse hated the idea of dealing with another one.

"What's up, Tom?" Pouring a Styrofoam cup of strong coffee from the pot Martha kept fresh and full, Jesse tossed his sheriff's Stetson on top of a filing cabinet and perched on a corner of his desk.

Carruthers put the newspaper aside and exhaled loudly. "People are going to be talking about the Brent thing again."

Dave Brent had been a county scandal, the first six months of Jesse's tenure as sheriff. Dave was a long-time deputy, the only one of his staff Jesse could call a real friend. And he was serving a ten year murder sentence at LaGrange Prison.

"People will talk about Dave Brent until he says who was with him the night Ray Bailey was shot." Jesse sipped coffee and waited for Tom to tell the rest of it.

"He'll never do that now," the attorney said at last. "He's dead."

Jesse put the coffee down, his chest constricting with surprise and shock. He'd told no one about his plan to work Dave Brent back onto the county police force, once the man got out of prison. The first step was promoting a pardon from the Governor's office, and Jesse had already written half a dozen politely pleading letters to the capital at Frankfort. "How did it happen? When?"

"This afternoon. Couple hours ago." Tom unwrapped a long black cigar, a habit everyone knew was meant to make him seem older than his twenty eight years. "Throat was cut in a fight with another inmate. Man named Enochs Porter did it, maybe 'cause Dave used to be a law officer. I suppose he might've had some cousins arrested by Dave before he went to LaGrange, or something."

"Goddamnit," Jesse sighed. "Anybody talked to Dave's family yet?"

Carruthers nodded, holding a match to his cigar. "The warden at LaGrange did." Grimacing, the young attorney exhaled loudly. He managed to smoke six of the cigars every day but never pretended to like them. "Then he called to tell me about it. I was scheduled to be a witness at a parole hearing next month. The warden wanted to let me know I didn't need to go now."

Jesse wondered how his deputies would react to the news. Dave Brent was respected and well liked. Every man on the sheriff's payroll had tried to talk Dave into naming the person who could provide an alibi for him. He'd gone to prison without naming the woman who'd been with him, in a motel room, the night of the killing.

"You want me to talk to the other guys?"

Jesse shook his head. "Martha'll take care of that."

Carruthers stood and blew noxious smoke toward the floor. "Guess that's it then." At the door he turned to face Jesse again. "This is a damn shame. I liked Dave Brent. I was going to *beg* that parole board to send him home."

"We all liked Dave," Jesse muttered.

The county attorney acted as though he wanted to say something else, but after a long moment, turned to leave. He almost knocked down Martha Compton, trotting from her radio into Jesse's office.

"Lord have mercy, Elmer Brent's gone crazy!" Martha panted, out of breath. "He's over to Virgie White's, waving a pistol, threatening to shoot her." The dispatcher leaned against the door frame, fanning her chubby face with a stack of dispatch forms. "One of Virgie's neighbors seen what was going on and called."

"Who's responding?" Jesse dropped his coffee cup into an overflowing wastebasket, reaching for his hat in the same motion.

"Larry Daniels is on his way," Martha replied. "And one of the city policemen."

"Get them on the radio," the sheriff directed. "Tell them not to do anything until I get there."

Rushing past Martha and a wide-eyed Tom Carruthers, Jesse jogged down the court house steps, hearing distant sirens converge on Virgie's. His siren and flashing lights helped him reach Tyler's Trailer Park, just inside the city limits, before dust from Larry Daniels' hurried arrival had time to settle. Jesse parked behind the deputy's cruiser and studied the scene before him.

Larry and a city policeman named Armstrong crouched behind their respective vehicles, pistols aimed at the tiny porch of a rust streaked mobile home where Virgie White cringed in a plastic lawn chair. Behind the terrified woman, Elmer Brent faced the lawmen calmly, a faint smile on his face, as though he was welcoming Sunday company.

Jesse got out of his car and gazed over the vehicle's roof. Elmer Brent was over eighty years old. In the forties, before marrying a woman from the Pentecostal Church and settling down to raise nine children, Elmer had been a moonshiner. In those days, he'd been feared by federal and state lawmen alike. County gossip said he'd shot three men in those hard times, killing one of them.

Jesse tried to keep his legs from shaking as he faced the old man. "Has he shot anybody?"

"No, but he's got a gun, Sheriff," Larry Daniels hissed. "Shoved into Virgie's back."

"We can take him," Freddie Armstrong said. "I could hit him in the head from here, easy."

Jesse shook his head. "You boys drop your guns down out of sight. Let's see if we can get this done without anybody getting hurt."

Jesse walked around his car and stopped. "Looks like we got some talking to do, Elmer," he called. "How about if I come close enough we can do it without yelling?"

"I *want* you up close, Sheriff." Elmer Brent's voice was hoarse with tension. "Close enough to hear what this whore says about the night you all claimed my boy killed Ray Bailey."

Jesse almost ducked as the old man raised his pistol, but Elmer didn't aim the weapon, used it only to wave the sheriff closer. "Leave your gun in the car, then come on."

Jesse released the snap on his holster, turned and tossed the magnum onto the passenger seat. Facing the porch again, he took slow steps closer. The nearer he came, the more the young woman in front of Elmer worried Jesse. She looked only a few seconds away from panic. "Be easy, Virgie," he said in a low voice. "Everything's okay."

"That'll do," Elmer Brent said when Jesse reached the porch steps. He lowered the hand holding the gun, and the woman winced as he shoved it into her back. "You talk up now, you whore."

"What do you want me to say?" Virgie's voice was shrill and desperate. "What am I supposed to tell him?"

"Tell the man you was with Davey when they say he killed Ray Bailey, that he never left that room you was in a'tall." Elmer shoved with the gun again.

Virgie nodded her head, her eyes blinking rapidly. "It's like he said, Sheriff. Whatever he says, I agree to it."

"All right." Jesse looked into her eyes, willing the woman to calm herself before she did something reckless, arousing Elmer even more. Looking at the old man Jesse continued, "She's said it, Elmer. Can you put the gun down now?"

"My boy's dead." The old man's eyes glistened, and he brought a sleeve up to wipe at them. "Did you know? Did you hear they've killed Davey?"

Jesse nodded. "I found out not ten minutes ago." He shook his head. "I'm sorry, Elmer. You know I am."

"This one same as killed him," Elmer snapped. "Letting Davey go to prison without saying nothing to save him."

Jesse looked at the wordless plea in Virgie White's eyes, took a deep breath and let it out slowly. "Elmer, you've got to put that pistol down." He put one foot on the steps. "Shoot somebody and *you'll* go to the penitentiary. Who'll be left to help Patsy with Dave's kids?"

It was the right thing to say. The old man's shoulders began to shake, and harsh quaking sobs racked his body. Jesse went onto the porch and took the gun from Elmer's unresisting hand.

Realizing she was safe, Virgie White rose out of the lounge chair, leaped off the porch, and turned to face the sheriff.

"You all better lock up that crazy old son of a bitch!" Looking at Elmer, she raised her voice even louder. "I never had nothing to do with your boy since we was in high school. God almighty, he was a *cop!*"

Virgie wrapped thin arms around her body, as though to still the trembling that had invaded her limbs. "I was going with Tommy Rankin when Dave got in trouble. Tommy'd've *killed* me if I messed around on him. Especially with a cop!"

14

Larry Daniels left the shelter of his car and retrieved Jesse's gun from the front seat of the cruiser. Reaching behind his back where handcuffs hung ready, Daniels asked, "You want me to take him in, Sheriff?"

Jesse shook his head. He'd seen the old man's eyes roll into his head, felt the sudden relaxing of the frail body. "Get an ambulance," he said. "Something's happened to Elmer."

CHAPTER THREE

Lorena didn't vent her grief in a cathartic wailing, a shrieking hysteria of denial.

Instead she took a cup of strong, sugary tea to her kitchen table, settled into a wicker-bottomed chair, and stared at walls painted a cheerful yellow, seeing nothing. A parade of silly thoughts passed through her anguished mind, each foolish notion a scene played out in a chill, a private theater of loss.

She and David would never dance together.

They'd talked about it, planned a score of trips they never got around to taking. They meant to go to Lexington or Louisville, to find a smoky tavern miles and hours from Hawkes County. In a hidden place David and Lorena would drink beer until they were giddy with alcohol and one another. They'd move around a dance floor as a couple, without worrying about who might see them.

Lorena and David made sweet plans, but never managed to get further than the nearest available bed, back seat or flat piece of ground in the woods where they could find thirty minutes of privacy. Lorena's hunger for David Brent's touch burned hotter than slow romantic waltz fantasies.

When David insisted he couldn't dance, Lorena promised to teach him, certain he'd be graceful and agile whenever and wherever they found their dance floor. In their moments alone he showed an innate sense of how to move with her, where to put his hands, when to push, when to yield. She was confident those instincts could be used to mold David into a wonderful dance partner.

Lorena sipped her tea, not caring that it had grown cold as her own soul.

There would never be a Sunday morning when they woke slowly together, a time she could bring the day's first cup of coffee to their bed, black and strong enough to refuel passion they'd turn on one another all over again. At the end of their hours together there had always been a hurried, guilty rush to get David home before daylight.

Their hours together were over.

Forever.

The expensive lawyer whose office was near the prison assured Lorena there was an excellent chance David would be a free man by Christmas. That holiday, she grudgingly admitted, would belong to the dull wife Lorena hadn't quite persuaded David to leave. But she had sworn before God the New Year would be hers. She'd have him by Spring, she'd have him for Sunday mornings, she'd have him for dancing. She'd have him forever.

She'd even planned further.

In the event the lawyer's persuasive gifts were insufficient to bend the parole board, Lorena meant go to the police herself, tell them the truth. *She'd* been with David Brent that night in the motel. The pitiful charade he insisted they play out had gone on long enough. Lorena wouldn't allow the man to talk her out of honesty again. In her lonely lover's vigil Lorena had even sworn to identify Ray Bailey's killer, if that's what it took to bring her man home.

And suddenly her secret plan, all the plans they'd made together were gone.

Lorena had a child to take care of, a home to manage. She had her flowers, and her friends. She wouldn't say anything now. There was no reason to tell anymore.

There was no reason to do anything.

Her voice a husky whisper, Lorena sang the song in which her mother had found a name for her daughter. *The years drift slowly by, Lorena. The snow is on the grass again.*

She'd kept her name secret for years. The night she told David what her mother had called her, she blushed and couldn't look at him.

The sun's low down the sky, Lorena.

He didn't laugh, or tell her it was old-fashioned, or talk about her reasons for hiding the name.

The frost is where the flowers have been.

Instead David whispered the syllables of Lorena's birth name into her ear as they made love.

Only then, remembering the sound of his voice so close, how his breathy utterance tickled her ear, did Lorena cry, sobbing and cursing any God who allowed her David to die at LaGrange Prison, instead of sending him back to her.

CHAPTER FOUR

There was room for Jesse in the ambulance, after two medical technicians loaded Elmer onto a stretcher and slid it inside. It was a tight fit, squatting between machines the paramedics ignored. They didn't do much more than put a blanket on Elmer, but Jesse noticed how often they touched the old man.

Every now and then one medic or the other leaned close to offer reassurance, urged Elmer to hold on, insisted things were all right. A siren blared traffic out of the way and the ambulance rocked as though the driver had the accelerator mashed against the vehicle's firewall. Unable to see outside, Jesse wondered how fast they were going, how much the paramedics really believed things were all right.

At the emergency room, after doctors and nurses swarmed to and around Elmer, Jesse wandered the halls until he found a bank of pay phones in the lobby. He tried his home number, found it busy, waited three or four minutes, and tried it again. For a while he stared at the phone, wondering if his wife was talking to someone in Norfolk again, an old lover, a lawyer, someone with a house for sale.

When he still couldn't get through, Jesse called Martha Compton, asked the dispatcher to keep trying his home number until she was able to tell Margaret he'd be late getting home. Martha said the deputy, Larry Daniels, would fetch his car from Virgie's and leave it in the hospital parking lot.

Then Jesse called Dave Brent's house, surprised he remembered the number and didn't have to look it up. Dave's younger brother Paul answered after only one ring. Jesse identified himself and gave a brief account of what happened at Virgie Warner's.

"I'll be there quick as I can," Paul said.

"You be careful," Jesse cautioned. "Patsy doesn't need you in a car wreck on top of everything else."

When the connection was broken the sheriff felt ashamed, telling the kid not to drive too fast, coming to a father who might be dying. If Jesse'd been in the youngster's place, he'd have found out just how fast his car could go. Putting the receiver back on its hook, he wished he'd been able to get through to Margaret.

Paul Brent arrived fifteen or twenty minutes later. By rights Jesse might have gone home then, with someone else there for Elmer, but he stayed on, staring at the television in the visitor's lounge without trying to make sense of images on the screen. He didn't think he *could* leave until he knew if Elmer Brent survived the stroke.

Jesse felt Paul's eyes on him from time to time. The young man didn't say much after Jesse told him things hadn't changed since their telephone conversation. For the first hour or so there were other people in the waiting room, some of whom engaged their sheriff in time-killing conversations. Paul's taut silence didn't seem so bothersome in a room full of idle chatter.

Trips outside to smoke cigarettes, beyond the lounge that didn't have ashtrays, let Jesse escape the tension briefly. About the time he would have been sitting down to dinner on a normal evening, people whose friends or family were being treated in the emergency room drifted away, until only Jesse and Paul were left.

As the only witness to Paul's mute vigil, Jesse felt like an intruder, seeing things not meant for his eyes. Jesse was sure the youngster expected him to say something, but had no idea what it might be. So he stared at the television, avoiding Paul's eyes, hoping for encouraging news about Elmer.

When the doctors said they'd allow one visitor at a time, for five minutes in every hour, Jesse was surprised Elmer asked to see him first. He was in a dim room, surrounded by a clutter of clear plastic tubes and blinking lights, his face sagging oddly to the left.

"I'd a'done things different if I'd thought it through." The old man's voice was hoarse and rough.

Jesse shrugged. "Don't think about it, Elmer. Just get well enough to help Patsy and Paul."

"You think that Warner tramp was there the night Ray Bailey was killed? Think she had anything to do with it?" Elmer's eyes were piercing and clear, staring up from starched hospital sheets.

Jesse shook his head. "No reason to think so."

20

"*Somebody* was there. Somebody knows Davey never killed no one." Elmer sighed loudly. "Do you reckon I'm going to die over this?"

"Doctors don't seem to think so," Jesse replied.

"Make me a promise, Sheriff," the old man demanded. "Clear my boy's name if you can't do nothing else." He reached for Jesse's hand, held it in a grip cold as a hard November frost.

Elmer held on tightly until Jesse nodded and told him, "I'll do what I can."

"Then I don't believe I'll die just yet." Elmer twisted his half-paralyzed mouth into a parody of a grin. "I believe I'll hang on just to see what you do about it."

Jesse left Elmer and let Paul visit his father. The younger man returned with a doctor, who assured them Elmer would sleep the rest of the night. "His situation won't change much before morning," the doctor told Paul. "This would be a good time to go home and get some sleep."

After the doctor left them, Paul turned to Jesse. "They say he'll live. Might have a limp though, when he gets out of here." The younger man grimaced and shook his head. "If Pop can't get around, if he ends up a cripple, that'll kill him sure."

"Men like your daddy are tough." Jesse meant to offer comfort, but didn't know words for anything other than trite, useless phrases. "He's survived a lot in his life. Sometimes a stroke that'd kill you or me is just a temporary nuisance for men like that."

Paul looked away. "If Pop lives, I reckon you'll be taking him to jail." His voice was resigned, his young eyes dulled by the pain of a brother's death and the problems with his father. Paul Brent looked like a man sleepwalking through a nightmare.

"I don't think we'll have to do anything like that." Jesse hoped the smile on his face was encouraging. "Virgie Warner won't take anybody to court over a gun being waved around. It's not the first time that kind of thing has happened out there." Fully a third of the "domestic disturbance" calls answered by Jesse or his deputies were at Tyler's Trailer Park. "How's Patsy doing?"

Paul shook his head. "When I left the house she was crying again." Paul's voice was quavery and his eyes were red and watery. "I didn't have no idea Pop would do something like this. He's been drinking off and on since Dave . . . " The voice nearly broke, but Paul stared at the ceiling until he regained control. "Since Dave went away.

I noticed when Pop left the house, but figured he was just going after more whiskey."

Paul was the youngest of Elmer Brent's children, an unexpected baby born when Elmer was almost sixty. Only Paul and Dave had stayed in Hawkes County, the other children scattering to the greater prosperity of factory towns in Indiana and Ohio. Until his older brothers and sisters arrived, Paul was left alone to deal with Patsy's grief and Elmer's rage. Jesse was glad to remember one small thing he could do to lighten the boy's burden.

He lowered his voice so the nurses periodically hurrying by wouldn't hear. "Dave had some life insurance with the county. I've got the policy in my office. If you take it to Patsy, she can cash it in."

"Life insurance?" Paul stared quizzically and echoed, "With the county?"

"They buy a policy for all the deputies," Jesse explained. "It's a group deal, and I never dropped Dave's coverage."

"Didn't nobody notice?"

"If anyone cared about the county paying for the insurance, they never said anything." Jesse had spent hours shuffling paper, working creative accounting on his department budget to keep the policy in force. "People liked Dave. They'd want his family taken care of."

"How much money are you talking about?" Paul seemed bewildered by the news, but Jesse thought some of the worry pinching his face was gone.

"Thirty thousand dollars," Jesse told him. "Not a fortune, but it'll help with expenses. And Patsy won't have to pay taxes on it."

"I'll tell her when I go back to Dave's house."

"I'll give the policy to Martha Compton tomorrow morning. You or Patsy, either one, can get it from her." Jesse wished he'd had someone fetch the insurance file from his office. He could have given it to Paul instead of just telling him about it. "If there's anything I can do, you call me, hear?"

Paul nodded, and Jesse left him in the waiting room. The youngster showed no signs he was going anywhere, and Jesse knew Elmer Brent's son would spend the night on one of the hospital's uncomfortable benches.

Larry Daniels had parked Jesse's cruiser just outside the emergency room. The late afternoon sun that warmed the day was gone, and the night air was chilly enough Jesse turned on the heater.

He took the radio microphone off the dash and contacted his office, to let them know he was back in the car.

Olive Lester, the wife of one of his younger deputies, worked as a night dispatcher. "We never was able to get hold of nobody at your house, Sheriff," she reported. "Martha wanted me to tell you that." Jesse acknowledged the transmission and told Olive it didn't matter, he was on his way home anyway.

Leaving Midland, steering toward his farm eight miles outside of town, he muttered out loud. "Goddamnit Dave. Why'd you leave such a mess?" Jesse was as certain as Elmer that Dave Brent hadn't killed Ray Bailey, that he'd gone to prison protecting someone else.

Dave's conviction was based on entirely circumstantial evidence. Ray Bailey, a bootlegger in dry Hawkes County, was shot inside the former filling station that was his place of business. About ten o'clock one evening, the killer walked into the dingy cinder building where Bailey sold illegal liquor and beer, fired a pistol three times and ran away into darkness.

Two blocks away, a group of college students heard the shots and turned toward the noise. All of them agreed the man who ran looked like Dave Brent. None was willing to say it *was* Dave, but they were unanimous in remembering a strong resemblance.

Buddy Upchurch, one of Jesse's deputies, was the first officer on the scene, and found a gun they later determined belonged to Dave Brent. The pistol was abandoned close enough to Ray Bailey's body the wooden grips were stained with the bootlegger's blood.

Jesse had gone looking for Dave himself that evening, but the deputy wasn't home. Patsy, pregnant with a child she'd miscarry two months later, shyly admitted they'd been having occasional problems. She told Jesse once in a while Dave didn't come home at night.

No one saw Dave until he reported for work the next morning. After initially refusing to talk about where he'd been, he offered a thin alibi. He said he'd spent the previous night in a local motel, less than a quarter mile from where Bailey was killed. He admitted someone had stolen his gun, but swore he hadn't left his room until he dressed to come to work.

The motel confirmed Dave Brent had checked in and out. While no one saw Dave leave, there was no way to prove he hadn't walked the few blocks to Ray Bailey's filling station. Helen Pruitt, a motel maid, told Jesse about cleaning the room after Dave checked out.

It was been obvious two people had stayed there. Helen blushed, describing stains on the bed. She remembered finding used condoms and a nearly empty lipstick tube in the wastebasket. And she said the room reeked of a particular perfume scent, an odd odor she hadn't encountered before.

Jesse retrieved the lipstick from the motel dumpster, and confronted Dave with the maid's statement. His deputy refused to identify the person who'd been in the room with him, and the only legible fingerprints on the lipstick were from Helen Pruitt. Dave went to trial for the killing of Ray Bailey without ever saying who was with him the night of the shooting. Helen's story leaked quickly, and during Dave's trial Midland buzzed with speculation over the identity of the unknown woman in the motel. With Dave's death there would be more talk.

A Chevy Cavalier lurched out of a driveway, and Jesse stopped thinking about Dave Brent to pay more attention to his driving. A decal in the car's window indicated the driver was a student at the college. The kid deserved a chewing out at the least, but Jesse was in no mood for hearing lame collegiate excuses for reckless driving.

He kept his hand away from the switch controlling the lights on the squad car's roof, and when the Chevy made a left turn into a fraternity house parking lot, Jesse mashed his right foot to the floor and tapped his horn once. The Cavalier's driver lifted a hand in a careless wave.

Dave Brent had only talked to Jesse one time about the woman who could have provided his alibi. The conversation took place after the trial, while Dave was waiting to be transported to LaGrange Penitentiary. Jesse had carried a six pack of beer into the jail, and he and the former deputy drank it together while Dave talked about being "in love." Jesse hadn't said much. Dave had ignored all the earlier pleas that he change his mind, and after the trial it was too late.

"This prison thing is just something I got to get through," Dave had murmured toward the end of their talk. "It's how I got to pay for everything I'll do later, leaving Patsy when the kids are big enough, disappointing everyone." Dave had smiled sadly. "Ain't nothing free, Jess. We got to pay for everything."

Eight miles east of Midland Jesse made a right-hand turn off U.S. 60, onto a newly paved lane that led to his farm. Bulldozers had recently gouged at what had been a tobacco field for as long as the

24

sheriff had memory. He lifted his foot off the accelerator, let the car coast past the barren plot and looked with distaste at red-flagged stakes lining the lane. They marked where Carl Edwards meant to put concrete curbs and sidewalks.

The housing contractor planned to build either twelve or fifteen small frame houses—he was never definite about the number, though the county building inspector was supposed to be kept apprised of such things—where the Turner family once farmed. Given the reputation of Carl Edwards, Jesse expected the new homes to be built cheaply and so close together it might be possible to stand in one and hear conversation from the next.

The bulldozers had knocked down a high chestnut oak Len Turner always plowed around. The two hundred year old tree shaded seventy five or eighty square feet of grass. It was where generations of Turners found shelter from the sun for a noon meal, or let its broad limbs deflect rain when a sudden shower caught them at work in their fields.

Jesse cursed Len's involvement with ex-sheriff Bradley Smallwood's marijuana operation. Now Len was serving time in a Federal penitentiary, while his wife Darlene sold his farm piecemeal to support their family.

Jesse was elected to office when Bradley and his brother Noah went to jail. Nearly killed exposing his predecessor's corruption, Jesse was initially elated at the score of arrests that followed. But during a series of trials that sent men to prison who'd merely been struggling to save farms from foreclosure, the taste of victory became a heavy, rotting lump in the new sheriff's gut.

While he drove away from the new housing development, Jesse didn't look in his rear-view mirror. Turning into his driveway, he recognized Rita Bailey's van, parked behind the house, next to Margaret's Ford.

If ever there was an odd pairing into friendship, it was the connection between the sheriff's wife and the widow of the man a deputy was accused of killing. Rita was in her early thirties, at least fifteen years younger than Margaret, but age didn't seem to matter to them.

After her husband's death Rita decided she wouldn't continue living in the house they shared, but her seventeen-year-old brother Bobby required a residence with special accommodations. Margaret had sold real estate in those days; in finding a house for Rita, found herself a friend.

Climbing out of his car, Jesse wondered if he might be able to talk to Rita about Margaret's recent odd moods.

CHAPTER FIVE

Margaret Surratt kept one eye closed as she lifted a heavy pitcher to pour frothy liquid into a pair of glasses. Two rum-heavy daiquiris were already fuzzing the edge of her vision, and she was determined to get back to the table without making a mess on her counter. Margaret had almost stopped thinking how awful the next few days were going to be.

Pleased at managing the transfer of glasses to table without spilling a drop, she refilled a plastic flask clamped to Bobby Stillwell's wheelchair. Rita's brother sipped orange juice, chewing a straw to a useless ribbon while his sister downed daiquiris with Margaret.

Bobby was seventeen years old, and dependent as an infant. Intellectually he was bright as a typical five year old. A muscle disorder Rita said was permanent and progressive had ruined his legs, made his speech all but unintelligible. Still, the boy radiated a mindless happiness as he caressed the graying head of Casey, Jesse's aging German shepherd.

When Margaret initially met Rita, Bobby walked as well as anyone, but by the time their acquaintance blossomed into friendship Bobby was spending more and more time in the wheelchair. He didn't seem to mind. He appeared to enjoy sitting with Rita and Margaret, attentive to the conversation passing between them, showing no resentment at not being part of it.

"We better slow down on these things." Margaret slumped into her chair. "Either that or say 'Screw the whole sad, bleeding world' and have a bunch more. If you and Bobby stayed the night you wouldn't have to drive home. We could make daiquiris till the sun came up."

Rita declined the invitation with a shake of her head, tossing short, straight-cut hair away from her eyes. "Bobby gets fussy if he can't sleep in his own bed." Raising her glass, Rita intoned sarcastically, "Here's to the goddamned media, keeping friends close in Hawkes County. You don't know how glad I was to have your house to run to, Margaret."

Their pleasant afternoon began with tears from a panic-stricken Rita, after her red van pulled into the driveway. Once her brother's wheelchair was on the ground, instead of pushing him toward the house Rita leaned against the vehicle and turned toward the hills beyond the barn, where the forest was a cold blaze of high autumn color. Her head down, Rita stared at the ground, not the orange and burnt umber trees on the ridge.

When Margaret came outside, her friend's makeup was a tear-streaked ruin. "My God. What's happened?" Margaret asked. Rita Bailey did not cry easily. Hawkes County still remembered how she buried a murdered husband with dry eyes.

Rita sobbed once, then pulled the tears back inside herself, an act of will Margaret found sadly familiar. Jesse maintained the same iron control on *his* feelings. "I swear to God, if those reporters start up again, the way it was when Ray died . . . " Rita's words trailed away, the threat incomplete.

Puzzled by a reference to a long ago carnival of television cameras and strobing lights, a daily litany of rude questions shouted as Rita attended Dave Brent's trial, Margaret asked, "Why would *they* start bothering you again?"

Rita bent her head. "David Brent was killed today. This morning. A reporter called, told me it was some kind of knife fight." Then Rita *was* crying, openly and loudly. Margaret opened her arms, pulled her friend close. "I can't do this all over again, Margaret! Not again!"

Fear and alarm passed across Bobby's face, but when the dog Casey came trotting from the barn he smiled. His unflagging attentions were a joy for the shepherd, and she ran to put her head in his lap. Bobby's eyes softened and he smiled while the dog whined and wagged her tail.

Margaret's vision blurred with her own tears. Whenever he came to the house Jesse's chief deputy had been awkwardly shy, seldom looking her in the eye, never addressing her more intimately than "Miss Margaret." She hadn't meant to intimidate the younger man, but it took only her glance to bring a hot flush to Dave Brent's face.

Margaret's tears weren't for Dave Brent though. "Jesse," she muttered.

Rita pulled free of Margaret's arms, daubing at her eyes with one hand. "What about Jesse?"

Margaret fished a tissue from her skirt pocket and wiped at her eyes. "The last time a friend of Jesse's died was in a fire, on an aircraft carrier, off Vietnam someplace." Margaret blew her nose and replaced the soggy tissue in her pocket. "When Jimmy Winkleman died Jesse went crazy for a while. It was awful, the way he hurt and wouldn't say anything."

She and Rita walked slowly to the house, still touching one another while Rita pushed the wheelchair. Before long Margaret had the blender turning out pitchers of daiquiris, and soon both women were numbed to their individual pain.

"If they don't have drinks like this in heaven, I'd just as soon go to hell." Rita lowered her glass and daubed a napkin over the foam mustache on her lip. "I wish you'd show me how to make them."

"I learned about daiquiris when Jesse was stationed in New Orleans." Margaret smiled, remembering. "'75 and '76, I guess it was. These things are an art form down there."

At the sound of a car in the driveway Margaret raised her eyes to the high broad windows Jesse had installed because she wanted to live in a house that was *their* house. She'd made other changes as well. Long before she was done with her remodeling, the house had only a passing resemblance to his parents' old home-place or the dreary dwelling he'd inhabited alone.

In a moment the front of a county patrol car entered her field of vision. "I'll just be a minute." Margaret took a can of beer from the refrigerator and went to meet her husband. His eyes would tell her if another wave of the helpless hurt she remembered from Jimmy Winkleman's awful death was imminent.

She found Jesse on the back porch. He'd taken off his shoes and sat motionless on an old glider, staring off toward the barn. Casey had followed Margaret outside, and he idly scratched the old dog's throat, his eyes vacant and tired.

"Are you all right?" She gave him the beer, kept the door open with her body, not quite going out onto the porch.

"What's wrong with the phone?" He snapped the top on the can and took a long swallow. "People have been trying to call you all afternoon."

"I took it off the hook." She told Jesse about a television station in Louisville phoning Rita, frightening her into expecting a phalanx of reporters. "I figured if they called *her* they might have this number too. I wasn't up to dealing with that."

"People in Louisville will forget about Dave before he's even in the ground."

"Well he's not there yet, and they haven't forgotten." Margaret frowned, remembering the afternoon. "Rita was a mess, thinking the media was going to start all over again with her."

"A woman named Virgie Warner lives down in Tyler's Trailer Park." Jesse raised the beer can again. "Elmer Brent went down there with a pistol today, threatened to shoot her if she didn't help him prove Dave was innocent."

Standing in the doorway, Margaret listened while Jesse told how a city policeman had wanted to shoot Dave's grieving father down, described the old man's sudden collapse. As her husband talked, she experienced a flash-fantasy of Jesse's death, was immobilized by the thought of losing him. Jesse smoked too much, he needed to lose fifteen or twenty pounds, he was a *sheriff*, for God's sake.

"What's wrong?"

Margaret refocused her eyes, shaking off the horror that was playing behind them. Jesse was staring at her, a puzzled look on his face. "Nothing." She sipped from the daiquiri she'd brought with her. "Is Elmer going to be okay?"

Jesse shrugged and said the doctors at Midland General seemed sure he'd live, though he might have trouble walking later. "I wish you wouldn't take the phone off the hook. Either that or let me get you a cell phone so I can get hold of you when I need to." His voice was accusatory.

Resisting the urge to defend herself, Margaret took a deep breath and murmured an apology. "I'm sorry. I wasn't thinking about anything but Rita. Anyway, cell phones don't work well out here." When she'd sold real estate Margaret had tried one of the devices, and soon learned the farm was in a "dead spot" for any sort of radio signal.

Jesse raised the beer can to his lips and emptied it. He sighed and stood up. Margaret stepped aside to let her husband pass, hoping he would touch her before going inside the house, hiding her disappointment when he didn't. She heard him in the kitchen, opening the refrigerator for another beer.

"Margaret told me about those reporters, Rita." Jesse's strong voice carried through the house to the porch. "If you want, I can call that TV station, ask them to lay off."

"You don't have to do that," Rita demurred. "I'll get through it. I expect they'll forget about me now anyway, except for maybe one or two of them."

Margaret came in the kitchen in time to see Jesse lean over a grinning Bobby. The disabled boy adored her husband. "Whaddya think, Robert?" Jesse asked. "Should we go see if Sam's hungry?"

The boy's smile broadened and his strangled vocalizations communicated complete happiness. "Let me change clothes and we'll take something to that worthless old mule." As Jesse left the kitchen Margaret wanted to follow, but kept her seat..

"I love watching Jesse with Bobby," Rita said when Jesse was gone. "Bobby loved spending time with Ray, whenever Ray wasn't too busy." Rita grimaced and shook her head. "That wasn't often, but Bobby took what he could get. He misses having a man around."

Margaret lifted her glass, but the daiquiri had gone warm, and the taste almost made her gag. "Sometimes I wonder if Jesse and I shouldn't have had kids."

"Why didn't you?"

Margaret sighed. "He was in the Navy. It didn't seem right to have children when we were moving every three or four years. If he was stationed aboard a ship Jesse wasn't around for months at a time. It's a rough way to make somebody grow up. But I wonder sometimes if I didn't cheat Jesse somehow."

"You know what?" Rita didn't seem interested in her drink either. "I think Ray is really and truly dead, all the way dead, because he and I never had babies."

"God we're getting maudlin." Margaret forced herself to smile. "Let me freshen these things."

As she moved to the blender Jesse came back in the kitchen, his khaki uniform replaced by faded jeans and a denim shirt turned almost white by countless washings. He put his second beer on top of the refrigerator, rummaged inside for a handful of apples. "Know what I remembered about Dave Brent this afternoon?"

Jesse's eyes were bright with unshed tears, and Margaret wondered if her husband would actually cry in front of two women.

"He was the first person I talked to about how an old man named Otto Stevens skinned me, selling me that mule. I bought Sam thinking he could be saddle broken, but Lord, that son of a bitch was too old and too mean for riding years before I came back to Hawkes County."

Jesse looked at Rita. "I ran into Dave at Ray's place, when I stopped to get some beer. We sat talking a long time about people Ott Stevens hustled in trades. That was the first time I had something to laugh about in a long time."

Margaret hoped Rita wouldn't break the mood. Jesse was talking about something that mattered, not just telling a story. Real tears hung in her husband's eyes. When he spoke again his voice was a husky rasp.

"Dave came out here a lot after the business with the Smallwood brothers." Jesse sniffed once, then took a loud breath.

Margaret watched his unshed tears disappear, the same way Rita had shoved her hurt away. For Jesse, tears were adversaries, rather than a lubricant that eased pain. "I wish to hell someone would just go ahead and *cry*!" she snapped.

Jesse and Rita stared at her blankly. "Rita, you show up and act like I wasn't supposed to notice you looked scared to death." Margaret turned toward Jesse, unable to stop the words bubbling from inside her. "And your *friend* was killed. Nobody's going to fall apart if you cry for him."

"Don't, Margaret." Jesse's voice was tight with anger. His grief was gone, at least for a while. "Don't start with that psycho-babble about feelings. Not now."

He put the apples in Bobby's lap. "Hold on to these, partner," he muttered, though without a seatbelt Rita's brother would be hard pressed to keep himself in the wheelchair, let alone hang onto the apples. Jesse rolled the boy away from the table, and a moment later the back door slapped shut.

The women sat without speaking until Margaret said, "One of these days the pressure that man carries around is going to blow like oil wells in old movies. He'll give himself a heart attack."

Rita sighed. "You want to go to Lexington one day next week, get away from all this?"

"And do what?" Getting out of Midland for a few hours was appealing.

"Maybe go to some malls, shop till we drop and all that."

"I don't know," Margaret said, getting up to fetch fresh drinks. "I wouldn't mind seeing a movie or two, but I don't care about malls. This close to Christmas they'll already be packed."

"Okay, we'll go to the movies," Rita conceded. "Two of them."

As her friend prattled on about what might be playing in Lexington, Margaret stood at the window, watching Jesse and Bobby approach the barn. Sam knew they were bringing food, the sole gesture from a human that wouldn't provoke a kick or bite from the ancient mule. When her husband suddenly hunched over, his body shaking, Margaret was alarmed, until she realized it was only tears giving way. "Good," she said to herself.

"Then it's a date?" Rita said, mistaking the utterance for approval of whatever she'd said about Lexington.

"Sure." Margaret didn't bother to correct the misunderstanding. She was thinking she should stop making phone calls to Norfolk, stop imagining a life other than this one. Turning from the counter with their glasses, she said, "Want to hear what Jesse told me about something Elmer Brent did today?"

CHAPTER SIX

While most of Hawkes County slept, for hours Lorena lay motionless in her bed. By and by, it became clear that even her iron will couldn't sustain an obstinate determination sleep would come, if she was patient. Each time blessed oblivion seemed close, a new memory of her David emerged, and Lorena snapped wide awake again, her pillow clammy and chill against her face from hours of nonstop seeping tears.

By the time she cast the covers aside to feel in the dark for slippers, the bedside clock showed a quarter past two. Lorena wrapped a flannel dressing gown around herself before stepping from the bedroom to the hallway. Pausing at her son's door, she listened to his regular, deep breathing, then left him to sleep on.

Drifting through the unlit house to the back door with cat-like confidence, as she crossed the threshold Lorena clenched her teeth at the wind keening off the Appalachian ridges. A cold front, moving across Hawkes County, sent up an eerie distant wailing in the trees like the mourning of lost souls on the hilltops.

Lorena's haven and pride lay fifteen yards behind her house. She hurried across wet grass, slippers saturated long before she reached her destination. Glass panes of the greenhouse, rimed with frost, looked like stacked blocks of ice in the moonlight.

Breath fogged around Lorena's face until she slipped through double-insulated storm doors, into tropical humidity. The fecund odors inside were welcome evidence of life, of a place where death was transient and meaningless. "Hello darlings," she whispered. "Mama's come to see you. "

Years before talking to plants became a trendy eccentricity, Lorena believed flowers thrived on vocal encouragement. She spoke to her blooms and bushes constantly, told them when they looked

34

especially lovely, encouraged every drooping stem, offered congratulations for every new bud.

Half-reclining on a sofa where she and David had made love more times than she could count, Lorena thought she sensed a trace of his smell, under the reek of humus and water, stem and leaf, a suggestion subtle as a haunt. Closing her eyes she settled deeper into the couch and welcomed the fragment of ghost.

Sometimes Lorena had stretched full length on the sofa below her lover, lifted her splayed legs and whispered "Fuck me *now!*" Never before had she used such words with a man, but what passed between herself and David was too primal for euphemisms. They didn't make love, they thrashed and wrestled and *fucked*, and Lorena did things that shocked her even as she did them, or wantonly arranged her body so David could do them.

Merely thinking about David made her slick beneath the thick robe, ready for his touch. Her mouth twitched with the beginning of a smile. David liked knowing the mere thought of his touch could make her squirm like a schoolgirl only half-suspecting what's about to happen.

On one visit to the prison, Lorena told David about getting wet when she remembered the things they'd done. Above David's shy grin his eyes flashed delight and pride at her revelation of his power, even at a distance. Dear God, she thought. What a distance it had to cross now.

Pushing thoughts of David aside for a moment, Lorena wondered how much trouble Sheriff Jesse Surratt would cause.

Inside a gas station on the outskirts of Midland, waiting for a bored high school boy to take her money, she had listened as three or four men clotted around a coffee pot, gossiped about new interest in the Bailey killing. The men ignored her, as one of them, married to an emergency room nurse at Midland General, repeated a story from his wife. She claimed she overheard the sheriff make a promise to Elmer Brent that he'd confirm, after all this time, Dave Brent's alibi.

Lorena shook her head fiercely, thinking about it. Jesse Surratt wouldn't discover a damned thing. She'd see to that. Lorena had always been willing to march into the courthouse, tell everything she knew, if the telling would bring David home. But he argued the consequences would be too severe, always talked her out of telling.

And now he was gone.

There was no reason to do anything of the sort.

Lorena could have saved David from prison, by acknowledging she was the woman in the motel room, the only person apart from David himself, who *knew* he didn't kill Ray Bailey. After they heard pistol shots and realized David's gun was missing, Lorena had begun to gird herself for the repercussions.

Then David reminded her of obligations to her son. She couldn't afford to be implicated in what had happened. David promised he could use his position in the sheriff's department to take care of everything. He was so damned reasonable, so convincing. Lorena found herself agreeing with her lover, and began removing all traces of herself from the tacky motel room.

Then she went home.

After his arrest, David mailed a note to Lorena, telling her not to say anything. Even in prison, during her frequent visits he insisted she keep silent. "It's only for a little while," he lied. "This isn't all that different from being in the service. And it's better than what would happen if you told."

Lorena saw his haunted eyes, and knew her David was in a place worse than any army barracks. Sometimes she almost managed to hate him and the Baptist conscience he couldn't quite escape. David believed in a primitive sort of God who was perfectly willing to make certain His erring children were punished. David accepted everything that happened after the killing, believing it was divine retribution for their having found one another, payment for falling in passionate, impatient adulterous love.

In the warmth of the greenhouse, Lorena missed David terribly. She'd always missed him, but there had been the relief of the ridiculous visits, of quick kisses stolen in a dingy visiting room amid the chaos of wailing children, unhappy wives and tearful mothers. There had been the anticipation of what would happen after his release.

Lorena cried herself to sleep on the sofa, remembering their bittersweet visits. It was nearly daylight before she woke and went back to her bed.

CHAPTER SEVEN

After twenty three years of Navy reveilles, Jesse Surratt seldom slept past 5:30. The clock radio near the bed, red letters glowing in pre-dawn darkness, was for Margaret, who set it for 8:30 and hoped the thing's monotonous drone would rouse her by nine.

Skin goose-pimpling as he rolled away from warm covers, Jesse reached for a bathrobe tossed over a chair, pulled the belt tight and headed for the kitchen, toward the aroma of fresh coffee. So far as Jesse Surratt was concerned, the person who mated a clock with a coffee maker so that waking up to fresh coffee was easy, deserved a Nobel Prize.

The shepherd Casey, asleep under the kitchen table, raised her gray muzzle when Jesse turned on the light. She didn't come out to greet him. Before Margaret came back, the dog generally slept at the foot of Jesse's bed. Sometimes it seemed her eyes carried a hint of reproach for her kitchen exile. Casey watched him for a moment, then curled back into sleep.

Beyond the windows a security light, installed after Jesse's predecessor in the sheriff's office turned murderous, showed a carpet of frost stretching into darkness. He took a cup of coffee to the back room. It was still fairly warm outside when he and Margaret went to bed, and there'd been no need to use the woodstove. Wednesday looked to be a "warm coat, high fire" sort of day, though.

Kneeling to shake ashes off the grate, Jesse grimaced at the thought of approaching winter. He intermingled half a dozen sticks of kindling with wads of newspaper, then covered them with two lengths of split oak. Jesse briefly wondered why he hadn't stayed in San Diego, where it was always warm, where he could have easily found a civilian job with the Navy Department. He'd be sixty in two years, old enough to make the prospect of approaching snow and cold weather an ache.

Flame blossomed from the well-seasoned wood not long after Jesse touched the paper with a lit match. A few steps from the back door firewood was stacked head high and five rows deep under a three-sided shed. It ought to be enough to carry them through winter, but he decided it would be a good idea to slip onto the hill behind his barn soon and cut a few more sticks. Having too much firewood was a more comfortable problem than not having enough.

Hooking a finger through the handle of his coffee cup, Jesse walked to the bedroom to fetch his cigarettes. Lighting one, he eased his weight onto the mattress. Margaret would sleep through the intrusion, wouldn't notice light spilling from the living room. Being able to look at his wife without embarrassing her was a rare luxury. Whenever Margaret caught him studying her face, she blushed, then self-consciously protested his stare.

Jesse liked looking at his wife. Time had etched strength and character onto her face without coarsening her delicate features. The bright-eyed college girl who married Jesse had been pretty; age made her beautiful.

When he leaned to brush her forehead with his lips, Margaret's arms came up, wrapped around him and pulled Jesse close. She rocked slowly in sleep, the way she'd once held a very young West Coast sailor newly and madly in love with her. She'd have no recollection of the moment when she finally woke. Gently disengaging himself, Jesse wondered how he would live if Margaret left again, and wondered how to make her life full enough to stay.

In the first months after coming back to him, she'd busied herself with remodeling the house, making it reflect her preferences, not those of Jesse's mother. When there were no more additions to be made to their home, Margaret became a successful Realtor for an agency in Midland. The last deal she brokered involved the property where Carl Edwards was building a collection of cheap houses. Jesse hadn't voiced his disappointment that a housing development was raised so close to their farm, but Margaret had to have known how he felt.

She soon lost interest in real estate and resigned from the agency. Afterward it seemed to Jesse his wife spent all her time reading. She moved two bookcases into the living room to hold volumes she'd read once and meant to open again. She gave the others away, to Rita or the public library.

38

Margaret had no close friends other than Rita Bailey, no interest in the politics of the sheriff's office. Nothing seemed likely to keep Margaret in Hawkes County. Jesse would have given up an index finger to find a way to make life with him full enough Margaret would never think about going away.

Sighing, he went back to the kitchen, snagging a magazine off the coffee table as he passed through the living room. He sat in the kitchen and read *Time* magazine reviews of three movies he'd never see. At the sound of the bathroom door closing he looked up, surprised. Margaret almost never got up so early.

"I'm going to throw that blender *away*," she muttered as she poured a cup of coffee. "Then I'm going to forget I ever knew the word 'daiquiri.' Got any recommendations for a murderous hangover?"

Jesse couldn't help grinning at her. He gestured at the empty chair to his left. "Sit down."

From the bathroom he fetched two ibuprofen tablets, with a cup in which three inches of water dissolved a couple of Alka Seltzer pills. "Wash the pills down when the water stops bubbling," he said. "And after you finish the coffee, fill the cup again,"

"At least it was for a good cause," Margaret said after she swallowed the ibuprofen, grimacing at the taste of the water. "If you could have seen Rita when she got here . . . " Turning dark eyes on Jesse she asked, "And how are *you* doing?"

Jesse settled back into his chair. "Don't ask me to talk about Dave. Not yet." Margaret took a deep breath, then released it, a loud signal Jesse recognized as a sign of temporary surrender.

"I want to tell you what I did yesterday," Jesse said. "Before I got the call from Martha Compton about Dave."

He drained off the rest of his coffee. "In the morning I had a budget meeting with three county councilmen, a couple of hours where we fought over every nickel I need to run the sheriff's office. After that I planned to get caught up on paper work, but soon as I got the reports laid out on my desk, I had to go out to Tracy Kidwell's place. He's feuding with Ted Jarnigan over a property boundary and somebody needed to see they didn't shoot each other over half an acre of worthless scrub."

Jesse propped elbows on the table and leaned his face on his hands. At his feet the shepherd whimpered in a dog dream. "You think Casey's sick? She didn't eat this morning."

"Casey eats breakfast when you're gone." Margaret reached for Jesse's pack of cigarettes, lit one, and stubbed it out after two puffs. She'd been trying to quit for weeks. "Did you know she comes to bed with me, after you leave for work?"

"She used to sleep there."

Margaret smiled. "I know. Now she comes back after you're gone, and we commune about middle-aged lady problems."

"You're not middle aged," Jesse said.

"Oh yes I am, Jesse Surratt. So is Casey, and neither of us is ashamed of it. Now finish what you were saying."

Just talking about the routine of his day made Jesse feel tired. Any taxpayer with a problem, however minor, could claim blocks of his time. "After Jarnigan and Kidwell, I came back to town and took Ruby White's oldest boy home. Larry Daniels caught him breaking a window in an empty house and put him in a detention cell for a few hours."

"What are you trying to tell me?"

"Wait." Jesse raised his hands. "I'm not finished. After that I was sick of everything in the courthouse. I spent three hours shooting a pistol on Carson Ridge, until Martha called about Dave."

"And?" Margaret pressed

"And maybe I might forget about another election. All those people I ran for office with, in such a hurry to clean up Hawkes County? They aren't crooked like the Smallwood bunch, but they *are* politicians now. And I'm not." Jesse slumped lower in his seat. It had been, for him, a long speech.

"Are you asking me for permission to stop being sheriff?" Margaret relit the cigarette she'd extinguished, and this time she let it burn. "When Rita told me what happened to Dave I had this idea, or vision, or something. It was almost like dreaming awake, that you might get killed. God, Jesse, I don't *want* you to be sheriff."

Jesse left the table, brought the coffee pot back to refill their cups. "If I start spending all my time at home again, how do you think that'll be?"

"I don't know." She tilted her head back, and blew three quick, perfect smoke rings. "But I'd be willing to find out."

Jesse wanted to tell Margaret about Elmer Brent asking him to finally discover who really killed Ray Bailey, but he was tired of talking. He didn't want to think about promises to an old man who might be dying, especially promises he couldn't keep.

"I ought to go on, take a shower." Jesse stood behind Margaret, lay his hands on her shoulders so she couldn't turn around. If she looked at him, he was afraid the words he needed to say would be choked off, unspoken. "Please don't leave me again."

Margaret shook off the restraining hands, moved into Jesse's arms as she stood up. "We wrecked it, the first time, didn't we?" she whispered against his neck. "Do you suppose we might be grown up enough to keep it going now?"

Jesse shrugged. He would have promised Margaret anything at that moment, but words seemed empty.

"I'm not going to leave you, Jesse," Margaret whispered. "Not now, not ever. I'm home."

When he let her go, to Jesse's relief Margaret didn't seem inclined to talk any further. He went off to the shower, was soaping himself and wishing he could stay home when Margaret pushed the flowered curtain back, her robe a pool of fabric at her feet.

"How late would you like to be this morning?" she asked.

"I've got all the time in the world," he whispered, surprised his voice didn't crack like a sixteen-year-old's. He always felt adolescent awkward when he looked at Margaret naked.

"Then I'll come in there with you." Margaret stepped into the tub, took the soap away from him and began doing wonderful things with her hands.

When Jesse glanced at his watch later, only an hour had elapsed. Minutes spent with Margaret could be incredibly elastic. Sometimes an hour felt like a day. Other times it was as though the hands on his watch had done a lap around the dial in triple time. Rolling off the bed he reached for his trousers. "Would you call Martha while I get dressed? Tell her I'm on my way."

Margaret sat up and stretched, raising her arms, breasts rising. "Want some coffee to carry with you?"

He watched her pad off to the kitchen without covering herself. Jesse knew he looked his age. There was gray on his head and his chest. He had a belly, and when he looked at his hands he saw his years in the way the veins were more obvious. The changes time worked on his wife's body were far more minimal.

41

When Margaret came back in the room she set a steaming mug on the dresser. "Martha says go for seconds, if you're not too tired."

Jesse stared. "You told her what we were doing?"

"I didn't have to." Margaret lay on the bed, looked up with her legs immodestly parted. "A woman knows when another woman's been well and truly taken care of, Jess. Just from the tone of voice."

Jesse gazed for a moment at the dark thatch at the juncture of Margaret's white thighs. Smiling, he began to unbutton his khaki shirt. "I don't think I'm too tired."

CHAPTER EIGHT

Steering his cruiser out of the driveway an hour later, Jesse felt hopeful about his marriage—and his life—for the first time in weeks. Running late meant a mountain of paperwork would be piled on his desk, but knowing Margaret wanted to stay made up for any problems caused by one morning's tardiness.

Giving up politics to stay home was a tempting thought, and Jesse was glad he'd mentioned it to his wife. Money would be tight if he gave up the sheriff's job, but they could survive on his Navy pension and their savings.

By the stop sign on the highway, three men unloading a backhoe from a flatbed truck stopped their work to wave at the sheriff's cruiser. Jesse figured they were about to dig new water lines with the machine. Looking at the muddy construction site left a sick feeling in his stomach, but he lifted one hand off the wheel to return the waves. Carl Edwards' notions of progress weren't the fault of backhoe operators.

Near the Jerry's Restaurant on the outskirts of town, Jesse tapped his turn signal and steered into the crowded parking lot. He was already late. Another few minutes wouldn't hurt, and he was hungry.

Most small towns in eastern Kentucky have a Jerry's, and the one in Midland was typical. Part of a regional chain, the restaurant nevertheless felt like an old-time country diner. The elderly widow who ran the kitchen somehow made the restaurant's homogenous menu seem like home cooking.

The restaurant's windows were fogged, but Jesse already knew who was inside. The morning crowd seldom changed. Before going in, he fished in his pocket for two quarters and pulled a Louisville *Courier Journal* from the machine near the door.

Settling in a booth, he smiled at the waitress who brought an insulated plastic carafe of coffee to replace the empty one already on the table. "The usual, Sheriff?" she asked, already writing the order on her pad by the time he nodded agreeably.

Pouring a cup of coffee, Jesse unfolded his newspaper. Before he had time for even a quick scan of the headlines, there were three interruptions by men eager to hear the sheriff's version of what happened at Virgie Warner's trailer. Two others asked who was taking a collection for Dave's family.

"Call Martha Compton," he told them. "She takes care of everything that matters in the office. She only tolerates me being there because I stay out of her way."

The men laughed, knowing as well as their sheriff there was more than a little truth in the statement. Sheriffs would always come and go with electoral whims but Martha was permanent.

As the men left, Eddie Byrnes, a foreman at the county highway garage, slid into the seat opposite Jesse. "We got to talk about snow," Eddie said, pouring a refill for his coffee from Jesse's pitcher.

"What's the rush?" Snow on mountainous county roads wasn't likely to be a problem until after Christmas.

Eddie frowned. "We ain't got but one plow for the whole county," he said, stating a fact Jesse was well aware of. "And it's got an electrical problem nobody's been able to fix. None of the lights on the damn thing work, so we can't use it before dawn or after dark."

"What do you need to get it taken care of?" Jesse moved his newspaper aside as the waitress brought his eggs, hash browns, and a fresh supply of coffee.

"Hard to say," Eddie answered. "I called the state garage and they sent somebody to look it over. He couldn't do nothing with the damn thing neither. Prob'ly need to have a man sent out from the factory."

"Call Phil Evans. Ask him to get the county council to turn some money loose." Evans, an M.D. in general practice, had a flair for politics and was part of the reform slate with which Jesse had run for sheriff. "Tell Phil you talked to me already. We can't do without a snow plow."

"I'll try and get to his office this afternoon." Eddie slid to the end of the bench seat, then turned to face Jesse again. "One of the hospital nurses is married to a man on my crew. Says she heard you telling Elmer Brent you'd look into the Bailey killing again."

44

Jesse shrugged. He could hide something like an insurance policy on Dave Brent's life, but there were few real secrets in Hawkes County. "I'm thinking about it. You think Dave killed Ray?"

Eddie scowled. "I never did think he done it, Jess. Damn shame what happened too. Dave was a good boy."

Eddie stood up but before leaving he pleaded, "Reckon you could talk to Phil ahead of me calling, let him know we *got* to have money for that plow? If we wait till the snow flies it'll take weeks to get a factory rep here."

Jesse nodded. "I'll call him from the courthouse."

Eddie was hardly gone when Tracy Kidwell rushed to occupy the vacated seat. Still fuming over Jesse's intervention in his land dispute with Ted Jarnigan, Kidwell gruffly demanded, "You going to run for re-election, Sheriff?"

"Why?" Jesse directed most of his attention to breakfast. "You thinking about trying for the job?"

Kidwell scowled. "Some of us would like to talk Blaine Ingraham into running."

Jesse frowned. Kidwell's friend Ingraham, nearly ready for retirement from the state trooper barracks by the interstate, was a bully. And Blaine was a coward. He'd want to know there wouldn't be serious competition in a race before openly admitting interest.

Most Kentucky troopers were good lawmen, happy to lend professional expertise to county sheriffs. The one time Jesse called to ask Ingraham's advice about an investigation into the theft of someone's car, Ingraham only half-covered the telephone mouthpiece before complaining about "that amateur over at the courthouse."

"I'll let you know when I make up my mind." His eggs finished, Jesse refilled his coffee cup before opening his paper again, dismissing Kidwell with a curtness just short of open insult.

Left alone, Jesse spotted a brief announcement on page six, a ten or twelve line story most people would overlook. A man named Enochs Porter was alleged to have fatally stabbed a fellow prisoner at LaGrange State Prison. Dave was described as a former deputy sheriff, serving a ten-year term for killing a Hawkes County businessman. There were no references to the fact almost no one believed Dave had done the killing.

Jesse left the paper and two dollar bills on the table for the waitress, and went to pay his check at the register. He was glad no one else wanted to talk to him. The achy knot in his throat would make speech difficult.

It took less than ten minutes to reach the courthouse, where Jesse found Patsy Brent perched on the edge of a wooden bench outside his office. Motionless, she stared at the wall, eyes focused on a personal infinity. Absorbed in her private reverie, Patsy didn't acknowledge Jesse until he stepped in front of her.

"Good morning, Patsy," he said gently, not wanting to startle her.

She raised her eyes slowly, like someone coming out of a trance. Patsy had quit high school at sixteen to marry. Not yet thirty years old, she was a widow with four school-age children.

"Paul said I should come." Patsy's voice was hardly more than a whisper, and Jesse wondered if a well-meaning physician had prescribed some strong tranquilizers to help her through the next few days.

Jesse took Patsy's arm and gently steered her toward his office. "You didn't have to wait outside." He glanced toward his radio dispatcher. "Martha, would you fix us some coffee?"

"I needed to be by myself for a little while." Patsy let Jesse lead her to the sofa near his desk. "At home everybody watches me so close. They're afraid I might do something crazy, like Daddy Brent did." She sat quietly while Martha brought Styrofoam cups to the couch.

"Are you making it all right, Patsy? Can I do anything?" Jesse put one of the cups in Patsy's icy hand, making sure she had a good grip before letting go.

Tears welled in her eyes. "Lord, Jesse, it's hard," she whimpered. "For three years I never thought past the day when Dave would come home, and now I don't know what to do, what to plan for. I don't know how to talk to my kids."

"How's Elmer doing?" Jesse asked.

A not-quite-smile lifted the corners of Patsy's mouth. "Daddy Brent's a case, ain't he?" She sipped gingerly from the steaming cup. "I went by the hospital before I come here. He says you're going to find out who killed Ray Bailey. Did you really tell him that?"

"I'm not sure what all I told Elmer." Jesse sighed and sat down next to her. "That old man scared me to death at Virgie's, waving that gun around, then falling over like God reached down and turned him off."

"Could you find out who done it? After all this time?"

"I don't know." Jesse leaned back and crossed his legs. "Dave could have told us the name, and never said a word." Jesse shrugged his broad shoulders. "Never said a word to me anyway. I don't suppose you know something you haven't already told us?"

Patsy shook her head and put her coffee cup on the tile floor. Settling deeper in the couch she exhaled loudly, eyes glazed with exhaustion. "When Daddy Brent told me you was going to look for whoever killed Ray Bailey, I almost called you up." Patsy took a deep breath and then looked Jesse in the eyes. "I meant to tell you to let it alone."

"Is that what you want me to do?" Jesse hoped it was.

"Dave run around some." Patsy's weak smile appeared again. "Mama Brent warned me, before we got married. She told me Brent men made good husbands, once you got used to their girl friends." The half-smile on Patsy's face broadened a bit. "She claimed Elmer slipped around some even after he got religion."

"I never knew anything about . . . " Jesse began.

Patsy cut him off. "If you're fixing to tell me Dave didn't tom cat, don't. I knew about it. All I thought of when Daddy Brent said you meant to clear Dave's name was I didn't want to know who she was."

Patsy stared off into space. "Especially if it was some little whore like Virgie Warner. If you was to find out who was in that motel room with Dave, I'd hear about it, wouldn't I?"

Jesse nodded. "Most likely."

"What I decided was this, Sheriff. My babies deserve to know their daddy wasn't a killer. My husband didn't a bit more shoot down Ray Bailey than you did."

When Patsy stood up she nearly kicked the forgotten cup of coffee across the floor. "Find out who done it if you can, Sheriff. Dave's kids are owed the truth." The new widow stepped toward the door and turned to face Jesse again. "They're owed it no matter what that truth is. You find out who done it."

Jesse went to the filing cabinet by his desk, opened it and took out the life insurance policy, wrapped in a red plastic folder. "I think all you've got to do to get this money is call the agent. There's a name and phone number on the front."

Patsy looked at the policy for a while before putting it in her purse. "I thank you, Sheriff," she said. "If you need to talk about anything Dave ever done, come to me. I'll tell you whatever I can. I won't hide nothing." She stepped toward the door, then turned again. "One more thing. At the funeral, will you help? Be a pallbearer, I mean?"

Jesse nodded.

"It's tomorrow." Patsy's voice cracked, hands fluttering like broken birds around her words. "Paul can tell you details. Call him."

When Patsy was gone Jesse drank another cup of coffee, wondering what he could do that would satisfy Elmer Brent. Martha Compton looked in as though she wanted to say something. "What is it?"

"I hope you *do* find out who it was," the dispatcher said, and turned back to her radio.

That pretty much settled it, Jesse thought. Three years in the sheriff's office taught him if Martha Compton believed the sheriff ought to do something, sooner or later he'd end up doing it. He finished his coffee, then retrieved the file on the killing of Ray Bailey. "I'll be out for a while," he told Martha. "I'm gonna go see Crow Markwell."

CHAPTER NINE

The old man was paying a high price for allowing a length of firewood to fall into the yard, for letting it lie there all night instead of restacking it. But about ten o'clock the previous evening Crow Markwell had been half asleep when he came onto his porch. He meant only to fetch enough wood to warm his house, and ignored a section that rolled into the yard. When he came outside after breakfast, Crow was certain he'd seen a copperhead crawl underneath it.

Snakes should have been gone after the frost, but a stretch of unseasonably warm days had some of them out and about. The yard around Crow's house was kept neat, the grass cut short, just so he'd more easily spot a hated snake. Copperheads loved nesting in wood above all else, and Crow had unwittingly provided this one a place to go.

The old man regretted sleeping so late, staying in bed until the day warmed. With normal October weather the thing would have been sluggish and easy to kill. But the sun would have energized it. A well-sharpened garden hoe lay across Crow's lap, and he kept his fingers wrapped around the handle, ready to strike if any part of the snake's anatomy showed.

Crow considered using the hoe to turn the slab over, but was afraid the snake would get away. He had speed enough to hit the thing once, and turning the wood meant putting the hoe in a position from which it couldn't strike. Taking a chance at exposing the snake might give the damned thing an opportunity to escape. So he sat, waiting.

One of his three fox hounds, a long legged bitch called Glenda, bayed in the dog run. In a moment her kennel mates Jack and Billy called as well. Their voices carried an uncertain tone, showing they were only pretending. Jack and Billy had no more idea what had aroused Glenda than Crow did. Unlike the old man, they were unwilling to admit it.

"Hush," he called, and the dogs quieted, except for Glenda's impatient whine. Crow's pride in his animals was stronger for knowing they obeyed because they wanted to please him, not because he might rush into the kennel with a raised stick like some men.

Before long Crow heard what had excited Glenda. A police cruiser was laboring up the hill road in front of his house. He was intimate with big-bore engines meant for high speed highway chases, and this one roared as it fought the steep incline. Crow wondered who was coming, but didn't get up.

If you took your eyes off a copperhead, *that* was the moment it escaped. His visitor would have sense enough to come around back when no one answered a knock at the front door, or would leave. Either way, Crow meant to kill a snake.

He was not unhappy at the prospect of a visitor, especially someone from law enforcement. They were forgetting him, down at the courthouse. Even him. False modesty did not compel Crow Markwell to deny he was the best deputy sheriff to ever serve Hawkes County.

An honest awareness of his one-time gifts aside—Crow's eighty-fourth birthday wasn't far off—every old man is sooner or later forgotten. It had been a long time since any of his successors came to visit. If Crow survived another decade—and he might; his grandfather lived to a hundred and three—he probably wouldn't have any visitors from the courthouse at all.

There was a tentative rapping at the front door, a spate of silence, then a louder pounding. A moment later, Crow was pleased to see Jesse Surratt stroll around the corner of the house. A visit by some young deputy would have been pleasant, but Crow genuinely liked the county's new sheriff.

He was tired of waiting for the snake to move. "You know what a spud bar is?" he asked Surratt. Without looking to see if his question was acknowledged, Crow added, "There's one a'leaning in the shed. Get it, but don't walk close by that piece of wood. There's a damned copperhead hiding under it."

In a moment the sheriff was back with the long pry rod. "Wait." Crow stood up, legs and back tight from a long period of sitting without movement. Holding the hoe at the ready he nodded, and Jesse Surratt turned the wood. There was nothing under it. "Son of a bitch," the old man muttered.

"You're starting to see things, Crow," the sheriff teased. "You want a ride to the nursing home?"

"It was there. I *know* it was there." Crow lowered the hoe and leaned on the long hickory handle. "Prob'ly got away when you barged in uninvited. If I get bit and die from that thing I'll come back and h'ant you, set at the foot of your bed every night and ruin your love life." Crow grinned. "What little bit of it there is."

"You might be surprised."

And then Crow Markwell laughed out loud at Jesse Surratt's blush.

The two men turned away from the piece of wood and stepped toward the porch. "Wait," the sheriff cautioned. "Over there, by the corner."

The copperhead was frantically trying to fit itself into a crevice in the house foundation. It was eerie, the way a snake knew when a man was looking at it. "You got a gun," Crow reminded the sheriff. "Shoot the damn thing."

"With a magnum?" Surratt responded. "Hit or miss, it'll make a hole in your house big enough to hide a dozen snakes."

Crow handed the hoe to the younger man. "Kill it with this, then," he said. "But by God if I had eyes to aim a revolver, I wouldn't get no closer than bullet range to any snake."

Crow watched as the sheriff made short work of the copperhead. "Little one," he said, bringing the hoe back.

"Little ones bite the hardest." Crow stepped onto the porch. "Have a seat. But get us some coffee first." The familiar curve of his porch rocker was a comfort and Crow allowed himself a contented sigh.

The sheriff brought two full cups outside, gave Crow one and sat on the edge of the porch, his back against the house.

Crow eyed the folder in the sheriff's lap but couldn't read the name on it. "You come all the way from Midland to fetch me a cup of coffee?"

The sheriff shook his head and looked serious. "You heard about Dave Brent?"

Crow nodded. The news had been on the radio when he woke.

"Funeral's tomorrow. Two o'clock," the sheriff said.

"I'll be there."

51

Surratt took a deep breath, held it a moment, then asked in a rush of words, "When you were a deputy, did you ever start digging around a case after someone had already been convicted?"

"Not quite like that." Crow leaned back in his chair, tilted toward the wall until he was looking eye to eye with Surratt. "But did your dad ever talk about the Reeders?"

"I don't think so."

"Big, *big* family," Crow remembered. "And in May of '46 I got called to their house. Floyd Reeder was dead in the front room, shot in the chest. Raymond, the oldest boy, said he done it. Claimed him and his daddy was drinking and got to fighting. The boy said he was afraid Floyd was going to hurt him bad. Raymond said that was how come he shot his own father."

"That wasn't what really happened?"

Crow frowned. Younger people had no patience, didn't know how to let an old man tell a story. "I took Raymond off to jail, and by rights I suppose he might of been electrocuted by the winter of '47. Floyd Reeder was a church-goer, didn't drink at all that anybody knew of. A jury would of been hard on anyone who killed a man like that, never mind it was his no-account son."

Crow shifted in the chair. "Raymond wasn't a'tall like his daddy. Hardly ever worked, laid drunk most of the time, and a jury wouldn't've needed more than an hour to convict him of capital murder. But somebody, and I never did know who, called while we was waiting for the trial to start."

Crow reached under his chair and found a pint of bourbon. Pouring a modest shot into his coffee, he offered it to the sheriff, and when Surratt declined, put the bottle away.

"Whoever called told me Raymond was in Paintsville all that weekend Floyd was killed. Said there was a dozen or more could swear he couldn't have got back from Johnson County before daylight Monday morning. Coroner said Floyd was shot no later than nine o'clock Sunday night."

"What'd you do?"

Jesse Surratt was interested now. But Crow wasn't about to hurry the story. Telling it was close as he was going to be to living such things again.

"I fetched Raymond from the jailhouse," Crow recalled. "Took him in handcuffs to the Reeder house and got all of them together in that room where Floyd died. I told the Reeders Raymond would end up dead too, if somebody didn't tell the truth."

The sheriff put down his coffee to light a cigarette. "What'd they do?"

"Nothing at first." Crow got the plug of tobacco from his pocket, cut a piece and fit it into his jaw before telling the rest.

Tension in the Reeder parlor had been so thick the air seemed too heavy for breath while Crow described the process of state-sponsored electrocution. He told how the condemned man's head was shaved, described the smell of frying meat that would waft across the execution chamber after Raymond was strapped in the oak chair.

That was when fifteen-year-old Florence began to tell how her father had been slipping into her room at night for three years. That last time, she'd taken a .32 caliber revolver into bed with her, and when Floyd Reeder came close enough, shot him dead.

The family had stayed up all night, washing the sheets from Florence's bed, calming the hysterical girl. When Raymond came home from his poker game and learned what happened, the boy said he'd confess, that it would be better than everyone knowing what really happened.

"Back then, incest wasn't common conversation like it is now," Crow finished. "R. D. Crumm was the prosecutor. After me and him and Judge Rudy Clay had a little talk, the murder charges got dropped. Word got out about what happened, though. Always does." Crow leaned out over the edge of the porch to spit. "I expect that's why all the Reeders went to *Dee*-troit a few years later."

"What I'm thinking about is different," Surratt said.

"The Bailey killing ain't all that different." Crow tipped and emptied his coffee cup and shot a satisfied grin at Jesse Surratt. He'd known all along what the sheriff wanted to talk about. "Would have been better if you'd got after it earlier."

"Dave Brent didn't want me to."

"He told you so?" For a moment Crow's mind was filled with wonder a man would go into a place like LaGrange Prison rather than alibi himself out.

"Elmer Brent thinks I promised I'd clear Dave's name." The sheriff sighed. "I don't know, maybe I did. But it doesn't matter what I said to Elmer. What do *you* think? After all this time, could I find out anything?"

"Truth don't go away, just because nobody's been told it. The truth is always around someplace." Crow's cup was empty and he went in the house for a refill. He brought the pot outside with him, and took care of the sheriff's cup before sitting down again. "Didn't you have witnesses?"

Surratt opened the file on his lap, but didn't bother looking at it when he began to talk. Crow figured it was a fair bet the sheriff had the narratives on the pages all but memorized.

"Ray was killed in a back room at the filling station where he bootlegged. Three blocks away half a dozen college kids were standing around, trying to get up the nerve to see if Ray would sell them some beer. All of them said they heard three shots, and then a man who looked like Dave Brent ran outside."

The sheriff shrugged. "Nobody talked to those boys till the next day, though. They had time to convince each other what they'd all seen."

"But they all said it was Dave?" Crow interrupted.

"They said the man *looked* like Dave. He had on a University of Kentucky sweatshirt like one Dave wore a lot, and he was about the same size. There was a bright light outside, and one of those kids said he was about ninety percent sure it was Dave."

Crow wondered if another few drops of bourbon in his coffee would put him to sleep. He decided he didn't much care if it did, and reached for the bottle. "Seems like I remember Dave Brent claimed he was at a motel all night, though."

"I talked to the motel maid right after it happened. Nobody saw him go anywhere, but he could have slipped out for a few minutes. Whoever was in the room with him would know for sure if Dave left."

"How'd you know another person was there?" Crow asked.

The sheriff grinned. "You know Helen Pruitt, how religious she is? Helen cleans rooms at that motel, and when she told me what the sheets were like the poor soul's face turned red as fire."

Crow didn't care about the maid. "Who searched the room though?"

"*I* did," the sheriff said. "And found not a thing but a tube of lipstick and six empty beer cans. The lipstick tube was about empty too. Helen had taken the trash out to the motel dumpster. Hers were the only prints we could get off it."

"And that was all there was?"

"Except for the perfume smell."

"Perfume smell?" Crow prodded.

"Helen said she'd never smelled anything like it. The odor was still strong the next morning when I was in the room. Sweet, flowery. Nice, but different. It was a new one to me too."

The sheriff put the file down. "I asked Dave a dozen times who was with him, but he never told."

"Let me think a minute," Crow said, and then got up and walked into the yard, as far as the grass was cut short. He urinated against a small maple tree. His father always said a man was healthier for peeing outside.

When the retired lawman was comfortable in his rocker again, he said, "If I wanted to know who was in that room with Dave Brent, I'd find out who had contact with him at the prison. People with a secret that big to share will need to talk it over once in a while."

"I could call the warden at LaGrange."

Crow nodded. "Do that. But then go see him. You'll learn more looking him in the eye than you will with a telephone call by itself."

They were silent for a while, and the warm sun made Crow a trifle sleepy. He was almost nodding when the sheriff said, "Margaret would like it if you came to dinner soon. Can I tell her to look for you?"

Crow grunted an assent. "I'll call her and figure out what night."

"I'll leave this file. I'd appreciate it if you looked it over, maybe see if there's something in there I'm missing."

"No need to hurry off."

The sheriff shrugged. "If I'm going to be chasing off to LaGrange I ought to get all my paperwork caught up today. That's where I'll be if you think of anything else, in the office."

"Just leave that file on the chair, Jesse," Crow told him. "I'll get to it directly."

Then the sheriff was gone, and Crow napped peacefully until a trespassing rabbit set Glenda and the others into a paroxysm of barking.

CHAPTER TEN

From his office window five stories above LaGrange State Prison, Harvey Gartland looked down on the barren concrete of the exercise yard. If he raised his eyes he'd see the minimal skyline of the town that over the years grew up around the prison. Lifting his gaze a few more degrees would show him trees along the bluffs of the Ohio River.

The first time Gartland looked through the window, in 1968, he was applying for a position as a guard. Warden Arnold MacMasters, who ran LaGrange in those days, brought Harvey to the office for a final interview. Five years after being tapped to hold the top job in the institution, Harvey Gartland knew things seemed much clearer as a guard applicant than as warden.

When he retired Gartland would become a piece of prison trivia, the last warden to have risen through the ranks, from tier guard to the office overlooking the exercise yard. He'd seen the list of candidates to replace him, compiled by politicians in Frankfort. The names on it belonged to ambitious men in their forties, with advanced degrees in "criminology" and "penology," career administrators and assistant wardens from other states.

Gartland wondered if any among them had ever walked day after dangerous day, unarmed, among killers and thieves, rapists and psychopaths of all colors and bizarre tastes. He doubted any of his potential successors could control dangerous men with only personal strength and force of will.

When Harvey wore a guard's uniform his state-issued thirty-inch hickory club was a weapon of last resort. He doubted that rule still held at LaGrange. His staff—now called "correctional counselors," not "guards"—was a collection of brutes and dimwits, no more impressive than the bureaucrats lining up for his job.

Gartland didn't care any more. All he wanted was his pension and freedom to never again enter the zoo called "LaGrange," management of which was made all but impossible by combined, contradictory forces of do-gooders, politicians and judges.

Taped to the wall near his desk, where he could reach it without getting out of his chair, was a page of declining numbers, from 1,000 down to zero. At the end of each workday Harvey drew a line through another number. When the downward count reached zero, it would be finished. Harvey had worked it as far as 578.

The intercom buzzed behind him. "What is it?" the warden barked without turning from the window.

"Sheriff Surratt from Hawkes County wants to talk to you. Line two," his secretary announced.

Gartland stabbed a button with a scarred finger, turning on a remote speaker rather than picking up the receiver. The inch-long scar on his hand was a reminder of the time a convict, his name long forgotten, bit while struggling to hold on to something Harvey didn't want him to have. "Speak," he rasped in the general direction of the speaker box.

There was a pause before an electronic voice announced, "This is Jesse Surratt, in Hawkes County. I'd like to ask you about . . . "

The warden wasn't interested in who the voice claimed to be. As far as he was concerned, for the time being that's all he heard, a voice. "Are you calling from your office, Sheriff?" Gartland demanded.

"Yes," the voice admitted.

"Pick a number between one and ten."

"What?" The voice was puzzled and impatient, with a slight shading of anger.

Gartland ignored the aggravated tone. "Between one and ten."

"Seven." The voice sounded sullen and resentful.

"I'll call you back," Gartland said curtly, stabbing again with the scarred finger, breaking the connection.

From a desk drawer he took a page of phone numbers, listing every police agency in Kentucky. When he found the Hawkes County Sheriff's number, he punched it into a gray console on his desk.

The warden was still making payments on the complicated apparatus. The man who sold it to him swore it was foolproof, showing Harvey the red light that would flash whenever the machine sensed a recording device or tap at the other end of conversations. It had gone off twice in the year Gartland owned it, and he considered his money well spent.

He picked up the handset when a woman answered at the other end. The remote box was convenient but it distorted voices, and the warden was a careful listener. "What's the number?" Gartland demanded when the sheriff came on the line.

"Seven," the voice said. "And what the hell was that all about?"

"Reporter for a TV station called the man I replaced, back in '92, claiming to be chief of police at Paducah." Gartland reached into a humidor on his desk for a cigar. "That other warden said some things a reporter didn't need to know, and I decided if I ever had this job I'd always know who I was talking to."

"Are you satisfied you know now?" Sheriff Surratt sounded ready to vent the anger his voice only implied earlier.

Gartland applied a flaring kitchen match to the cigar. "Don't get all wound up, Sheriff." The spent matchstick chimed musically, dropped into a crystal ashtray by the phone. "All it took was making sure you knew the magic number. Besides, now I'm paying for this call. So what can I do for you?"

"You can talk to me about Dave Brent."

"What about him?" Gartland swiveled his chair to look into the yard where Brent died. The senseless killing was another reminder it was nearly time to retire.

If the guard Simpson had been where he was supposed to, out in the square close to the prisoners, Enochs Porter wouldn't have had time to do such a thorough job on Dave Brent's jugular. Yet Gartland couldn't fire Simpson without filling out half a ream of forms and reports. And even then he'd probably be over-ruled by the State Employees' Merit Board.

"For starters I'd like an explanation of how he came to be killed," the sheriff said. "A former law enforcement officer like Dave should have been in protective custody the minute he got to LaGrange. How come he wasn't protected?" Surratt's voice was sharp and hot, his anger no longer hidden behind polite façade.

Harvey Gartland shook his head, though there was no one in the room to see the gesture. The hick complaining at the other end of the line might run a few deputies in Hawkes County, but he didn't know a thing about prison reality.

"Protective custody is a misnomer, Sheriff," he explained. "In their infinite wisdom the courts require yard privileges, exercise, law library visits and all the rest of it for every prisoner. Any man walking around LaGrange with other prisoners can be killed. That's what happened to Dave Brent. Another convict, also in 'protective custody' killed him."

"But why?" The sheriff sounded less angry and more exasperated. "Do you know why?"

"I think I do, as a matter of fact." Gartland sighed loudly and slumped lower in his chair. "Dave Brent snitched on a dirty guard." The warden was still angry about what had happened, and the anger kept him talking. "Somebody, another convict probably, broke into a file cabinet in my office and figured out Brent had been talking to me." Gartland paused a beat. "Might've been a guard who broke into my files though."

"You've got crooked guards?"

"Jesus, you need me to draw a picture?" Harvey was beginning to wish he hadn't accepted Surratt's call. "Cocaine dealers who get busted in Louisville or Lexington, when they come here they don't necessarily want to give up wine, women, and song. Know what I mean?"

"Not really," Surratt snapped.

"These drug guys have more money than they know what to do with." The warden exhaled smoke at the window. "My staff isn't paid any more than your deputies, Sheriff. The dopers manage to bribe a few of them."

Gartland used the cigar as a pointer, emphasizing his words with piercing gestures. The hick sheriff couldn't see them, but the pointing was a habit for Harvey. "This staff is three times larger than when I started working here, and not a tenth as effective. It's made up of people I can't even do a decent security check on because of privacy laws and other bullshit invented in the seventies." Gartland gave up and dropped his cigar in the ashtray.

When Harvey spoke again the fire was gone from his voice. "Some of my guards, who incidentally are now called 'counselors,' belong on the other side of these bars, Sheriff, and I can't do a thing about it.

They're protected civil servants, and it's easier to lance a boil on your own ass than fire the sons a bitches. But if I find out who fingered Dave Brent, that'll be a sorry pup before I'm finished with him."

There was a long silence at the Hawkes County end of the line, and then the sheriff said something that surprised Gartland. "You all don't have a market on institutional crookedness," the sheriff admitted. "You probably know about bootleggers and sheriffs in dry counties."

Everyone in Kentucky above the age of sixteen knew a bootlegger couldn't operate without the cooperation of local law enforcement. "I know how it is," Harvey said.

"I didn't, not at first," the voice continued. "When I got elected sheriff I meant to shut down the bootleg payoff. Dave was the one who explained why I couldn't. 'You got a Navy pension,' he told me. 'Your deputies got eight dollars an hour and families.' I guess you and I have both learned to live with things we'd rather do without."

"You're lucky I don't have this phone bugged, Sheriff." Gartland studied the machine on his desk. It could discreetly tape any conversation held on it.

Surratt ignored the warning. "Dave Brent didn't even do the killing that got him sent your way. I'd like to try and prove he didn't."

"Good luck to you then." Harvey had a feeling this was one hillbilly sheriff he could learn to like. "What do you want from me?"

"Can you answer some questions?"

"Depends on what they are," Gartland hedged.

"Did Dave have visitors at the prison? Apart from his wife?"

"Let me check." Gartland turned his chair away from the window and faced his desk again. He punched a password into the computer filling a third of the walnut surface. "It'll take a minute to get Brent's file up. Hold on." Harvey let the computer whir and click through its catalogue of prisoner names, and when Brent's came up, pressed the "Enter" button.

"Visitors have to be approved before they come inside the walls, Sheriff," the warden explained. "David Brent's wife and father were on his list and came here eight times in three years. Somebody named Linda Carroll came a lot more often. Three, sometimes four times a month, it looks like. Who's she, a sister?"

On a few occasions Gartland had been in the visiting area when Linda Carroll appeared. From the way she and Brent looked at one another, he was sure they weren't siblings, but had no reason to share that information.

"Dave's sister lives in Ohio, and her name is Lynette Oldham." There was silence on the telephone. "How do you spell that last name?"

"C, a, r, r, o, l, l," Harvey enunciated. "You know her?" He envisioned the sheriff scribbling notes in some ramshackle courthouse. Well hell, the warden decided. Might as well give the man something serious to write down. "Was she a rich friend or something?"

"Rich?"

"Somebody put a lot of money into Brent's personal account while we had him," Gartland said. "There's a total here someplace."

The number was on the screen, but the warden didn't say anything for a few seconds. Callers who didn't know how fast the computer worked could be persuaded to wait when they called for information. Sometimes it was a useful ploy.

"A shade over thirty thousand dollars was sent to Brent while he was here," the warden said when he judged the wait was sufficient. "A lot of money in a place like this." Gartland grinned. That would be something for the sheriff to chase down.

"I'll look into the name," Surratt said.

"Call me any time you think I can help," Gartland said, hoping he would hear from this Sheriff Surratt again.

There was a pause, and then the sheriff said, "So Dave was set up because he was talking to you."

"By another prisoner most likely," Harvey admitted. "The guard we arrested was providing marijuana, whiskey, even women if one of those rich drug guys had enough money. A prisoner might have paid to have Brent killed."

The warden let the sheriff think on that for a moment. "Could have been another guard, though. Some of them are plenty pissed off one of their own is sitting in the Jefferson County Jail. A guard could have bought the killing as easily as a con."

"If you figure it out, would you let me know?" Surratt asked.

"I'll do that," Gartland agreed.

"Thanks," the sheriff finished. "And you know something? I wouldn't have your job for double pay."

The warden punched the button that shut off the phone and glanced at his watch. It was three o'clock. Swiveling in his chair, Harvey Gartland reached to put a mark through another number. "Five hundred and seventy seven," he said to no one, and got up to leave.

CHAPTER ELEVEN

The blare from Margaret's clock radio wrenched her from an unpleasant dream, a reminder of the years she and Jesse were divorced. In the dream she was in Owen Vinson's bed again, trying to explain why she was leaving. "I shouldn't be here, Owen," she told him. "I don't even like you very much."

"Of *course* you like me," Owen argued. His voice was self assured, patronizing in a way that made Margaret want to slap his smooth, pink face. "It's *Jesse* you don't like. He wouldn't talk to you, remember? I *talk* to you."

In the dream, Margaret lifted her head from the pillow and tried to reach for her clothes, neatly stacked on a chair near the bed. She briefly suspected Owen was holding her down, but aggressive behavior was as alien to the man as keeping silent for an hour. Her limbs refused to obey, and the dream-Margaret wondered if she'd died and entered a personal hell where she was trapped in Owen Vinson's bed forever.

For once she was glad to be pulled from sleep by the alarm. A dream about Owen Vinson wasn't being unfaithful to Jesse, but it nevertheless carried an uncomfortable emotional weight. She groped for the button which would shut the clock's noise off for a while.

Reaching across the bed she found the other side empty, sheets already cool to her touch. A sliver of light spilled through a gap at the not-quite-closed door, and unreasonably happy television voices chirped in the living room. Leaving the bed's warmth to close the door would bring her fully awake, and she wasn't ready for that.

Pulling the sheet over her face, Margaret rolled onto her side, away from the light. A low liquid drumming came into her awareness. An autumn rain was falling through the oak tree just outside the bedroom walls. Easing back toward sleep, Margaret considered the words Owen Vinson spoke in her dream.

Jesse seldom talked about personal feelings, but Owen was happy to voice all of his petty resentments and fears. His pose of male sensitivity was fueled by pop psychology books he read compulsively and constantly. It took Margaret a while to realize what initially appeared to be frank disclosure was, in Owen Vinson's case, no more than a highly focused interest in the minutiae of his own personality.

Margaret was never all that comfortable in Owen Vinson's bed, but in the months before coming back to Jesse, found herself there with disturbing regularity. The last time, when she told him she was going back to her ex-husband, Owen cried softly. Then, as Margaret dressed, he asked if she thought her friend Evelyn—her married friend Evelyn—would go out with him.

When the alarm went off a second time, Margaret made herself sit up and turn the clock off, rather than use the snooze button again. She was not a person who greeted a new day by rushing into it. On mornings no pressing business required her to be up and about, Margaret could lie for an hour or more in an odd state of consciousness halfway between sleep and real waking.

Shivering, she hugged herself against the chill beyond the bed covers. She'd worn a flannel nightgown to bed. Warmed by Jesse's body, sometime in the night she'd discarded it. The garment lay on the floor, near the bed, and Margaret pulled it over herself before standing up.

Owen Vinson said he needed her, but when Margaret slept with him, he stayed on his own side of the mattress, never touched her unless he was fully awake. There were countless things Jesse wouldn't say out loud, but he was forever pulling Margaret close if she strayed too far in the night. His sleeping touches seemed more honest than Owen's declarations of need.

Opening the door to the living room Margaret winced at the light but pushed toward the kitchen and the smell of fresh coffee. She didn't need to look at the TV set to know Jesse was watching the Weather Channel. He had a farmer's preoccupation with climate, compounded by curiosity about temperatures in Naples or Hong Kong, San Juan or Honolulu, places the Navy had sent him.

At the coffee maker Margaret poured herself a dose of caffeine and leaned close to the big window above the sink. She saw a circle of misty rain, silvered by the security light above the garage. Their pleasant and long Appalachian Indian Summer had ended. The rain would rip all the colorful autumn leaves from trees on the ridges. Once full daylight arrived, they'd be skeletal yet beautiful, in a stark monochromed way. Margaret was looking forward to snow, to seeing the mountains in their winter dress again.

She drank half her coffee while looking out the window, refilled the cup and went to the living room. It was much warmer outside the bedroom. Jesse had kindled a fire in the wood stove, and heat was spreading through the house. He'd left their bedroom door ajar so some of the heat could reach where she slept.

Margaret settled into her usual chair, glancing at the televised display of a Caribbean storm system. "Is it supposed to rain all day?"

Jesse grunted affirmation. "We'll be lucky if we don't end up lowering Dave into a foot of water."

Margaret shuddered and looked more closely at what Jesse was doing. A short stick of wood was nearly hidden in his big-fisted grip. Discreetly, she observed the unexpected grace working in her husband's wide, awkward-looking hands.

The carving seemed impossibly small, nestled in Jesse's thick fingers, and he applied the knife with unexpected delicacy. After a few cuts he raised the carving to the light, turning it, smiling. When his eye caught Margaret's subtle stare, he looked away, sheepish.

"What are you making?"

Jesse put the wood on the end table and dropped the sharp knife into the drawer. "Nothing. Just fooling around."

Margaret studied the piece of wood, but the figure was too rough to know what it was becoming. After moving into the house, she'd found carvings scattered on shelves and in drawers, squirrels and dogs and cats and horses, a miniature Appalachian menagerie, filling shelves and table tops in every room. She'd talked Jesse into letting her place some in an antique shop near the interstate, on consignment.

They sold steadily, but as the tiny bestiary was depleted, Jesse didn't replace any of them. Finally Margaret stopped carrying the carvings away. "I haven't seen you use the knife in a long time," she said. "I like watching you work with it."

Jesse shrugged. "Just something to do with my hands."

Margaret turned her eyes back to the television, where a scrolling message described local weather conditions. The temperature in Hawkes County was forty three degrees, and the crawling words indicated it wouldn't get much warmer until after the weekend.

"Terrible day for a funeral." Margaret wished she could find words to make the burial easier for Jesse. The rituals and rites of death held an abiding horror for him, but she didn't know how to offer comfort against something he wouldn't talk about.

The telephone rang in the hall, and she went to pick up the receiver warily. Early morning phone calls to a sheriff's house seldom brought welcome news.

There was brief silence, then words came over the line in a breathy rush. "Tell the sheriff the woman with Dave Brent in that motel room was Faye Carmody."

Margaret heard a high pitched giggle before the connection was broken. Replacing the telephone on its hook, she sat down again. Jesse looked over expectantly, and smiled as Margaret repeated the message.

"Faye Carmody teaches English at the high school," he explained. "My God, she was teaching when *I* was in school. Couldn't have been over twenty-two or twenty-three years old and we already called her 'Old Lady Carmody.' She never liked me. I'm not sure she liked *anybody*."

"Get a little revenge, then," Margaret suggested. "Take Faye Carmody to the courthouse, sweat her in a back room. Make her tell you where she was the night Ray Bailey was shot." It was a small joke, but when Jesse laughed out loud the sound was immensely pleasing to Margaret.

"I don't think I'll fool with Faye Carmody." Jesse lit a cigarette, still smiling. "I believe I'm afraid of her yet."

Margaret breathed in smoke from his silvery exhalation. She wanted to quit, but so far had only managed to cut down. "Why do you suppose kids make calls like that?" Noting the time, she made a silent promise to wait ten minutes before lighting a cigarette of her own.

"Something to brag about at school, putting the sheriff on Old Lady Carmody." Jesse looked thoughtful and added, "And it means people are talking about Dave Brent. Kids get interested in whatever they hear from their folks."

"Rita's going to be at the funeral." Margaret looked away from Jesse's cigarette and sipped her coffee. "You don't think Patsy or Elmer will give her a hard time, do you?" It was odd, thinking of Ray Bailey's widow at the burial of the man who went to prison for shooting her bootlegger husband.

"They'll know she's not there to gloat." Jesse absently rubbed his chin, and Margaret wondered if he missed the beard he'd worn before he was sheriff.

"Rita wants to tell Patsy how certain she is Dave didn't kill Ray Bailey. I was glad to hear she wanted to go," Margaret confessed. "I hate being in a crowd by myself."

"I'll be there. And everyone likes you. You know that, don't you?"

"It's not a question of being liked." She was supposed to wait another seven minutes for her own cigarette, but reached for one anyway. "Those people have been in Hawkes County all their lives, most of them. They've got twenty or thirty or whatever number of years together to talk about. I don't have that with them."

Jesse took a deep breath. "I thought you liked Hawkes County."

Margaret would have to very careful not to provoke Jesse's tendency to leap to the defense of his county and its people from anything he perceived as outside criticism.

"I *do* like it. It's home now, and will always be home," she said. "But you'll be a pallbearer, and I thought it would be nice to sit with someone I knew well. I was glad when Rita said she planned to be there." Mashing the cigarette into an ashtray, Margaret told herself she had to wait a full hour for the next one.

Jesse lumbered from his chair with a dismissive grunt, stiff as a testy bear. "If you got out more often you might have something to talk about when you see people," he said as he walked off to the bathroom.

Margaret bit back an angry reply. She *wouldn't* snap back at Jesse. In a day or two, perhaps the emotional resonance from Dave Brent's funeral would begin to fade, and her husband would be his normal self again. She waited until he finished his shower before going to take one of her own.

When Margaret came to the bedroom, Jesse was at the closet, wearing his dark blue suit and a white shirt. He was touching his ties, running fingers over the dozen or so she'd bought for him. "Which one, do you think?"

She lifted a length of maroon silk. "This is nice."

Jesse snatched it off the rack and put it around his neck. "Sorry if I was out of line a little bit ago."

He made the knot too tight, as he always did. Margaret stepped closer and loosened the strip of cloth. "You'll feel better if you don't choke yourself."

"Is Rita coming here, are we picking her up, or what?"

"She'll meet us at the funeral home." Margaret inspected Jesse's image in the mirror. He looked nice in a suit, even when he insisted a coat and tie felt like a clown costume. "She wanted her own car in case anyone objected to her being at the service."

Margaret reached into the closet for a conservative black dress, trimmed in white lace. She hadn't worn it, or any other nice dress, since she stopped selling real estate. She'd been secretly looking forward to dressing up for a day, even for something as dreary and dreadful as a funeral.

Stepping into the dress Margaret turned so Jesse could zip it. She only needed a few minutes at the bathroom mirror for her makeup. A little blush, a daub of color on her lips and she was ready to go.

Jesse waited by the back door, and as they stepped off the porch, opened an umbrella for her. He held it directly above her head, not crowding under its sheltering canopy himself. "I hate rain for a funeral," he breathed. In the car Margaret put her left hand close to his, and after Jesse slipped the police cruiser in gear, he wrapped his fingers around hers.

Jesse braked briefly at the driveway's end, then turned onto the lane leading to the highway. Where the narrow road curved to the left Margaret glanced at a dozen or more red flags hanging limp in the downpour. Movement on the hill above the embryonic housing development caught her eye.

"Who'd be walking around up there?" She peered through the rain-spattered window. "I wouldn't think even Carl Edwards would try to work in this rain."

Jesse peered past her at the solitary figure above them. "Mark Turner," he declared. "Len's boy."

Water beaded on the glass, and the drizzling rain made it difficult to focus on detail, but it was obvious the boy looked directly at them, lifted his right arm and raised the middle finger in a rude salute.

"Why would he do that?" Margaret asked.

"I put Mark's daddy in prison," Jesse said. Len Turner had been involved in the marijuana distribution ring run by the previous sheriff and his brother. "And then my wife sold his family's farm away."

At the stop sign on the highway Jesse turned left, toward town, and Margaret was glad to put the image of Mark Turner's solitary stroll over what had been his family's property behind her. "I still feel bad about that deal with Carl Edwards."

"If you hadn't made it, some other agent would have. There was no way the Turners could hold onto so much land, not with Len in jail."

Margaret had been proud when Edwards Construction expressed interest in the property. It was her biggest commission in the two years she sold Hawkes County real estate, and she'd been flattered when Carl Edwards chose her as his agent, bypassing local people who'd been in the land business for years. Even so, she understood why Jesse couldn't share in her pride, could only mourn the loss of another Hawkes County farm.

Len Turner was barely holding onto his acreage before he began helping Bradley Smallwood with marijuana. And the flat land bordering the highway was perfect for houses. It wasn't easy to find level ground in Appalachian Hawkes County.

Margaret hadn't realized the construction site would look like a muddy scar on the land, or that Carl planned to build so many houses there. "I wish Len Turner hadn't been selling marijuana."

"He wasn't selling it, he only trucked it to Lexington and Cincinnati," Jesse corrected.

Margaret thought sadness and pain were innate to Hawkes County. When she first came to live there, Jesse told her stories of the county's history. If his tales were true, people there had always been desperate, forever teetering on the brink of poverty and failure.

It didn't seem right, that people living in such a lovely place existed on the edge of desperation.

CHAPTER TWELVE

Rita Bailey was waiting for Jesse and Margaret at the funeral home's front door. She explained she'd be leaving as soon as the service was over. "That's if the new widow doesn't run me off first," she said.

Inside, tier upon layered tier of roses, arrayed in the limited confines of Oswald and Son Mortuary Chapel, fogged the building with a sweet miasma so thick taking a deep breath made Jesse Surratt nauseous. He made a silent promise to himself that real soon he'd find time to set down on paper plans for his own funeral.

It wasn't important what happened to his body once he was through with it. But he could ensure it wouldn't lie in a room so full of roses their scent was sickening. It was one favor he could do for whoever had to dispose of his remains.

From the chapel's arched entry, when Jesse glanced at the coffin, only Dave Brent's hands were visible, folded across his middle. Jesse decided the note about his own funeral would say the box should be closed. The macabre things morticians did in hidden rooms never made defunct flesh look more lifelike than hard wax.

People spoke to them as Jesse and Margaret made their way toward the casket, greeting the Surratts warmly, ignoring Rita altogether or acknowledging her with puzzled nods. Jesse responded to the voices without thinking, murmuring phrases that sounded reedy and thin inside his head.

From a seat behind the casket, Reverend Wayne Stuckey leaned forward as Jesse led Margaret and Rita closer. The Smallwood brothers, and many of the other men who worked in their illicit drug operation had been members of Stuckey's Brushy Creek Old Regular Baptist Church. The minister's mourning face changed when he looked at Jesse, who sent so many of his flock to prison.

Jesse saw something nasty in the minister's heavy-lidded stare. Perhaps it was a perverse hope the new sheriff would embarrass himself at the coffin, fuel a tale of ridicule the reverend might carry back to Brushy Creek's narrow-minded congregation. Jesse stared back at the preacher, met his stare with an unflinching gaze he hoped was a bit intimidating.

Staring down the reverend gave Jesse a brief reprieve from seeing what was inside the flower-bedecked metal box, but the preacher's cold eyes soon shifted elsewhere. Tensing, Jesse looked down at the approximate image of what had been a good friend. He could find no rational reason for standing so close to something that sad and awful.

Dave Brent was thinner than when he'd gone to prison, and while there didn't seem to be any gray in his hair, the color was pale and washed out. His eyes were closed, but the mortician's pose in no way resembled a sleeping Dave Brent.

At the courthouse, three or four deputies usually ate sack lunches in the County Attorney's conference room, where Dave habitually dozed off, mouth open, snoring. Once someone kneaded a piece of sandwich bread into a tiny ball and tossed it at Dave Brent's open jaws. When he woke, they all swore a fly had flown between his teeth.

Retching and strangling at the bit of bread, Dave rushed to a men's room, and it was weeks before anyone admitted what really happened. He swore he'd never nap in the conference room again, though he did. And when he slept, Dave Brent looked nothing like the thing in the box.

Jesse felt a dull anger instead of grief. "That was a good man, goddamnit," he heard himself mutter. Wayne Stuckey's flush at the impious words was gratifying.

Margaret leaned against him, unshed tears glistening in her eyes. Jesse suspected the tears were not for Dave so much as for the dark place he wouldn't let Margaret near. He didn't know *how* to let her approach that part of himself, though it would have been lighter, if she shared it. He carried grief, anger and pain in a solitary way that was comfortable only in its familiarity.

Their years together in Norfolk had driven Jesse and Margaret to a series of marriage counselors, well meaning babblers who tried to check the rush toward dissolution of the marriage. But Jesse hadn't been able to do the things they—and Margaret—demanded.

He still couldn't.

Jesse wondered why the undertaker buttoned Dave's funeral shirt ridiculously high, and understood suddenly: under a carefully knotted tie and stiff white collar lay the awful mark where Enochs Porter sawed at Dave's neck with a homemade knife.

Sickened, Jesse turned away and found himself facing the front pew. Elmer Brent held the hand of a grandson seated between himself and Patsy, his other arm stretching across the shoulders of twelve-year-old Marnie. The little girl's pained grimace was the image of an angry Dave Brent. A light-weight wheelchair was folded and leaning against one end of the pew, and Elmer looked pale and weak. His eyes were strong though.

Elmer and Patsy stared over Jesse's shoulder, at Rita Bailey. Jesse searched for words that would ease their awkward encounter, but Rita stepped forward before he found them. "Mrs. Brent," she whispered. "I know your husband didn't shoot mine. I *know* it. None of this should have happened, and I'm sorry."

Patsy came off the pew as though it burned. If he could have moved more quickly, Jesse might have laid hands on Patsy to keep her anger off Rita. But there wasn't time to intervene, and he stood motionless and mute, expecting something awful, until Patsy put her arms around Rita Bailey and hugged the other widow.

When they parted, Patsy raised a frayed tissue to reddened eyes. "I don't reckon it was easy for you to come here and say what you did, but I'm pleased you done it."

Nineteen year old Robby Oswald, the "son" in Oswald and Son Mortuary pulled an astonished Jesse away from the women. "Pallbearers sit separate, Sheriff."

Robby ushered Jesse into a curtained area at the side of the chapel, where five other men who would carry Dave's coffin were seated in two rows. Three were deputies. Dave's brother Paul was another, and the fifth was a stranger.

He settled in with his deputies, facing stiffly forward until Paul whispered, "Sheriff?" Jesse turned as the youngest of Elmer Brent's children leaned toward him. "This's my sister Lynette's husband, Reuben Oldham." Jesse reached to shake hands and muttered a bland greeting. "Daddy told me to tell you he'd like to speak to you after this is all over," Paul added.

In his front pew, Elmer Brent craned his neck to look toward the pallbearers. He stared till Jesse nodded, then turned toward a spate of fresh racking sobs from his daughter-in-law.

"They let Daddy out of the hospital to come to the funeral," Paul whispered. "He had to promise to use a wheelchair, but he says he won't go back, even after this is over."

Buddy Upchurch, the balding deputy to Jesse's left, touched the sheriff's arm. "Jess, if that story's true about you meaning to find who killed Ray Bailey, I want to help." Buddy clenched his jaw tightly. "Me and Dave was good friends. If I can help clear his name, just tell me what to do."

Jesse nodded. "I appreciate the offer, Buddy. I'll be in touch when I need you." He felt like a liar, talking as though he actually had a plan of action.

Conversation buzz in the chapel faded as Reverend Stuckey moved to the small podium behind the casket. Jesse bowed his head with everyone else, as the clergyman prayed in a solemn, gravelly voice.

Instead of following the words to the long invocation, Jesse sat wishing he'd never run for sheriff of Hawkes County. And he should never have told anyone, least of all Elmer Brent, that it was possible to do anything about a cipher so old as the killing of Ray Bailey.

Jesse felt more anger at Dave Brent than anything else. If Dave had only told the truth when he was arrested, put a name on the bimbo who shared that seedy room in a hot-sheet motel, none of this would have happened. He'd be alive to hunt and fish with Buddy Upchurch, to comfort his children instead of leaving that job to an invalid father.

He'd still be Jesse's friend.

At a chorus of soft "Amens" Jesse raised his head. Reverend Stuckey sat down while four men, one cradling an electric guitar, came forward. The musician strummed a chord, made a small adjustment in his tuning, then nodded at the others.

The quartet from Brushy Creek Baptist Church launched themselves into the old hymn *Farther Along*, and Jesse Surratt found unexpected comfort in the music. Whatever solace religion offered had evaporated by the time Jesse Surratt was old enough to shave, but there was something pleasing in the old lyrics. It was much easier to dismiss Reverend Stuckey's convoluted theology than to deny the appeal of the hymn.

The bass singer seemed to find his vocal limit, crooning "Farther along we'll know all about it," but on the next line, "Farther along we'll understand why," slipped several notes even deeper on the scale. The singer smiled, as though the reach of his voice surprised him as much as anyone. He was enjoying working his voice, and there was a pleasure in witnessing his delight.

The quartet had a similar effect on the crowd. Heads nodded in time with guitar strums, and when tears came to some eyes, they didn't seem so gloomy as those invoked earlier by the solemn organ.

Jesse scanned the faces turned toward the music. Whatever happened in a community as small as Hawkes County brought the same people together again and again. Wayne Stuckey had been a member of the grand jury that indicted Dave Brent after Ray Bailey died. Somewhere in the chapel, at least a few members of the jury that convicted Dave mourned along with his family.

Dave Brent's mulish silence before and after his trial locked all of them into a dance no one wanted to perform, and they had come together to perform the last steps at Oswald and Son.

One person wouldn't be feeling the same frustrations. The one soul who benefited from Dave's conviction was the man who pointed a gun at Ray Bailey. There was a good chance the shooter was in the chapel. Jesse wished someone looked guilty enough to be picked out of the crowd, but he saw only sorrow in the pews around him.

The lone exception was Margaret, seated midway to the rear, next to Rita Bailey. Her brows arched in a bewildered frown, and a smile touched Jesse's lips as he watched his wife's reaction to the guitar and the quartet from Brushy Creek. Margaret had never seen an Appalachian funeral, or heard a guitar strummed in a room dedicated to death. She would see and hear stranger things than an electric guitar before Wayne Stuckey finished.

Their song complete, the quartet stepped aside, allowing the minister to replace them on the podium. Referencing the Gospel of Luke, Stuckey read the story of Lazarus—not the man raised from the dead, but the beggar denied crumbs from a rich man's table—before putting down his Bible. He gazed placidly at the mourners for a moment, then began to speak.

Anticipating the familiar rhythms, Jesse nearly smiled when Reverend Stuckey began speaking in the cadences of old-time Baptist preachers. Punctuating his speech with loud exhalations of breath, the old man shouted, "And so my poor mourners (unh!), you don't need to worry none about David Brent (unh!). David is safe (unh!) and he doesn't hurt (unh!), he's with the Lord (unh!) at a far richer table (unh!) than any man can set upon this mortal earth (unh!)."

Stuckey's depiction of the world as endless disappointment was interspersed with elaborate descriptions of a heaven where Dave Brent waited for those who mourned him. Stuckey became more animated when he described a hell into which everyone who didn't follow his stern God would be cast.

Jesse grinned openly at the Reverend, knowing if Stuckey was consulted about tossing souls to hell, the sheriff of Hawkes County would have a long way to fall. As the sermon went on and on a subtle restiveness came over the listeners, and few of them missed seeing Oswald Senior pointedly tapping his watch. Reluctantly, Stuckey waved the singers forward again, without the guitar this time.

Lining up behind their pastor, they began *Almost Persuaded*, an altar-call hymn. Stuckey urged unsaved sinners to make the occasion of Dave Brent's death a reminder of their own mortality. "Find Jesus now (unh!)," he beseeched. "Don't think (unh!) you can put Jesus off (unh!) the way you put off (unh!) visiting the sick and afflicted (unh!), or the call you don't make to a poor mother (unh!) until it's too late (unh!)."

Over Stuckey's shoulder the quartet could be heard: "Almost persuaded, come, come today." The harmony was tight and lovely, and Jesse felt a nostalgic pull toward a time it had seemed possible to believe.

"Almost persuaded, turn not away," the quartet pleaded. The Reverend's bellow for salvation forgotten, Jesse sat missing his youth, when even people like Wayne Stuckey seemed to know something.

The rhythm of the minister's speech sped up, a primitive counterpoint to measured phrasing from the gospel singers. Soon he was pacing behind the casket, his voice shifting from patient entreaty to harsh, adamant demand.

No one moved to take advantage of Stuckey's invitation to "bend your sinner's knee (unh!) to meet Jesus right here (unh!) and right now (unh!)." Jesse couldn't remember anyone ever coming forward at an Old Regular Baptist funeral. With some relief, he remembered the altar call came at the end of the service.

Leaning forward to see how Margaret was taking Stuckey's performance, Jesse almost laughed out loud, despite the anger and sadness simmering inside him. Her wide eyes were fixed on the minister, her mouth open in an expression of bemused wonder, her head oscillating an almost imperceptible shake, a nonverbal but eloquent expression of "I don't *believe* what I'm seeing . . . "

Stuckey hushed and took his seat, wiping his brow with a white handkerchief so bright it gleamed like salt crystals. The singers swung into *Amazing Grace*, while singly and in small groups, mourners left pews to file past Dave Brent's coffin a final time. Jesse hung back, hoping the box would be closed before the pallbearers were called to pick it up.

A hand settled lightly on his shoulder and when he turned Robby Oswald looked apologetic. "Phone call, Sheriff. Some man says it's important he talk to you."

Jesse followed Robby through the side door to an office off the main hall, where a light on a desk telephone blinked. He picked up the receiver and pressed the light. "This's Jesse Surratt."

"I won't ask for the magic number this time, Sheriff." It was a moment before Jesse recognized Harvey Gartland's voice. "I'm sorry to pull you away from your deputy's service," the warden said. "But I heard something I felt like I ought to pass along."

"What's that?" Jesse didn't mind leaving the chapel. By the time he hung up the telephone and got back there, the dreadful box would surely be closed.

"Nothing more than loose talk, probably. You never know though." Gartland cleared his throat. "I told you we had plenty of people pissed off, about Dave Brent turning in that crooked guard. One of my inmates claims three or four very mean people are saying somebody's going to pay for what Brent did."

A fit of coughing seized Harvey Gartland. "I don't reckon our local thugs will make a connection between Brent and anybody down your way. But I thought I'd let you know."

"I appreciate it." The warning was a weak rationale for a telephone call, for interrupting a funeral. "What else you got?"

"You don't miss much, do you?" Gartland sounded amused. "You remember we talked about someone named Linda Carroll?"

"The woman who visited Dave at LaGrange?"

"One and the same. About twenty minutes ago I found out we got a picture of her." The warden paused, but Jesse didn't speak. "Did you hear what I said, Sheriff?"

"A picture." There was an ashtray on the desk, a piece of pristine black onyx. Jesse lit a cigarette. "How'd you get a picture?"

"We kept a secret camera in the visitor's room for a while, to record the goings-on Brent told me about. Contraband changing hands, that sort of thing. It's not a good likeness. Shows mostly the back of her head." Gartland cleared his throat. "I can fax it if you want. You all got a fax machine down there?"

"Oh hell, Warden, since us ridge runners discovered shoes and paved roads, electricity and all sorts of civilization has come in." Jesse remembered Crow Markwell said he'd learn more visiting LaGrange Prison than with a phone call. "Look here. You hold onto that picture and I'll come and get it myself."

"I'll do it," Gartland said. "Anything else I can do for you?"

"Have you sent Dave's personal stuff home to his family yet?" The heavy tones of the organ resumed in the chapel, reminding Jesse of his morbid obligations.

"We were looking at getting them in the mail this afternoon."

"Hold on to them," Jesse said. "I'll drive up first thing tomorrow. Ought to be there before noon."

"Good enough." Gartland paused. "Sheriff, keep your eyes open the next few days. Like I said, I don't imagine threats made here could have anything to do with you or anybody else down there, but these are serious bad guys, and they're mightily pissed."

"Thanks for the call, Warden. I'll see you in the morning." Jesse hung up the phone, mashed his cigarette into the ashtray and walked back to the chapel.

He took his place with the other pallbearers, and together they lifted Dave's casket onto a wheeled apparatus. It rolled easily to a side door, where the open hearse waited outside. A cold, wet wind blew off the ridges, and Robby Oswald shivered as he followed them through the double doors.

"Rain at a funeral is an awful thing, Sheriff." Robby turned a crank that lowered the casket so it could slide into the car. He pointed to a Cadillac limousine. "You all will ride to the cemetery in that car yonder."

Then there was nothing to do but wait under an awning while mortuary employees transferred banks of flowers into a van parked behind the hearse. Oswald Senior moved around his parking lot, attaching magnetized flags to vehicles that would be going to the Brent family plot.

"Sheriff?" Helen Pruitt, the maid from the motel where Dave Brent spent his last night as a free man, stood at Jesse's elbow. "Can I talk to you?"

Jesse stepped away from the other pallbearers, far enough he and Helen could talk privately. "What is it?"

"Maybe nothing," she said, looking at the ground. "But remember when you asked about who was with Dave Brent in that motel room that night? And I told you about a odd perfume?"

Jesse nodded.

Helen took a deep breath. "I smelt it again, Sheriff, when we was going past the coffin. Just for a second but I'm sure I smelt it. That woman was in there."

Jesse stifled an impulse to fire questions at Helen Pruitt. She appeared scared enough. Snapping questions would only frighten her further. He almost touched the woman's arm, but held back. Putting a hand on Helen might make her even more nervous. "Could you tell who was wearing the perfume?"

The maid shook her head. "The smell was only there for a second, and they was so many people close I couldn't tell who had it on."

"You're sure it wasn't the flowers?"

Helen shook her head. "Before I come to see you, I went to ever' single bunch, and sniffed them good. None of them smelt anything near the same."

Jesse stood without moving. His idle fantasy the killer might attend the funeral had almost turned into a full fledged premonition. Having the bimbo there was almost as good. "Did you notice anything else?"

Helen shook her head, and Jesse saw an almost imperceptible shudder pass through her thin shoulders. "I was scared, Sheriff, knowing that woman was so close, someplace."

"Are you going to the cemetery, Helen?" Jesse wanted to send the maid through the crowd looking for the perfume again. He'd have her stand where every man and woman at the graveyard would have to pass close.

Helen shook her head. "I got to be to work in thirty minutes."

"Helen, I need your help," Jesse urged. "You know something important."

The woman only stared, fear bulging her eyes. "I couldn't do nothing like that, Sheriff, even if I didn't have to work. What if that woman tries to hurt *me?*"

"No one will hurt you," Jesse promised. "I'll stand right beside you."

Helen Pruitt looked into Jesse's eyes briefly, then hung her head low. "I ain't a'going to do it," she whispered.

Jesse sent the frightened woman to her car. He watched as she climbed into a battered Toyota, knowing he could have forced Helen to come with him to the graveyard. But when he promised she'd be safe Helen Pruitt's eyes reflected every lie any man ever told her. It looked as though she'd heard quite a few, and wasn't about to trust another one, not even the sheriff of Hawkes County. She'd be useless at the cemetery.

Jesse turned and walked slowly to the black vehicle reserved for the pallbearers. As he passed the wheelchair where Elmer Brent waited to be helped into another limousine, the old man reached from under a black umbrella and grabbed the sheriff's arm. "I heard what she said, Sheriff. You can use what Helen give you to clear my boy's name."

Jesse nodded absently, wishing things were so simple.

He would go through some motions, though they were empty ones. At the cemetery he'd circle the crowd, sniffing perfumes, without the faintest idea what it was he meant to find. And in the morning he'd go to LaGrange .

CHAPTER THIRTEEN

The ceremony at the cemetery lasted a miserable, interminable hour, and Lorena was sorry she'd decided at the last moment to come to the final part of the funeral. She was alone with her ache and hurt, even while standing elbow-to-elbow with others mourning her David. The presence of a chilled and damp crowd no more eased her pain than did the dripping trees under which they all stood to avoid the worst of the rain.

Cold seeped through her shoes even before everyone had left their cars. By the time they all huddled around the clay-streaked ditch that was the grave, Lorena was shivering. A chill breeze penetrated her clothing, and she felt as though the tears she wouldn't shed publicly might, if released, make ice trails on her cheeks.

Mossy nineteenth-century grave markers leaned precariously over low places in the ground, among more contemporary headstones and bowers of fading plastic Decoration Day bouquets. Lorena remembered sunny days with David, when they slipped to the cemetery to make love. Those days, the Brent burying ground was pleasant as any park. In chill rain it was only a depressing icy clearing in the woods.

The fat minister, in love with his own voice, must have felt the cold as keenly as anyone. He hurried through the graveside service, his closing prayer ten or twelve sentences instead of an endless entreaty like the one in the chapel. Even the gospel singers refrained from inflicting their horrible hymns on the funeral party.

Lorena had dreaded the cemetery, feared the sight of David's casket suspended over a dark hole hacked in hard rocky ground. If she was going to lose her composure, react in a way that would threaten her secrets, it seemed likely to happen at the cemetery.

Following the hearse from the mortuary, passing through Midland at a dismal pace, then trailing slowly up the steep, narrow lane to Brent plots on Caney Ridge gave Lorena time to think, a piece of time in which to gather strength. She had maintained a social mourner masquerade through enough harsh moments at Oswald and Son's to know her poise would survive the graveside rites.

In the overheated mortuary Lorena hadn't flinched from facing David's gray metal coffin amid a profusion of floral tributes, remained calm while loss mauled her heart. Seeing the stern marks prison put on her man, she felt like she was truly facing for the first time the high price fate exacted for secrets. Looking at his thin face outside the steel horror of LaGrange Prison for the first time in three years, too late to offer comfort, was as bad a moment as life could ever offer.

During visits to LaGrange, David smiled and worked hard to camouflage the impact of imprisonment. Lorena's perceptions during those minutes couldn't be trusted. A simple look in her direction made her feel as though her David's brown eyes pierced her soul.

The prison visiting room—always furnished with more bodies than chairs—was a hot riot of strangers' sweat and perfumes. David distracted her with discreet, forbidden touches until she stopped seeing or smelling or hearing LaGrange Prison and her imagination ran to fantasies of their life together after his release. Those were her memories of prison visits, David's bright eyes, laughter even in that savage place, and subtle caresses.

When she looked into the coffin Lorena couldn't deny the sweet touches and laughter were really dead. For the first time, she noticed how much weight David had lost, was mindful of his unnatural pallor. David was a pasty pale husk, a stranger to sunlight though he had loved the outdoors. The morticians had failed. Their makeup hid David's suffering no more effectively than oil could camouflage water.

Seeing the widow standing over David's children like a jealous she-bear was a bad moment. Lorena caught herself wondering if David would have left his family after all, if he could have abandoned the little girl whose face was a smaller, softer version of his own. For the first time, Lorena wasn't altogether confident he would have done so.

That frightened mouse of a motel maid, telling Jesse Surratt about the perfume, created the worst moment of all. To free her man, Lorena might have told the truth to the sheriff, to a jury, or anyone else who could send David home. But after leaving him in a wretched, cold piece of ground on Caney Ridge, she'd never do any such thing.

She hadn't hesitated about wearing the scent. David loved it, happily buried his face wherever she splashed it, tracking its flowery redolence over every inch of her body. It was a comfort, wearing it one last time, but for a frightening few minutes she was afraid it would be her undoing.

Within moments of the funeral party's arrival at the cemetery, every mourner knew what Helen Pruitt told the sheriff. Elmer Brent babbled to anyone who'd listen how Sheriff Surratt meant to look for "the *hoor* that let my Davey die in prison," and for a time it seemed possible he would find her. The sheriff had circled carefully, blankly unaware of how he was diverting attention from the final business at the grave.

It was bitter cold on Caney Ridge, a thin breeze making a numbing rain cold as melting ice. At the end Jesse Surratt looked terribly disappointed. Under her wool coat, Lorena shivered during the sheriff's search, and it wasn't only wind and rain that made her tremble.

When the mourners walked away from the grave, Lorena stood by her car for a moment and looked back. Only the preacher and Patsy remained close to the coffin, in what seemed the loneliest spot on earth. Lorena wondered what sort of marker the Brent family might put over their husband and father, her lover.

Driving home, she decided if an appropriate stone wasn't raised immediately, she'd buy one herself. Making arrangements so no one could trace them would entail risk, but Lorena would not allow David to lie in an unmarked grave, or be remembered with nothing more than a chalk-white Veteran's Administration stone.

When she arrived home Lorena gave money to the elderly neighbor who had stayed with her son. He was asleep, and when the sitter was gone, Lorena hurried across the wet lawn to her flowers. The double-paned walls of the greenhouse enclosed a spot of summer, whatever the climate beyond. It was the last place she could feel close to David. Lorena settled onto the old sofa, surrounded by earth and life, and in a while she felt sweat pooling between her breasts.

It was over. Following him to the cemetery meant her glorious connection with David Brent was forever severed. Her brain knew it.

Her body rejected the idea out of hand.

Some treacherous and libidinous part of her summoned an image of David Brent the night she surprised him with twenty-five candles scattered among her plants. Glass walls reflected and echoed the wavering flames into infinity, and David had been pleased as a child on a new playground when he discovered her gift. Lorena let him find her on the couch, a silk kimono spread open.

If the only real love of her life was truly over, why didn't her body know it?

Lorena sat for a long time, crying softly, wondering why her body wouldn't admit it was over.

CHAPTER FOURTEEN

Walking away from the graveside service, Margaret was glad Jesse had left the car's engine running. The cold drizzle touched her to the bone, and slipping into the warmth of the police cruiser was wonderful. Settling into the seat she wished they could go straight home, but they were more or less obligated to stop at the Brent house for a little while.

Jesse eased the car to the right, away from a boulder pressing out of the hillside. "Did you hear what Helen Pruitt told me? At the mortuary?"

"Elmer was talking about perfume and the whore who was wearing it. You were supposed to find her. Did you?" At the highway Margaret fastened her seat belt.

"I wasn't even sure what I was looking for. The Pruitt woman wasn't real specific." Jesse turned his head to look at her. "Did *you* notice anything unusual? An odd smell or anything like that?"

Margaret shook her head. "All I noticed was that awful preacher. A funeral is supposed to comfort people. Yelling at us to find Jesus before *we* wind up in a coffin ourselves didn't strike me as comforting."

A minute or two from Patsy Brent's house Jesse said, "I know this isn't fun for you, being a half-stranger to so many of these people. But I'm glad you're with me. I'm not sure how I could have done this if you weren't here."

Margaret reached for her husband's big hand and squeezed it. She knew Jesse needed her, depended on her, but it was a rare pleasure to hear him actually say so.

As they parked near a small frame house outside of town, couples and families were leaving other cars for the walk to the Brent house. The rain had stopped, and most of the men stayed outside to smoke and talk while their wives carried pots and platters heaped with food into the house. One of the men asked, "You coming back out, Sheriff?" and Jesse nodded.

Patsy Brent met Jesse and Margaret just inside the front door and led them to a bedroom. "You all can put your things in here." She gestured toward a bed heaped with damp coats.

Margaret slipped out of her overcoat, lay it across the others and turned to find Jesse staring out the window. Or rather *at* the window. "Why's this window only a foot off the floor?" he asked.

"Marnie wasn't but three years old when Davey built this house." Margaret strained to hear Patsy's whisper. "He put that window down low so she wouldn't hurt herself, climbing on chairs to see outside. He can't stand to see a child hurt. Any child."

Patsy trembled with fresh sobs and Margaret found herself holding the grieving woman. "He's so *good* to us, even when we don't do for him the way we should," the new widow wailed. "We don't even visit at the prison near as often as we ought to. Dave says we're to treat his time there like him being in the service was, a time when he's away is all he wants it to be."

Patsy's speaking of her dead husband in the present tense, as though he still breathed, was unnerving. Margaret glanced toward Jesse, who stood in the doorway.

"How often did you go to LaGrange?" he asked gently.

The widow lifted her hands, then dropped them back to her side. "Just holidays, and not even all of those. That prison is an awful place, Jesse. I'd of still gone every Saturday except Dave doesn't . . . " Patsy's voice faltered. " . . . Didn't want me to." She pulled away from Margaret and dug in a pocket for a fresh tissue.

"Did he have other visitors?" Jesse asked.

Patsy shook her head while blowing her nose into the tissue. "We're the only kin Dave has." She managed a wan smile. "You all go out and get something to eat. I'll be all right now."

"I spoke with the warden today," Jesse said. "He's going to hold Dave's personal things, instead of mailing them. I'm picking them up tomorrow."

Patsy nodded and edged toward the door. "I appreciate that. I know Dave would too."

"Do you have a list of what he had up there?" Jesse pressed. "So I'll know if I got everything?"

"They wouldn't let him have much." Patsy sighed as she led them through the doorway. "They give me a list of what we could send, mostly things Dave didn't care about. They said we could send books, but Dave wasn't much of a reader."

In the hallway Margaret let Patsy go on ahead, and pulled at Jesse's arm. "What are you up to?" she asked, keeping her voice low so no one else could hear. "It almost sounded as though you were going to start interrogating Patsy back there."

Jesse's eyebrows lifted. "Was I that obvious?"

"Maybe not." Margaret took his hand, lifted it to her cheek. "But something's going on. Will you tell me what it is, later?"

"I promise I will." Jesse squeezed her hand. "We won't be here long."

Margaret followed him to the kitchen and a table heaped with food. A smiling elderly woman handed out paper plates inside wicker holders, and Margaret wordlessly trailed after Jesse, accepting small portions of whatever was offered. He led her to the living room, where they sat together on a worn sofa.

Jesse ate like the farmer he still was at heart, quickly and efficiently, as though chores were waiting. In five minutes he cleared his plate, praising each mouthful, to the delight of an admiring audience. When an older woman—it was only women in the living room—urged the sheriff to get more, he declined with a smile and a satisfied pat of his belly. "I don't believe I could handle more than a cup of coffee."

One lady offered to fetch it for him, but Jesse got off the sofa and walked toward the kitchen, leaving Margaret alone. "Get you another plate, Mrs. Surratt," someone said. "Lord knows we got a'plenty."

In a minute or two Margaret followed after Jesse and found the kitchen empty. Peering through a window in the back door she saw him in the yard, surrounded by grinning men who were clearly pleased he had joined them. Someone she recognized as a deputy discreetly handed Jesse a pint bottle. Wishing she could go into the back yard for a drink, Margaret filled a Styrofoam cup with coffee and turned back to the living room.

Conversation in the circle of women centered on childbirth and raising babies. With nothing to contribute, Margaret sat mute and miserable. The only person she recognized was Martha Compton, but the dispatcher was across the room with another group, and only smiled at her. Margaret was glad when Jesse came back and apologized for the fact he and his wife had to leave.

Patsy went with them to the bedroom, thanked Jesse again as they put their coats on. "I think Dave would have liked how we buried him. All his friends came, and he would have liked it, don't you think?" Patsy didn't cry, her grief depleted for the moment. It would refill, Margaret knew, over and over.

Jesse reminded her he'd be bringing Dave's personal things from the prison the next day, and then they were drifting toward the front door. Outside Jesse took Margaret's arm as they walked toward his car. "I'm glad that's over with."

"Getting Dave's things isn't the only reason you're going to the prison, is it?" Jesse opened her car door and once she was seated, closed it without answering.

Sliding behind the wheel he told her, "Patsy says the family didn't visit Dave at prison. But somebody—the warden says it was a woman—came up there pretty frequently."

"Do you know who it was?"

Jesse shook his head. "I've got a name, Linda Carroll. Does it sound familiar to you?"

The syllables were blank sound to Margaret. "I can't remember hearing anyone around here called that."

"Me neither. The warden found a picture of her though. That's one reason for going to LaGrange, to look at it. If I go through Dave's things, maybe I'll find something useful." Jesse sighed. "I think whoever killed Ray Bailey is still walking around Hawkes County. That misery in Patsy's house is happening because the wrong man went to prison."

"But that's what Dave wanted to happen."

"I don't care." Jesse set his jaw stubbornly. "Just because the county got a conviction, all of us, including me, forgot somebody got away with murder."

Late afternoon sun broke through the clouds, making wet pavement bright as molten metal. Jesse flipped his visor down and Margaret rummaged in her purse for sunglasses. "But you don't have any idea who this woman at the prison was?"

"No, but she's got money. A lot of cash went into Dave's personal account while he was there." Jesse steered around a pothole and hoped he'd remember to call someone on the county road crew about it. "I think she was with Dave the night Ray was killed."

"Why don't you take pictures of women with police records to the warden? Compare them to what he shows you?"

"That's a good idea." Jesse reached to squeeze her hand. "If I get a name, it's just a matter of twisting her a little bit for information." Jesse slowed the car, approaching their turn off the highway. "This could be easier than I thought. Your idea about the pictures might . . . "

Glass exploded in the back seat as the crack of a rifle reverberated off the hills. Jesse straightened the steering wheel, pressed the accelerator hard and the county car seemed to fly. He turned to look back, scanning the ridges.

Margaret noticed their drift off the road, but there was no time to shout a warning. The car went off the pavement, crossed the narrow shoulder and dropped into a ditch. Less than a hundred yards from where the bullet smashed into the back seat, they stopped.

Looking over her shoulder, Margaret saw both the rear windows were gone. A small piece of glass had lodged in the collar of her dress, scraping her skin every time she moved. She raised her hand to remove it but Jesse pushed her down and shouted, "Stay on the floor!"

Margaret huddled under the dashboard, and over her head Jesse reached into the glove compartment to retrieve his pistol. "Are you hurt?" he demanded.

"I'm okay," Margaret said. "But it's awfully crowded down here. Can you move the seat?"

Jesse reached for the adjustment lever and the seat lurched backward. It was more comfortable, but if someone was coming for her, or for Jesse, Margaret needed to *see*. She tried to raise herself but Jesse pushed her down with one hand and grabbed for the police radio with the other.

Margaret listened as Jesse demanded another car be sent to assist them, but her mind was full of the need to get off the floor and *see*. "Let me up," she pleaded when Jesse hung the microphone on the dashboard.

He shook his head. "They might shoot again." In the distance a siren wailed, a banshee shriek echoing off the ridge. "When I spoke to the LaGrange warden he warned me something like this could happen."

"Why didn't you say anything to me about it?" Margaret felt her face flush with anger. If someone was going to shoot at them, Jesse ought to have told.

He avoided looking at her eyes. "I didn't think there was anything to it. And I didn't think it would have anything to do with me—with us."

While Jesse kept watch to the rear, Margaret managed to slip onto the seat next to him, evading the hand reaching to keep her on the floor. She let her gaze drift over the hillsides and considered the fact that someone had fired a gun at them from up there. She wondered how long it would take for her to accept the fact someone actually *shot* at her.

Other cars had stopped, and their drivers were beginning to cluster together in the road. A young man reached the cruiser, knocked on the window and asked how badly they were hurt. "I can't have people standing around like this," Jesse said, touching her face lightly with his fingertips. "Will you stay in the car?"

He was close to pleading, and Margaret nodded agreement. The siren was much closer, and before long another county car skewed to a stop in the middle of the road, red and blue lights flashing. After Larry Daniels got out Jesse left Margaret, and went to stand with his deputy. She was relieved to see Jesse kept Larry's car between himself and the hill from which the shot had come.

"We got to get these people out of here," she heard her husband shout. Daniels began directing traffic, ordering those who had stopped to proceed on.

Jesse came back to Margaret and put his head in the open window. "Why don't you take Larry's car and go home? I'm going to be here a while."

Margaret wasn't going anywhere without Jesse, and told him so.

"Be reasonable, Margaret," he argued. "We've got to get a search started on that hill. There's nothing for you to do here."

Margaret took a deep breath, and her racing heartbeat seemed to slow a fraction. Jesse's eyes were wide with worry and adrenalin-laced excitement, and she knew she didn't need to make things more difficult for him.

Jesse conferred with Daniels, then returned to the squad car. "I'll drive you home. I need to call Gartland at LaGrange anyway. We'll take Larry's car and he can get a wrecker out for this one."

Margaret didn't mean to cringe as she left the safety of one police cruiser for the cover of another, but couldn't help ducking as she scurried across the highway. Some part of her insisted another round was already on its way from the unseen gun. When she reached Larry Daniels' unscathed car, Margaret slumped in the seat and wished Jesse would do the same.

He drove to the farm, and while he made his telephone call to the LaGrange Warden, she busied herself with the coffee maker. Staring out the window, she saw Sam the mule waiting expectantly by the barn gate. It was 5:30, the hour Jesse arrived home from work. He always carried apples to the ungrateful animal who would, given opportunity, kick or bite the man who fed him.

Sam was a mean brute, but he looked pitiful, waiting for the treats he wasn't going to get. Turning from the window, Margaret banished the mule from her thoughts.

Jesse strode into the kitchen and wrapped his arms around her from behind. "Gartland's running a check to see if anyone's missing who might've come down here to shoot at me." Margaret felt breath on her neck and wished Jesse would never leave her alone again. "This is crazy. Dave got killed because he snitched on crooked guards. That doesn't have anything to do with me. With us."

"What are you going to do now?" Margaret leaned into her husband's body, yearned to burrow inside his warmth and not come out until she felt safe again.

"I need to help with that search." Jesse rocked her in his arms. "They're sending city policemen and all the deputies out. The state police post is sending some of their people too."

"You'll be careful?" Margaret clenched her eyes shut, trying to blank out mind-pictures of Jesse being hurt, the same way she closed the begging mule from her thoughts. The thought of Jesse hurt was harder to make go away than ignoring Sam.

She felt his nod, his chin brushing her hair. "I don't think we're going to find anything. Whoever shot at us is long gone. He's not sitting up there waiting for us to find him."

"Or *she's* not," Margaret corrected. "If your mystery woman doesn't want to be found, couldn't she have done it?"

"It's possible." Jesse hugged her tighter. His right arm eased away, and when it encircled her again the hand held a pistol. "I'll leave the .38 for you." When Margaret didn't touch the weapon Jesse laid it on the counter.

"If you need anything, call the office. There'll be dozens of cops up the road. The dispatcher can have someone here in less than a minute."

He hugged her tighter before stepping backward. Jesse didn't put on his uniform before leaving, but Margaret noticed he strapped the holstered magnum pistol he wore as part of his uniform around his waist.

After Jesse backed the police vehicle out of sight, Margaret looked at Sam again. Standing in a damp chill, the sun having gone behind clouds again, the mule had no way of knowing everyone's routine was altered. She took three apples from the refrigerator and picked up the .38. The pistol a cold, alien weight in her hand, Margaret walked to the back door and stepped onto the porch. And stopped.

She couldn't force her feet to leave the safety of the house, couldn't make herself take that first step onto the grass. Shadows on the hills were lengthening, and anything might be hidden in the mottled forest.

Sam brayed an angry complaint, but Margaret couldn't move. When she went back in the house she turned the television up loud so she couldn't hear the mule. She stared at an inane comedy, waiting for her husband to come home, the pistol still in her hand.

CHAPTER FIFTEEN

"Sons a bitches." He spoke in a whisper, but where the only other sound was the rustle of a small breeze in the pines behind his perch on the hillside, even a whisper seemed loud.

Crouched behind a cedar tree, he looked down at the sloping field below, where there were already more cops than he'd ever seen in once place. More police cruisers arrived as he watched. He grinned down at them. At the rate they were going, in a couple hours every squad car in Kentucky would be parked along U.S. 60.

For a long time no one moved closer to the ridge than the open meadow bordering the highway. After a while the sheriff came back, without his old lady this time. It was obvious Surratt would be in charge of the search, and he looked anxious to get started.

Policemen crowded around Surratt like an oversized football huddle. The shooter was much too far away to hear words, but everybody at the foot of the hill seemed to think what their sheriff had to say was important. Surratt could talk all day if he wanted. He and his police helpers weren't going to catch anybody.

They probably thought he was trapped, cornered on high ground. Twenty or thirty yards behind his hiding place, the hill became sheer vertical cliff. From below they'd think there was no way to retreat or escape. It'd be funny, when they got around to searching and didn't find a damn thing except blackberry briars and rocks.

He resisted an urge to put another round into a police car, maybe take out a set of blue and red lights. The day had gone back to overcast and gloomy though, and the Winchester's muzzle blast would give him away, show the cops exactly where their quarry sat watching. The lawmen all carried magnums or nine millimeter pistols. If they fired toward the rifle's flash one of them might get lucky.

Whenever he decided to go, escaping would be a piece of cake. The shooter wasn't in a hurry to leave though. The show below him was funny as any movie, and the shooter could watch for a long time, until his pursuers were practically tripping over him.

Surratt arranged his forces into a straight line extending across the open field. When the cops began moving, they looked like men hunting rabbits, studying the ground around them as though expecting to find what they were looking for in waist-high weeds near the road.

It would have been great if there were some surprises for them to find, maybe a trip wire tied to a few shotgun shells. No one would get hurt, at least not seriously. And it would be a hoot, watching cops scatter as half a dozen rounds of twenty gauge birdshot went off around them.

He saw it happening in his mind, and couldn't help snickering at the picture of three or four dozen cops pissing all over themselves to get out of the way. It was a long time before he managed to stay quiet again.

The line of bodies stretched as the cops drifted further apart. They meant to climb the face of the hill without leaving any part of it unexamined. The dumb asses actually thought they were going to catch him. The shooter couldn't help himself. He started laughing again.

Glancing to the right, he took a reassuring peek at the hole in the mountain, wide enough he could worm his shoulders through, so narrow it was unlikely anyone who didn't know the hole was there would ever find it. A few feet beyond the opening a meandering low tunnel passed through the mountain, with an exit on the opposite side. It was a ventilation shaft, from one of the small coal mines that once pockmarked Hawkes County.

The shooter turned his attention back to the policemen. He ought to have spread kerosene in the weeds, forced them to walk through a curtain of fire to find him. There was probably a way to make a fire starter out of a battery and a few grains of black powder.

Half a dozen other ideas flitted through his mind. If he'd taken time to plan things, the deputies and state troopers would have paid for every step up the hill. The idea of putting a .30-30 round through Jesse Surratt's car had come to him late in the afternoon though.

There wasn't time to do more than find the right place on the hill and wait.

The cops were coming up the slope too quickly to suit him. "The hell with it," he whispered. Turning, he shoved the Winchester's muzzle into the ventilation shaft's entrance, thumbed the hammer back and pulled the trigger. His body hid the flash of light, and the crack of the rifle was muffled. Spinning around again, he wondered where all the policemen had gone.

Fully half a minute passed before the sheriff's head lifted above a patch of weeds and briars. Then more cops were peeking from where they'd dropped at the sound of another shot, a few rising warily to their feet. "Anybody hurt?" The sheriff's voice carried easily in the mountain dusk, sounding so close it startled the shooter. "Somebody get a head count."

"Who *was* that?" someone else called out. "Did one of *us* shoot or was it on the hill?"

"Where'd it come from?" another voice demanded. "Any y'all see where it come from?"

It took the better part of twenty minutes for the cops to satisfy themselves the shot wasn't from any of their guns. Then they started climbing again, though some didn't look any too happy about being there. This time they moved much more slowly, and some kept pistols in their hands, pointing up hill.

When the police lines moved another thirty yards, and reached the really steep part of the grade, the shooter thought about firing again, but didn't take the risk. "Should've made some of them kerosene bombs, though," he told himself.

Twenty minutes later, a full hour before anyone was likely to walk within fifty yards of his hiding place, the shooter slipped feet-first into his hole like a rabbit, pulling a heavy flat stone over the shaft's entrance. He didn't turn on his flashlight until he was deep inside the familiar passage.

CHAPTER SIXTEEN

Forty-two policemen from various jurisdictions in or adjacent to Hawkes County searched for the sniper until three in the morning. They were like blind men hunting black cats in the dark, and no one argued when Jesse Surratt told them it was time to go home.

Once he reached his house, Jesse collapsed into sleep until he climbed stiff and scratchy-eyed from his bed at 6:30. Margaret hadn't set the timer on the coffee pot. Once the thing was loaded and bubbling, Jesse looked out the window at a misty Appalachian dawn, events of the previous evening playing through his mind like a bad movie with a disappointing end.

They'd doggedly scoured the hill from its base to the cliffs at the top, without finding so much as a spent cartridge. After a fifteen-minute break in the midnight chill, the lawmen came down even slower than they'd climbed, flashlights guiding their descent. Exhausted and frustrated, they reached the highway with nothing to show for their efforts.

Before they disbanded, there was disagreement about whether a shot was actually fired from the hill or had come from some other place. Albert Fitch, an aging deputy from Mather County who joined the search after hearing about it on his police radio, ended the arguments.

"I ain't got but one thing to say, boys," he muttered before he got into his car for his long drive home. "I been shot at before. I wasn't here for the first round, but I guaran-damn-tee you, that second time, the gun was on this hill someplace."

The aroma of perking coffee pulled Jesse from his staring stupor. Chilled, he went to the stove room and found the fire reduced to a bed of glowing coals. Stacking wood on the embers, he watched flames grow under the seasoned oak. While the last of the coffee dripped into the pot, he filled Casey's bowl with dry food. The dog eased stiffly from under the table, sniffed at the bowl and whined disappointment.

Jesse inspected the refrigerator, found a package of sliced ham and took three pieces to the table with his coffee. "Maybe this weekend we'll go up in the woods," he told Casey. "Just you and me, the way we used to." He tossed a piece of ham over her head, and the shepherd snapped it neatly out of the air. "While I cut wood you can make some rabbits live hard."

Casey sat on her haunches, tail whisking the floor, catching pieces of ham until Jesse's hands were empty. Then she curled back into sleep under the table. Jesse refilled his coffee cup and switched on the portable radio by the toaster. At seven o'clock, a Midland station carried local news.

An announcer described the night's excitement as "random shots fired by unknown persons." Jesse didn't think they were random. He was sure some connection existed between the LaGrange warden's warning to be careful in Hawkes County, and shots fired two hours later.

Taking his coffee to the living room, Jesse tapped his office number into the telephone. "I need you to hunt up some mug shots I can take to LaGrange," he told Martha Compton.

"Which ones?"

Jesse answered her question with one of his own. "How many women have we arrested in Hawkes County? Since I've been sheriff, say."

Martha thought a while before answering, "Sixty. Maybe seventy. 'Course, I'm counting drunk drivers in that, and bad checks and lots of little things."

"Can you pull their records in an hour?"

"I'll try." Martha laughed. "When a judge's cousin or a county councilman's fishing buddy's sister gets booked, her likeness has a way of disappearing from them files."

"Do the best you can." Jesse checked his watch. "I'll see you in about an hour."

"This have anything to do with what happened last night?" In the background there was a burst of noise from Martha's radio. "Hold on," she said. "Let me take care of that."

While he waited Jesse Surratt gave silent thanks Martha Compton was on his staff. She'd worked at the courthouse for thirty years, could find in minutes items no one else would locate in a week.

"Well? Does it have anything to do with that shooting?" Martha asked again when she came back on the line.

"Maybe." Jesse explained his plan to show the photographs to the LaGrange warden, see if together they could identify the woman who was such a frequent visitor to Dave Brent. "If that woman didn't have a rifle out last night, she might know who did."

"Pictures'll be ready when you get here." The old woman paused. "I wrote a statement about what happened last night and signed your name. The paper sent a kid over for a copy."

Jesse grinned. His dispatcher was an excellent forger. It would take handwriting analysis to determine it wasn't his signature on the press release he hadn't yet seen.

After another burst of static in the background Martha said hurriedly, "Are we done, Sheriff? Buddy Upchurch's got a speeder pulled over and needs me to check on a license number."

"It'll do for now," Jesse acknowledged.

Hanging up the phone, he sat quietly until a tremor in the hand holding his cup threatened to spill coffee when he lifted it. Without Martha's distracting banter he couldn't ignore the emotional storm raging inside himself.

After he retired from the Navy, the farm was the only place on earth where Jesse Surratt felt safe. A few years later, when the corruption of the Smallwoods invaded his world, suddenly no part of it was secure. Now a different kind of craziness was much too close. In the corner of his soul where unvarnished honesty resided, Jesse Surratt wasn't sure he could stand another such siege.

He was angry, and he was frightened.

He'd been secretly relieved no one found the sniper. If he'd come face-to-face with someone who committed the mortal sin of endangering Margaret, Jesse might have lost his composure altogether. Her involvement with the Smallwood violence had been marginal; it was easy to convince her such things only happened once in a lifetime.

Jesse's fear that Margaret's return to his life would prove to be temporary could have serious implications for the sniper. If his rifle bullets ran Margaret off, God help the poor soul when the sheriff of Hawkes County found him.

Margaret stumbled into the living room, eyes red, as though her few hours' sleep hadn't been at all restful. When Jesse stood up she pressed into his arms, and he pulled the slim body tight against his own. His nose nestled in soft, scented hair, he wished had something comforting to tell her. "Sit down. I'll bring you some coffee," was the best he could do.

"I heard you saying to Martha you're going out of town."

Jesse nodded. "I'm sure last night was connected to Dave Brent somehow. Harvey Gartland might point me to the person who shot at us."

He paused for a moment. "I've got that picture of Dave's woman visitor to look at, and my own pictures to show the warden." Jesse pushed gently at Margaret's shoulders until he could see her face. "Why don't you go with me?"

When sheriff's business took him out of town, sometimes Margaret rode along, waiting at a movie theater or shopping mall until he was finished. "I don't think so," she said. "But I don't want to be by myself either. Maybe I'll call Rita, see if she'll come over."

"I'll have patrol cars check the house every hour or so," Jesse told her. "There'll be men on that hill again, probably all day long. You can get a dozen cops here, if you need them."

Margaret settled onto the sofa. "You promised me a cup of coffee."

Jesse fetched her a cup, and when his wife didn't seem inclined to talk further, went off to take a shower. When he came out Margaret's mood had changed. She was on the phone, laughing with Rita Bailey about waking her so early. "Then I'll see you after Bobby's had his breakfast?" She laughed again. "Right. No more daiquiris."

"Maybe I ought to stay home," Jesse blurted when she put down the phone.

"I thought you said this trip was important."

Jesse shrugged. "I could put it off."

"You're feeling guilty, aren't you?" Margaret carried her newly emptied cup to the kitchen. "You think you should have protected me from that sniper."

"I don't feel guilty," Jesse said, following her.

"You feel *something*," she insisted. "Even if you won't admit it, you've worked yourself into thinking last night was your fault."

"Bullshit."

Margaret put a drawl in her voice, her west coast notion of a southern belle's breathy whisper. "Oh do talk more po'try for me," she simpered, then her gentle eyes took on an ominous darkness. "Just leave that gun where I can find it."

While Jesse put on his dress uniform Margaret came to the bedroom door and tolerated his lecture about staying indoors. "I should be home before dark," he finished. "If I'm not, pull the drapes and stay away from lighted windows."

He carried his coffee cup to the kitchen sink, and Margaret followed. He stood behind her, Margaret leaning into his chest and belly. Despite decades of familiarity with her body, Jesse could feel a response where Margaret's bottom pressed against him.

Lifting his hands, he laced his fingers below the swell of her breasts. He wanted his wife to know he would protect her, that she was the most important piece of his world. But the words stayed in his throat, died without being spoken.

They stood quietly until Rita's van pulled into the driveway. Jesse put the .38 on top of the refrigerator, out of Bobby Stillwell's reach. "I'll be back quick as I can."

A pleased grin split Bobby's face when he spied the sheriff coming out the back door, and Jesse was sorry to be leaving so abruptly. "See you when I get back, sport," he said, ruffling Bobby's cropped hair.

"You're not going to work, are you?" Rita's words were freighted with disapproval. "Not after last night."

"I'll be back soon." Jesse wasn't anxious to hear what Rita Bailey would say if she knew he was going further than his courthouse office. Even Bobby's innocent face was reproachful as Jesse got into the replacement cruiser Martha'd had one of the night duty deputies bring to the house. A note taped to the steering wheel said damage to Jesse's personal car was superficial, and he could pick it up from the county garage in three days.

Martha was alone in the office. It was too early for complaining citizens and the 7:00 a.m. shift change of deputies was accomplished fact. The morning crew had already commenced patrolling.

Martha was talking on her radio and at the same time tapping a query into a terminal connected to a State Police data bank. She winked at Jesse as he took a cup of coffee to his desk without interrupting her. Settling into the creaking oak chair he scanned the messages stacked neatly in the center of his desk.

The only one important enough to return right away was Teddy Sparks' request for information on the hillside sniper. Teddy published Hawkes County's twice-weekly paper, the Midland Trail. He'd been supportive of Jesse in the past, though not so overtly as to upset any of the sheriff's potential rivals.

"Everybody talks to *me*," Teddy was fond of boasting. "If there's a man in Hawkes County I don't like, he doesn't know it." Despite a personal distaste for politics and the people who played that game, Jesse had an abiding fondness for the fat little newspaperman. He was a survivor.

"What do you know that you haven't told everybody else?" Teddy barked after Jesse got past the Trail's switchboard. "I already have Martha's press release, so don't bother reading that empty old thing to me."

"Don't have a thing, Teddy," Jesse admitted. "We didn't find anything last night. There'll be another search this morning. Maybe something'll turn up then."

"Any connection between that sniper and Dave Brent? Everybody's saying you're investigating the Bailey killing again." The newspaperman was silent for a few beats, but when Jesse didn't say anything, said, "Seems funny that right after you start nosing around somebody shoots at your car."

"I don't know if there's a connection or not." Jesse lit a cigarette and weighed how much he wanted to give Teddy Sparks. "I think there might be one," he admitted after a moment, and told the editor about the call from the LaGrange warden. "But I'd appreciate it if you didn't print that. Not yet anyway."

"The regular arrangement?"

"I won't talk to anyone else about it until you got the whole story," Jesse conceded.

"Okay, Sheriff," Teddy agreed. "By the way, when are you going to announce for re-election?"

"Filing deadline's a ways off," Jesse parried. He didn't want to talk about November yet. "I don't reckon I have to decide today."

"Some folks are pushing Blaine Ingraham to run."

Jesse sighed into the phone. "So I hear."

"I'd hate to see Blaine in your chair," the editor said. "And I don't think there's anybody else who could beat him."

"That's not like you, to be so plain spoken."

Teddy laughed. "Sometimes neutrality is so much bullshit, Sheriff," he said. "Blaine Ingraham's only a few degrees less shady than the Smallwoods. I'd hate to see the county take a step backwards by electing that fraud."

"I haven't made up my mind." Jesse stood up and carried the cordless phone to the window overlooking the courthouse yard. "I'll talk to you about it, once I know which way I'm going to go."

"Fair enough," Teddy said. "And good luck with the other thing. Most of us tried to forget Dave Brent was covering up for somebody. Be a shame if there was a killer still running loose in Hawkes County."

Wishing his reinvestigation of the Brent case wasn't common knowledge, Jesse turned off the phone and continued to stare out the window. Such a thing couldn't be kept secret for long in Hawkes County, but if he failed to turn over anything new, he was going to look awfully foolish.

Just in time to ask people to vote for him again.

"Here's them pictures," Martha said behind him. "I guessed low on the number. I found eighty-two women's photos in the files."

Jesse took the heavy envelope, hoping there was an image in it that Warden Gartland would recognize. At the door to his office he paused. "Have someone check on my house every now and then, will you?"

"I already got people doing that, Sheriff," Martha said. "You go on now, and get back home soon as you can."

Nodding obediently, he carried the envelope of photographs to his car.

CHAPTER SEVENTEEN

Harvey Gartland lit his sixth cigar of the day, ignoring, for the most part, the cacophony of droning voices in his office. The monthly meeting of his "security supervisors" had so far been fifty minutes of complaints about legislators who'd limited pay raises for any state employee to five percent.

"Hush," Harvey told a nearly illiterate ex-Marine named Hennessy. "Why don't you all aim your bitching at Frankfort politicians instead of unloading it on me?" Harvey toyed with his cigar. The ash grew in the silence, until the warden tapped it gently against his crystal ashtray.

Hennessy—nicknamed "Bull"—spoke at last. "Tell us what you want to talk about, Harvey."

"How 'bout the fact one of your subordinates was arrested last week, for taking bribes from inmates?" Gartland laced his hands behind his head and leaned back in his leather chair. "They got a good case against Clyde too. Took some interesting pictures in the visiting room."

The mentioning of Clyde Tolliver produced a tympani of shuffling feet. The five supervisors in attendance looked at the floor, at their hands, anywhere but into the hard, confident eyes of Harvey Gartland. "This morning I'd really like to know where Clyde is right now. And where he was last night."

"He's in jail." Hennessy seemed to be the only person in the room with enough courage to talk to Harvey.

"You sure?" Gartland puffed on his cigar, wreathing his head with tobacco reek. "You *certain* he's in jail, Bull? 'Cause if I do some checking and find out Clyde made bail and nobody told *me* about it . . . "

Bull nodded curtly, and a junior supervisor hurried from the room. One light on Gartland's telephone console illuminated immediately. In less than two minutes the light went out, and the man came back, grinning. "Clyde's still locked up."

Gartland nodded. "Now that we got that straight, somebody oughta find out if any of Clyde's buddies were out of town last night."

"Out of town where?" Bull asked sullenly.

"Somebody took a shot at the sheriff down at Hawkes County." Harvey looked around the table again. "Anybody hear about it, anything that wasn't in the paper?"

Nobody said anything, and Gartland decided he'd enjoyed as much staff meeting as he could stand. He waved his subordinates out of the room with a flick of his cigar. The last man out closed the door softly and Harvey was alone in the office he couldn't wait to give up. He grinned at his retirement calendar, amused at how easy it was to intimidate the thugs who worked for him.

Harvey believed an honest man could always intimidate a corrupt one. He couldn't fire prison employees, not when they were protected by civil service laws, but he could make any guard's life difficult. The warden controlled schedules, and three months of night duty with hard-eyed wretches in the special punishment block still called "the hole" was not taken lightly.

Harvey snapped open his briefcase and took out a handful of brochures collected by his wife Frieda, glossy flyers claiming no place on earth was better suited for retirement living than some Sunbelt Mecca or other. Frieda wanted to move where snow was uncommon as a mustache on a rooster.

Unfolding one of the things, Harvey liked what he read about Yuma, until he learned the old Territorial Prison at the edge of town was a museum. There was no way he'd consent to living in a town that memorialized a jail. He tossed the flyer into the wastebasket as the door opened and his secretary announced Jesse Surratt's arrival.

The warden stood up and reached to shake hands without moving around his enormous desk. "Have a seat, Sheriff."

Surratt settled into a chair. "I appreciate your taking the time to see me."

"Wasn't doing much anyway," Harvey said. "Just listening to my people bitch about their pay. I can give you at least as much time as they took."

The sheriff dropped a large brown envelope on Harvey's desk. "I'd like you to take a look at a few pictures for me."

"You catch the man who shot at you?"

"You know about that?"

The sheriff's surprise pleased Harvey, and he considered hinting at a personal source of information in Hawkes County before confessing, "Was a little piece about it in the Louisville paper this morning." The warden leaned back in his chair. "Didn't say a whole lot, just somebody fired a rifle at your car."

"That's about all that happened. Except my wife was in it at the time."

"Paper didn't get that part about your wife." A cold edge in the sheriff's voice convinced Harvey he wouldn't envy this shooter, when Jesse Surratt caught him. "Nobody hurt though, right?"

"Just a few scratches from flying glass."

"Clyde Tolliver didn't have anything to do with it. He's the guard Dave Brent helped me bust, and he's in jail. I'll know soon enough if any of his buddies slipped out of town yesterday." Harvey's cigar had gone out, and the warden struck a wooden match before adding, "I don't see much in the way of a connection though."

"Me neither." The sheriff shook his head. "More likely it has something do with the killing that sent Dave Brent to prison in the first place. You had an innocent man in here, warden."

Harvey nodded. "Everybody doing time is innocent, to hear these boys tell it."

"Dave had an alibi, a good one. But he wouldn't use it. He was protecting somebody." The sheriff glanced down at the floor. "When the killing happened, he was with a woman, in one of those no-tell motels that doesn't get much family trade."

"And you're trying to find out who she was?"

"Maybe she's the woman who used to visit him, Linda Carroll." Surratt squirmed a bit in an upholstered chair that looked comfortable but was actually a miserable perch. Harvey'd bought a pair of them on purpose. He wasn't particularly interested in letting anyone get too comfortable in his office. "On the phone, you said you found a picture?"

Harvey nodded and reached into a desk drawer for a grainy black and white photograph discovered while preparing Clyde Tolliver's prosecution. "I had it blown up, thought it'd make her easier to recognize." Harvey pushed the five-by-seven enlargement across the desk.

Jesse Surratt picked it up, studied it carefully. Watching his eyes, Gartland saw no flicker of recognition. "Know her?" the warden prodded when a full minute had gone by.

The sheriff shook his head. "Like you said, it's hard to tell much about her. All you can see is the back of her head, and she's out of focus."

"We weren't trying for her. The idea was to take a picture of something else." Surratt put the photograph back on the desk, and Harvey leaned to point with his finger. "That's Clyde Tolliver, in the uniform, just beyond where she's sitting. He's passing a quarter ounce of marijuana to an inmate named Osgood Lewis."

"And that's what you wanted a picture of?"

Harvey nodded. "Brent told me Tolliver was slipping other things inside the walls too. Razors, lighter fluid, harder drugs."

The sheriff looked down at the picture, and Gartland thought the man's eyes were seeing something besides the photograph. "Probably wasn't any of Dave's business."

Harvey sighed. "Could be Brent heard an inmate was going to get cut or torched, maybe for something he thought wasn't worth dying over."

"I still don't think it was worth Dave's dying." Surratt sat back in the chair again. Gartland figured the big man was trying to find a way to be at ease in the chair. Gartland also knew it couldn't be done.

After squirming a while, the sheriff asked, "You got any idea who fingered Dave as a snitch? Or paid Enochs Porter to kill him?"

Harvey shook his head, embarrassed at how little he knew about what went on inside his prison. He tapped ashes off his cigar and carried it to the window.

"Couple years ago I went to one of those 'penology conventions,' where people who run prisons get together and brag about themselves. Total waste of time, but it was held in Las Vegas, in February, and my wife wanted some sun."

Harvey looked down on the prison exercise yard and wondered how many men had died on its asphalt surface. Dave Brent was the third that he knew of. "Anyway, I met another warden, runs a state prison out west. A cocaine dealer had offered fifty thousand dollars for every year he was in custody, if that warden would authorize a private telephone in his cell."

"Did the man do it?"

Harvey shook his head, remembering. "He gave the dealer ten days in solitary for attempted bribery. Six months later, during a surprise inspection, he found out the man had his phone. Paid off at least three guards to get it."

Surratt lit a cigarette. "What's the point?"

"No point, Sheriff," Harvey said. "Just a story. But we've lost control of what happens inside these walls. And I can't wait to retire." The warden pointed out the window. "Your friend died down there in that exercise yard."

Surratt came to look down on the bleak concrete square. "Notice how happy he looked in that picture? Smiling at the woman?"

"He was always glad to see her," Gartland remembered. "I would have been too. You can't see it in the picture, but she had hair red as new fire and eyes the color of Navajo turquoise."

Surratt moved back to the desk, opened the envelope he'd brought and spilled its contents over the oak surface. "Could you look through here, see if you recognize her?"

"Anybody coming inside the walls has to show picture identification," Harvey mused, sorting through the collection of county mug shots. "Linda Carroll used a Kentucky driver's license. I ran a check on it, after we talked. It was a real good fake." The warden looked up from the scattered photographs. "She's not in this bunch."

"Was it her who put money in Dave's account?"

Harvey nodded. "Money orders," he said. "That's the only accepted deposit into those accounts. No checks, no cash."

"You try to have them traced?"

Gartland shook his head. "Can't do it. Companies that issue them can tell where and when they were sold, but nobody asks a buyer for identification. You can sign any name you want to. She always signed 'Linda Carroll,' and she bought them at convenience stores between here and the interstate." The warden shoved a cardboard box across his desk. "That's Brent's personal stuff."

"Any way to identify this Carroll woman in there?"

"Nope." Harvey wished he could help Surratt. "The box is stuff from his kids, mostly."

The sheriff put his mug shots back in their envelope. "Nothing else you can tell me?"

"I don't know what it would be, Sheriff." The warden wished there was. Harvey'd liked Dave Brent, and was close to liking the sheriff who was Brent's friend. "You might talk to the lawyer who was going to represent him at the parole hearing."

Surratt looked up from the envelope. "He hired a lawyer for that?"

Harvey searched through his Rolodex, found the card he wanted and pulled it free of the file. "This is the guy. And Corbin Young never works cheap."

"Dave Brent couldn't afford a high-dollar lawyer." Surratt studied the card as though answers to his questions would be found there, if he looked hard enough.

Harvey replaced the card in his file after the sheriff wrote down the telephone number. "The woman, maybe? Reckon she paid for it?"

Surratt stood up to leave. "I can stop at this guy's office on the way back to Midland."

Harvey held up a restraining hand. "That old man won't say a thing."

"I got a wife still shook up over being shot at, and I spent three hours getting here," Surratt snapped. "He'll talk to me."

"Corbin gave up a big Louisville practice four or five years ago; said the only people with enough money to hire him were dope dealers and crooked politicians," Harvey explained. "He only works cases he thinks are interesting."

"So?" The sheriff resealed the clasp on the envelope of pictures and stood up. "If something about Dave Brent interested him, I'd like to know what it was."

Harvey sighed, remembering his own impatience as a younger man. "Let me make a phone call, at least open Corbin's door for you."

Surratt sat down but Gartland noticed the sheriff had moved so he was perching on the end of the uncomfortable chair. He didn't intend to stay much longer.

Corbin Young's receptionist explained her boss was out but was expected back shortly. "Tell him Harvey Gartland's on his way over," the warden said. "I got a man with a few questions. I'll have him there around, oh . . . " Harvey looked at his watch. "1:30 or so."

"I didn't come here to take you away from your work," Sheriff Surratt apologized as the warden slipped into his jacket.

"This isn't work," Harvey said. "All I do in this office is mark time. Besides, Corbin Young won't tell you a thing if I don't go with you."

As they rode in the sheriff's cruiser through the tight cluster of buildings that was downtown LaGrange, Harvey asked Jesse Surratt what he knew about Florida. "My wife wants to live where there's no snow." He gestured out the car window. "Take a left on Main Street."

The sheriff slapped at the turn signals. "I'd shovel a lot of snow before I'd live in air conditioning from May to September."

Harvey nodded. "Maybe I'll keep looking out west." He directed the sheriff to the town parking lot, and led him half a block to Corbin Young's office. They were a few minutes early; Harvey turned into an adjacent diner.

"We got time for a cup of coffee and a smoke," he explained. "Corbin's wife died last year. Emphysema. He's down on tobacco, and I hate being where I can't smoke." When a waitress had taken their order, Harvey asked, "What're you going to do if you find out your friend was framed? It's a little late to do him any good."

"I know." Harvey read pain and regret in the sheriff's frown. "I was writing to the Governor about a pardon. Dave Brent was the best deputy Hawkes County had. I wanted him back in the department."

"Would have been quite a trick," Gartland mused. "Taking a convicted killer out of prison and putting him back on the street with a badge."

"I'd have done it." There was iron determination in Surratt's voice. "People liked Dave. They wouldn't have argued with me."

"You the kind of sheriff people are afraid to argue with?" There were plenty of Kentucky counties where the sheriff's department was a model of bullying corruption.

"I don't know what kind of sheriff I am," Surratt said. "I might give it up after this one term. It was Dave Brent who talked me into running in the first place."

For a few minutes Gartland listened as Surratt told about his brief war with the former sheriff, running for the office after the Smallwood brothers went to prison. Harvey had learned a little of what happened in Hawkes County through reading the papers, and five men who were convicted as a result of the Smallwood debacle were doing time at LaGrange.

Still, it was interesting to hear first-hand how Jesse Surratt defeated a crooked lawman, almost by accident. Most men who experienced such things spent the rest of their lives bragging. Jesse Surratt sounded sorry any of it happened.

"You reckon that lawyer's in his office now?" the sheriff asked after Harvey ran out of questions to ask.

Harvey smiled. "He's been sitting over there by the window for about ten minutes."

Gartland got up and brought Corbin Young to the table. Young was a tiny man, barely five feet tall, but Harvey had seen him work, and he was a giant in the quasi-theatrics of a courtroom. The warden snuffed out his cigar as the lawyer sat down, and was pleased Surratt extinguished his cigarette as well.

After making the requisite introductions Gartland explained, "Sheriff Surratt has some questions about your interest in his friend David Brent."

"Don't have any interest," Young said brusquely. "Whatever interest I might have had seems moot."

"Who hired you to represent him?" Surratt leaned across the table, looked ready to grab the lawyer's tie and pull him closer.

"That's none of your business." Corbin Young glared over his coffee cup.

"Sheriff Surratt's reopened his investigation into Dave Brent's case." Harvey sipped from his coffee, wished he'd ordered some sort of pastry to go with it. "Shots were fired at the sheriff's car yesterday. He thinks the person who retained you might know something about that."

The attorney frowned. "I don't see any reason to provide anyone with confidential information, merely to assuage the curiosity of a rural sheriff."

"What could be so confidential about . . . "

Harvey spoke up again, before Surratt had time to become contentious. "It's this way, Corbin: I'd count it a favor if you told the sheriff anything that might be helpful to his investigation."

Corbin Young shot a look at Harvey Gartland, a stare which softened to a grudging acquiescence. "Is that all you want to know?" Corbin asked. "Who hired me to represent your friend?"

"It'll do for a start," Surratt answered.

The old man raised his cup, emptied it and gestured at a waitress for a refill. "Whatever I tell you at this table will be the total of any information provided by me. I don't expose confidences to every hick lawman who happens to be a friend of Harvey Gartland."

Harvey was bored by Corbin's eccentric act, and Surratt was visibly bristling, ready to retort angrily. "There's no reason this has to be an argument," the warden said. He knew Corbin's behavior was all an act. If the attorney didn't mean to talk to the sheriff, he'd have never come to the table.

"I'll listen to his questions." The lawyer was silent for a beat. "I'll decide about answering once I've heard them."

"Who hired you to represent Dave Brent?" Surratt asked coldly.

Leaning over the table, Harvey Gartland felt like a referee. "Will you answer that one, Corbin?"

A small nod indicated partial surrender. "I can't give you a name. But it was a woman, very lovely, and very tough, it seemed to me."

"Are you playing attorney-client privilege with the name?" Surratt snapped. "I can talk to the county attorney back home, look into a subpoena to make you say it in a courtroom. Dave Brent was your client, not the woman who paid his bill."

"Don't threaten *me,* Sheriff. I never knew her name. We only met the one time." Corbin Young sighed and stirred his coffee. "She called, asked for help with an appeal to the State Parole Board. I told her I required five thousand dollars in advance, and she made an appointment to bring payment."

"Interesting case." The old attorney stared at Jesse Surratt. "Your ex-deputy ought never have gone to prison, you know. A first year law student could have successfully defended him."

Surratt ignored the remark. "Do you have a record of a check? A photocopy, a note of when and where it was deposited? Anything we can track backward"

Corbin Young sipped delicately at his coffee, then put the cup down gently. "She paid cash. I reported the income, paid taxes on it and don't have anything to hide." The old man moved his chair backward a bit. "And I don't believe I can help you any further."

"Would you look at some pictures before you go?" Surratt asked.

Young acknowledged the woman in Harvey's photograph was almost certainly the one who brought money to his office. But he didn't find her in the envelope of mug shots from Hawkes County.

Corbin Young moved toward the door, then came back to the table. "If you find this woman, Sheriff, tell her she's due a refund. Less two hundred for the telephone consultation and office visit."

"Send the money to Dave's kids," the sheriff said tiredly. "They deserve it."

Gartland watched Corbin Young leave the restaurant. "If he knew any more I think he'd tell you."

Jesse Surratt lifted his hands, then dropped them. "We tried."

"Give me a ride back to the prison?" Gartland asked, feeling tired. "I got a calendar to update."

CHAPTER EIGHTEEN

Jesse thumbed a toggle switch forward, and his chainsaw sputtered into silence. He put the tool down, settled onto a flint ledge jutting from the hill and mopped his brow with a bandana. The view from his stone seat had changed dramatically since Jesse last sat there to look back toward his house.

In August, amid summer forest and thickets of brush and briar he hadn't been able to see more than twenty yards in any one direction. But it was October, and Jesse could look all the way to the barn and beyond.

He smiled, pleased with what he'd done with his land, amazed it all happened in less than nine years. His father had believed in the "carry it behind the barn" method of storing useless artifacts like old tires and broken implements. Over the years the clearing to the rear of the building had become nearly impassable.

His first summer back in Hawkes County, Jesse carted truckloads of junk away. Now a pair of young steers grazed on high autumn grass, watched by—and occasionally harassed by—his mule, Sam. Jesse wondered if putting the sheriff's uniform away would allow him to become seriously involved with the farm again. Or would he die of boredom if he left the office?

He'd been warm enough while operating the saw, but it was different, sitting on a cold rock with a fall breeze moving through the hollow. He reached for the jacket he'd discarded soon after beginning to use the chainsaw. His cigarettes were in a pocket and he lit one, inhaling the smoke deeply.

A drowsing Casey looked up from a spot where sun was golden on a carpet of fallen leaves, then dropped her head as Jesse settled again. The dog's behavior was a sharp contrast to the exuberant squirrel chasing that had been her normal behavior on the hill, only a few years gone. Jesse wondered if there was a way he could arrange a place for Casey to ride on the tractor. Another year or three, the climb up the steep road might be too difficult for the dog. Jesse didn't think he could bear to leave her behind.

When his cigarette's ember burned near the filter Jesse crushed it under a boot heel, stood and inspected what he'd done with the chainsaw. Three twisted white oaks that would have never grown into marketable timber were on the ground. Properly seasoned, spit and cut into twenty-inch sticks, they'd heat Jesse's house for the better part of a month. First, though, he had to get them off the hill to his wood splitter.

Stretching muscles unaccustomed to such exertion, Jesse stored the chainsaw in a box behind the tractor seat and backed the machine up until the high back tires were a few feet ahead of the first of the trees. He stretched a logging chain from the oak to the tractor, got back on the machine, and dragged the log away from the branches he'd lopped off the top.

When the first tree was parallel to the second, he got down to rearrange the chain to hold both logs. Straightening, he glanced down the hill road and saw Crow Markwell easing warily around the barn, one arm behind his back. The mule Sam saw the retired deputy about the same time, and brayed a sharp protest at the trespasser.

Dropping his head to browse at patches of dry grass, the mule took what looked like random steps toward the old man. Crow waited until Sam was almost within kicking range before moving his hand from behind his back and showing a hidden length of two-by-four. Once—and only once—Sam had tried to bite Crow, who stunned the beast with a quick punch to his soft brown nose.

Neither Sam nor Crow had forgotten. Whenever the retired deputy came around, Sam sought a fresh opportunity to do damage to the old man. Crow was careful to deny the mule his revenge. After facing off with the man for a long minute, Sam cantered away, turning in the shadow of a tall oak to glare at the old man walking up the hill.

When he was close enough to be heard, Crow complained to Jesse, "Damn if *I'd* feed a animal that's only good for bites and kicks."

"I'll sell him, one of these days," Jesse said agreeably, knowing he never would. He admired the mule's unyielding defiance.

Crow stopped near the tractor and turned to spit a thin stream of tobacco juice. "Many people as that son of a bitch has bit, you could get rich raffling off the privilege of shooting him." The old man looked at the downed trees. "How many more you got to drag off?"

"Just these three," Jesse told him.

Securing the last tree went quicker with Crow wrapping chain while Jesse steered the tractor. When it was done the old man climbed behind the seat and they towed the white oaks close to the woodlot and Jesse's gas-powered log splitter.

Crow Markwell wasn't foolish enough to insist he could do the same work he'd done at fifty or even seventy. He sat on a stump while Jesse chain-sawed the trees into stove-length sections. Only then did the old man come close to the splitter. He took as his responsibility the lever controlling a hydraulic wedge, moving it each time Jesse lifted a section of trunk into the machine's cradle.

After a dozen pieces were split into quarters, Jesse leaned against the splitter, breathing hard. "You know any Carrolls in Hawkes County?"

The ex-deputy nodded. "Know a Carol Ferguson, Carol Kelly. Knew a Carolyn Shaw years back." Crow grinned. "That'n had the most beautiful blue eyes I ever seen. Hated being called just Carol though."

"I mean for a last name," Jesse interrupted.

"Oh." Crow tongued the wad of tobacco in his left cheek. "Used to be some Carrolltons living toward the head of Three Doves Creek."

"Any of them named Linda?" Jesse lifted another piece of wood onto the splitter.

Crow threw his lever forward, and when the machine grew quiet again, shook his head. "Carrolltons been gone a long time. And none of them was named Linda."

"That's too bad." If Crow Markwell wasn't familiar with a name, it was unlikely anyone had used it in Hawkes County for better than half a century. While they worked he told Crow what he'd learned of the woman who frequently came to the prison to see Dave Brent.

"A lady who carries false I.D. into a prison and ain't afraid to sign a fake name on money orders. That's a woman with a whole lot of 'I don't give a damn' to her." Crow frowned a minute. "Did you ask that warden if she might of been wearing a wig?"

While recounting the story of his visit to the prison Jesse had continued to lift lengths of wood into the splitter. Dropping the last one, he straightened and stretched. "I didn't think about it." He reached to switch off the splitter's engine. "But he didn't mention it either."

"Prob'ly wouldn't," Crow mused, and went back to his stump. "Men don't notice them things. A woman will though. Wonder do they have female guards at LaGrange now?" The retired deputy extracted a sizeable pinch of chewing tobacco from a foil pouch in his hip pocket, squeezing it into a tight ball before tucking it into his cheek. "Be interesting, what other women might of thought about this Linda Carroll."

"The warden gave me a picture. Can't see much, just the back of her head, but I'll show it to you when we go to the house."

Crow nodded. "You want to stack that split wood or leave it lay?"

Jesse frowned at the scattered slabs littering the ground around the splitter. "That copperhead out to your house the other day's got me seeing snakes everywhere I step."

"And them things do love sticks of wood left laying loose by a lazy man."

There was an unwalled open-frame structure nearby, under which stove wood could be left to season. Jesse began carrying and stacking the split slabs, three and four chunks at a time. Crow carried single pieces of wood to the stack, but after four trips returned to his seat and stayed there.

"Maggie was laying out pork chops when I stopped at the house looking for you." Crow Markwell never called Margaret by her full name.

Jesse nodded. "I thought I'd barbecue them."

Crow laughed. "After the T.V.A. brought electricity into Hawkes County ever' woman I knew said she'd never cook on a fire again. Wonder what your granny'd say if she seen you making a cook-fire for the fun of it?"

"I'd like to know what my dad would say if he could see how this place looks now," Jesse said, stacking the chunks of oak.

"I know what would of made him real happy," Crow said. "Seeing you and Maggie back together. He'd a'loved that."

Jesse got his sweat-damp bandana out again. "Dad never knew we split up."

"He knew you was going to. Told me so, that last time you and her was home together."

During his father's final illness Jesse had believed he and Margaret did a masterful job of fooling a dying man. A Norfolk lawyer was already drawing up papers they didn't sign until three weeks after his father's funeral.

"He knew we were getting a divorce?"

Crow nodded. "You were going to a ship in California, and Maggie wasn't saying nothing about moving, that last time. Joe figured it out."

"I thought we fooled him." Jesse wondered how his father could have looked so closely at death and found vision enough to see past a son's charade. "I never would have guessed Pop knew what was going on with us."

"Joe said something else," Crow continued. "Told me you all might split up, but he was sure you'd get back together sooner or later. 'Both of them young'uns is too damn stubborn to live with anybody else,' was how he put it."

Jesse collected more wood for the stack, feeling vaguely guilty about the long-ago deception. Hearing Crow's recollection of his father's observations from his deathbed was all he needed to know about it, for that day anyway.

But Crow wouldn't let it go. "Know what your daddy said about you and women? Back when you was getting married and divorced often as other men trade cars?"

There had been two wives before Margaret, a distant history Jesse found hard to remember, though he'd been the man who lived it. "You're going to tell me whether I want to hear it or not."

Crow spit between his feet. "Joe said you was like a flustered butterfly, flitting over and through a field of sweet flowers to land on a dog turd ever' time." Crow laughed out loud. "Your daddy thought Maggie was a regular rose of a woman though. So do I."

"And?" Jesse wished the old man would get on with whatever he meant to say. "What else?"

"People my age don't have to be polite, you know." Crow stared unflinchingly into Jesse's eyes. "We ain't got time to follow rules about what is and what ain't our business."

Jesse tossed the wood he was carrying onto the rising stack. He'd thought enough about death in the last few days, didn't want to be reminded of it further. "Hell, Crow, you'll outlive me; be a pallbearer at *my* funeral."

Crow ignored the improbable prediction. "You got a good woman, son. You doing anything to keep her?"

There was one more armful of wood to throw under the shelter, and as he bent to gather it Jesse felt suddenly tired, an exhaustion which had nothing to do with stacking wood. "I think she may be thinking about leaving already," he admitted. "She's got that vacant way about her, like when we split the first time."

"Then you need to do something about it," Crow said.

"I'm trying," Jesse muttered. "Honest to God, Crow, I'm trying."

"Try harder," Crow said bluntly. He looked at the neat rows of firewood. "Now let's go to the house and you can show me that picture from the warden." The retired deputy stood up and took a deep, loud breath. "But first you can feed me a few pork chops."

CHAPTER NINETEEN

David would have mocked Lorena's nocturnal visits to the cemetery. He maintained a hostile cynicism about any form of life after death, never mind his notions a harsh God punished adultery so fiercely. "This is the only time we get," he told Lorena once, lying on the old sofa in her greenhouse.

Moving his skilled and knowing hands over her body, he added, "And *this*, what you and me do together, is the best part of the time we get."

Shuddering under the pressure of David's probing fingers, losing herself in his strong arms and hungry mouth, Lorena had found it easy to agree about what comprised the best part of life.

Sometimes David went with his father to the family's cemetery, but he found no comfort there. "Mama's gone, she don't know when we come around," he told Lorena after one afternoon trip with Elmer. "And Daddy can't do nothing but cry around that place. I don't know why he wants to go so often."

In those happier, distant days, Lorena hadn't understood why going to the cemetery was important to Elmer Brent, any more than his son did.

But she was learning.

The first evening she visited David's grave, Lorena gained a peaceful few hours of feeling close to and alone with him again. Her freesias—delicate, odorous flowering bushes seldom cultivated in modern gardens—had been in new bloom, filling the greenhouse with the sweet redolence David loved. She impulsively carried some of the flowers to him.

Whenever she wore similarly scented perfume he was entranced and aroused as a high school boy. The perfume had to be imported all the way from London, and Lorena was ashamed of the expense, but witnessing David's delight was more than worth the cost of a tiny golden bottle.

Creating a floral arrangement for him—mature flowers set among tiny new leaves and freshly budded blossoms—eased the muffling fog of grief that was Lorena's whole world since David's death. When it was done she added a pair of tapered candles to her purse and drove to Caney Ridge, hiding her vehicle on an abandoned lane a quarter mile from the graveyard.

A path to the cemetery was familiar from illicit summer afternoon meetings in the woods, and she moved through the night confident, with no need for a flashlight. Pausing at a clearing where she and David had made love, Lorena wished she'd brought the blanket from her trunk. The evening air was chill, but it would have been pleasant to lie on mossy ground, wrapped in a thick quilt that still smelled of *him*, to lie there and remember.

David's grave was still heaped with dying bouquets from the funeral. Lorena cleared a space and filled it with her flowers. Without thinking, she began talking to him, the way she imagined old Elmer Brent talked to his dead wife.

Lorena explained to David the forgotten tradition of freesias, how before roses became popular they were the flower of lovers. Lighting her candles, she recalled a night every pane in her greenhouse reflected dancing flames, and understood why she'd brought the tapers. She said she loved him still, spoke out loud how she missed him, and cried for a long time without realizing it.

She might have stayed until dawn, lost in grief and pain as hot and bright as the blazes topping her candles, but lights swept across the tombstones, interrupting Lorena's vigil. A car stopped some distance from her, and half a dozen high school boys took a case of beer from the trunk. An over-amped radio and raucous laughter destroyed the tranquility of the Brent burying ground.

Busy dividing their cans of illicit alcohol, the boys didn't notice when Lorena slipped just inside the treeline. Standing on the unlit path, she turned to watch the adolescents approach the grave, attracted by the burning candles. She was pleased to see them withdraw somberly back to their beer and radio, without disturbing anything.

Lorena went home to her sleeping son, but two nights later she went to the cemetery again. She built another arrangement of freesias—six white ones surrounding a single salmon colored blossom—and this time included a fresh pair of candles as an integral element of her creation. No giggling teenaged boys interrupted her: she waited until well after ten o'clock before leaving the house, ashamed of leaving her son alone and unwatched.

After that she went to the cemetery nearly every night, as soon as he was asleep. If she could persuade the elderly lady who lived across the street to stay late, Lorena paid double for the inconvenience. If not she went anyway, guilty but unable to stay home.

Her mind was nearly made up to leave Hawkes County. She meant to talk about her decision where David could hear, to listen in her heart to what he might say about it.

David would have thought she was crazy for believing her heart could hear him. But Lorena knew about being crazy. She'd lived for years in a faraway place with lots of crazy young women. She didn't think she was like them, then or ever.

David was wrong.

Surely her heart could hear.

CHAPTER TWENTY

Margaret finished tossing a salad, then bent to slide the pan of made-from-scratch biscuits into the oven. After rinsing her hands at the kitchen sink, she reached for a towel and glanced out the window.

Crow and Jesse stood together near the barbecue grill, oblivious to anything other than their conversation. Wind shifted the smoke rising off the charcoal, and the men edged away, circling the grill, their expressions somber. Margaret had no doubt their conversation was about identifying—however belatedly—Ray Bailey's killer. They were talking about it when they came off the hill from cutting wood.

Jesse had been quite excited when Margaret confirmed his suspicions the woman in the picture from LaGrange Prison wore a wig. The hair looked too perfect to be natural, especially when Jesse said the photo was taken in a hot, stuffy room in high summer. He'd wanted to ask more questions, but she told him to leave her alone.

Tired of hearing her husband's theories, weary of his insisting the shots fired at his car were related to the Bailey case, it was a relief to have Crow Markwell there to listen for a while. She hoped the old man would convince Jesse someone else in Hawkes County might have a reason to shoot at a police vehicle. It was a certainty she'd never ride in another one, and wished she could say the same for her husband.

Margaret slid the salad—tailored to Jesse's palate with a double portion of onions—onto a refrigerator shelf. Sweet corn canned from Jesse's summer garden simmered on the stove, and the pan of biscuits in the oven was the only component of dinner not quite done.

When Crow had come looking for her husband, Margaret invited him into the house, hoping Jesse would finish on the hill and return to the house before the fragile old man—whose skin looked paper-thin, with a bluish cast in the right light—walked the steep incline to find him.

She had made coffee, and when she carried a cup to Crow in the living room, the old man looked into Margaret's eyes with frank curiosity. His silence reminded her of Avery Quentin, her grandfather. Crow Markwell had the same intuitive way of knowing things, without needing to hear them spoken. When she looked into Crow's eyes, she was sure he knew things she hadn't told him.

Margaret offered an inane observation the October evenings were growing cooler. Crow sipped coffee for twenty minutes and agreeably talked with her about weather. The old lawman didn't press Margaret to tell him anything—her grandfather never did either—but as he left to look for Jesse, she sensed his disappointment.

Fetching the pepper mill from her china hutch, Margaret regretted wasting those minutes with Crow Markwell. She might have told him how deadly boring her life had become after resigning from Loomis Realty. Jesse voiced a certain misery in being sheriff, but didn't find getting out of bed difficult, and there was more to his life than reading an endless stream of paperback novels.

Crow Markwell had never married, but had known plenty of sheriffs. He might have had something helpful to say about how their women coped.

After a quick inspection of her kitchen Margaret looked outside again. Jesse and Crow were laughing, finished for a while with serious talk. She needed to check the progress of the pork chops. Without a reminder Jesse might talk until they were charred bricks. Retrieving fresh cans of beer from the refrigerator, Margaret walked through the stove room to the back door.

" . . . was worse than worthless," Crow was saying as she stepped outside. "Except for making whiskey he was a plumb *do*-less son of a bitch."

Margaret stepped off the porch and gave Crow one of the cans. "Who're you talking about?"

"Didn't know you was there, Maggie." Crow looked at the ground, his face coloring. "Would of watched my language otherwise."

"Oh come on. I'm married to an ex-sailor, Crow." Margaret opened the other can and took a swallow before surrendering it to Jesse. "I don't think you know any dirty words I haven't heard a thousand times."

The old man lowered himself into a lawn chair Jesse had pulled close to the grill, a tiny smile adding more wrinkles to his creased, leathery face. "You know, it was a girl that taught me how to cuss in the first place."

"Who was she?" There was no one at Crow's house to hear his stories unless Margaret counted his three dogs. Once, talking about his life before she came back to him, Jesse said he used to talk to his animals—Casey, Sam, and Rufus, an old barn cat who disappeared two summers back—just to have an excuse to use his voice.

Jesse said talking to animals was the loneliest thing he ever did, and Margaret always encouraged Crow Markwell's recollections of a Hawkes County much wilder than the one she knew. Learning to swear was a new story, but Margaret would have pushed to hear it if Crow had told it a dozen times before.

"Her name was Annie Gillette," he said. "A little red-headed girl. At church she'd whisper the nastiest things I'd ever heard while the preacher—that was Luther Tate—talked scripture." Crow's eyes lost their focus as he prowled memory. "Annie had five brothers, and I don't reckon she ever learned there was things a girl shouldn't say."

"Were you her boyfriend?" Margaret prompted when the old man was quiet for a while.

"Not hardly." Crow laughed and shook his head. "Not with them brothers a'watching over any boy who come around her." He took a long drink from his beer.

Smiling toward the distance, the old man looked as though he hoped that little red-haired girl might come strolling from the barn. "Annie married one of the Buckners and moved to Indiana. They brought her home to bury eight or ten years ago, and one of her kids was a dentist. And she had a daughter who made a school teacher."

The smile faded. "Annie Gillette," Crow murmured, before sipping from his beer can again.

Margaret wondered how it felt to outlive all the people you cared about, hoped she would never have to learn first-hand. "Who were you talking about before?" she asked, hoping to move the old man's mind away from people who were gone from his life. "When I came outside you called somebody 'do-less.'"

Grease droplets sputtered as Jesse turned the pork chops over the coals and explained, "Crow was telling what a rounder Elmer Brent was, before he got married."

"Elmer was that." Crow set his beer onto the concrete floor by his chair. "And the son of a bitch couldn't . . . " Glancing at Margaret, he hesitated, but didn't stop to apologize. "That boy plain couldn't stay out of trouble."

Margaret smiled at hearing an aging grandfather like Elmer Brent described as "that boy."

The retired lawman leaned forward in his chair to take a plug of tobacco from a hip pocket. "I remember, in '48 or '49, Fred Johnson had a road house where U.S. 60 crosses the county line, and we got called out on a Saturday night to stop a fight. I got to Fred's ahead of the other deputies, but wasn't about to go in such a rough place alone. I parked the car, shut off the lights and waited for the rest to show up."

Jesse forked steaming pieces of meat onto a plate, and put the lid back on the grill. "Let's eat. You can finish telling us about it at the table, Crow."

Crow stood up hurriedly to follow Jesse into the house, and Margaret suspected he was afraid of losing his audience. "I was setting there in the dark," he continued, following Margaret and Jesse inside, "when all of a sudden Elmer Brent flew out the door, like somebody had hit him with a chair or something. He sort of rolled when he hit the ground outside."

In the kitchen Crow pulled a chair away from the table and eased down slowly, as though uncertain the seat would be there when he relaxed.

"Elmer rolled until he was a'laying up against a beat-up old DeSoto. There was sirens coming from off in the distance, and Elmer pulled himself up into that car and set up straight. When Tobe Fisher—he was sheriff then—got there he said to Elmer, 'What's going on here?' Elmer looked over at him, hands on the steering wheel and said, 'Damn if I know, Tobe. I just drove up myself,'" Crow's grin of pleasure at the memory turned into wheezing laughter.

"What's so funny?" Margaret asked. "Didn't the sheriff believe him?"

"*Couldn't* believe him," Crow said. "Elmer'd crawled into a car that'd been on blocks outside Fred's for two or three weeks. Tobe pulled Elmer out of the car to show him the wheels was gone and Elmer said, 'By God, I *thought* she drove a little rough.'" Crow's laughter turned into a weak cough, and it was a long time before the old man had breath enough to add, "That was another night in jail for Elmer Brent."

"Get you some of this meat, Crow." Jesse lifted the heaped platter across the table.

"Elmer Brent seems like such a sweet old man," Margaret mused out loud. "It's hard to think of him ever being in jail."

The old deputy nodded. "He was a bad one though, back a long time ago. Elmer's main problems came from making whiskey, not drinking it. After the war the rest of the country got prosperous, but around here there wasn't a whole lot of ways to make money but by making whiskey."

Crow cut a pork chop into tiny pieces. He wouldn't eat much, no matter how Margaret teased or cajoled or nagged. She thought about Avery Quentin again. "When I was growing up in California, my grandfather said some of the ones called Okies were actually from Kentucky or Tennessee. He said the moonshine they made was better than bourbon from stores."

"Some of it was," Crow agreed. "But bootlegging was a mean business. Wasn't so different from what's going on today with marijuana, I don't reckon. Them boys who worked for the Smallwoods? In forty or fifty years, they'll be sweet old men and people will say it's hard to believe they ever tried to kill Jesse Surratt."

Margaret shivered. In the first hour of her first visit to Hawkes County after the divorce, she found Jesse in handcuffs, held prisoner by one of Bradley Smallwood's hired thugs. The man who held a gun on her husband couldn't possibly have anything in common with sweet old Elmer Brent.

Jesse reached for a biscuit and speared another chop with his fork. "They say Elmer killed a man."

Crow nodded. "That was the time Andrew Patterson tried to take a still away from Elmer."

Margaret noticed the old man was only playing with his meal, decided she'd ask Crow what his favorite foods were and whenever he came to dinner, that was what she'd fix. "Did he go to prison?" She tried to imagine Elmer Brent, who doted on grandchildren and told funny old stories like Crow, in a gunfight.

"No, but he would've, sooner or later." Crow stopped even pretending to eat and pushed his plate away. "Grand jury called the business with Andrew 'self defense.' It prob'ly was, but ever'body knew something or other was going to send Elmer to the penitentiary before long."

The retired deputy leaned back in his chair. "That was before Maude Stuckey—she's a cousin to Wayne, the preacher at Dave's funeral—decided to marry Elmer and straighten him out. Maude was the best thing ever happened to him."

They took their coffee to the back porch, and after she settled into a chair Margaret only half-listened to stories Crow and Jesse told one another. The men's voices were only so much background noise as she watched lengthening purple shadows slip over the flint ridges around the house.

"Look at that mule of yourn," Crow said after a while. "A'begging like a big dog." Sam pranced near the barn gate, tossing his head, looking toward the humans on the back porch. "You'd think that miserable thing wouldn't have the conscience for begging when what he really wants is a piece of somebody's arm."

"Sam's only doing what he knows how to," Jesse murmured, leaving his chair to slip quietly into the house. He was back in a moment with a handful of apples. "Want to go with me to feed him, Crow?"

The ex-deputy snorted derisively, but got to his feet. "This man of yours ain't got a lick of sense when it comes to animals," he told Margaret. "You watch: before long he'll be setting out candy for the rats and telling everybody how rattlesnakes are play-pretties."

Margaret smiled, watching the men go toward the barn. She heard Jesse complain about stiff muscles from the wood cutting, and as their voices faded Crow was saying in the old days people thought carrying buckeyes in pockets helped cure an aching back.

The ill-tempered Sam greeted them with a loud bray, then lowered his big head to take apples from Jesse's hand. Margaret sometimes fed the mule herself, and knew how gently he could lift a treat from a palm.

She could be content, if all her hours were like these. But a night of stories and watching the hills was just a prelude to one more empty day. Margaret wished she was like her friend Rita Bailey, able to happily fill hours with pointless shopping in Lexington or Ashland malls.

And it wasn't as though shopping was all Rita had. Bobby lent purpose to her life. If Rita sometimes seemed flighty and silly, she deserved credit for taking good care of her brother.

Margaret wished there was something she could do—besides loving Jesse—that meant something.

She almost didn't answer the phone when it rang. She could have gotten away with denying she heard it. But if someone wanted Jesse, they'd call again and again. Acquiescing, Margaret went in the house, hoping the ringing would hush before she reached it, but the noise droned on until she lifted the receiver.

Martha Compton was at the other end of the line. The two women chatted politely for a few moments. then Martha asked for Jesse. "He's at the barn," Margaret said. "But I can get him."

"Maybe you don't need to." Martha paused. "This could wait till tomorrow. I'll see him in the office early."

"Should I give him a message?" Margaret offered. "Or have him call when he gets back to the house?"

The old lady was quiet for another long moment. After Jesse's election Martha had promised Margaret she wouldn't interrupt the sheriff at home unless it was important. "He'd be interested to know if people was telling a ghost story about Dave Brent's grave, don't you reckon?"

"What kind of story?" Jesse would want to know *any* story attached to the name Dave Brent, but Margaret was intrigued by the word "ghost" and hoped Martha would tell her more.

"My grandson, he's sixteen? Told me the kids are saying a ghost is at the Brent graveyard, leaving candles on Dave's grave." The dispatcher laughed out loud. "I told Roy I never heard of no spirit carrying candles, but some kids are claiming they're left there every night."

"I'll get Jesse."

Margaret put the phone down, went to the back door and picked up the old school bell she used to call her husband from the barn. She shook it vigorously until Jesse and Crow loomed out of the darkness.

"Telephone call," she said simply.

CHAPTER TWENTY-ONE

Crow noted the worried frown on Maggie Surratt's face as he followed the sheriff through the back door. He understood her displeasure, once he realized who was calling.

A former sheriff's daughter herself, Martha Compton wouldn't bother an off-duty member of the department without good reason. Her calls generally turned someone's quiet evening at home into unplanned, unpaid and, in most cases, unpleasant overtime.

Jesse stopped at the phone in the short hall connecting the kitchen with the living room. Crow walked past and settled on the sofa, the nearest seat to the door. Maggie sat in a chair and pretended to be engrossed in one of her books.

Crow leaned back to rest his head on the upholstery, a few inches nearer the conversation in the hall. He wasn't the least bit ashamed of eavesdropping, but saw no reason to be obvious. "That was a fine dinner, Maggie," he said.

She smiled, but kept her eyes fixed on the pages. Maggie was listening, just as hard as Crow was, to the sheriff's conversation. "You should come more often." Maggie lowered the book and sighed. In her eyes was a message Crow could not quite read. She wasn't a happy woman though. He saw that much.

"Anytime you feel like feeding a old man, give me a call." He allowed his eyelids to droop. "See how long it takes me to show up." The appearance of a doze was convenient when silence was preferable to talk.

"What else did he say about it, Martha?" Crow heard Jesse ask. The sheriff listened a while, then said, "I'd like to talk to Roy myself, if that's all right."

Crow didn't let a muscle on his face so much as twitch. An old man's eyes might let him down once in a while, like when he nearly lost that copperhead, but there wasn't a thing wrong with Crow Markwell's hearing. One of Martha Compton's grandsons was named Roy, and he wondered what the boy might have done to interest Jesse Surratt.

"I'll see you in a few minutes then." The phone dropped into place, and the sheriff called, "Crow? Margaret? You all want a cup of coffee?"

"I could stand one." Crow opened his eyes, sat a little straighter. "Would help me stay awake, driving home."

"Not for me." Margaret's voice was apprehensive as her eyes.

Jesse brought a pair of steaming mugs from the kitchen and handed one to Crow. "Feel like taking a little run out to Martha's before you go home?"

"Ain't in no hurry, if that's what you mean." The sheriff was going beyond asking for opinion, was going to actively involve him in his investigation. Crow tried to keep the sound of gratitude out of his reply. "What's going on there?"

Jesse sat at the other end of the couch. "Do you believe in ghosts?"

"I'll believe in anything you can show me." Crow lifted the cup of hot coffee. "I could believe ice cubes was in there, if I seen 'em." Crow lifted the mug and blew softly across the rim. "Nobody's ever showed me a ghost, though."

"Roy Compton told Martha some high school kids believe there's one hanging around Dave's grave, nearly every night."

Crow noticed Jesse kept his butt at the very edge of the sofa, anxious to go. Probably wouldn't even give a man time to finish a cup of coffee. "Is it supposed to be Dave coming back or what?"

"No, the kids say it's a woman. She leaves things too, candles and flowers."

"Don't sound like no ghost to me. Candles and flowers shouldn't hold much interest for a spirit." Crow looked at the younger man and grinned. "Sounds like this ghost might own a red wig and know about money sent to LaGrange Prison."

The sheriff stood abruptly. "That's what I figure."

Crow had guessed right; there wasn't going to be time to finish the coffee. Jesse stood up and asked, "So. You want to go to Martha's with me, talk to that boy, maybe look around the Brent cemetery before you head for home?"

Crow drank as much coffee as he could without burning himself. Aware Maggie was watching closely, he decided a meddlesome gesture was in order. "Want to go with us?" he asked her.

Maggie shook her head, looking past Crow to Jesse. "Will you be gone long?"

The sheriff shrugged. "I don't think so. Ten or fifteen minutes at Martha's, maybe an hour getting to the graveyard and looking around. You ready, Crow?"

"Ready as I'll ever be." Crow reluctantly put his coffee down and walked into the little hall.

Aware the sheriff wasn't following, he turned in time to see him carry a holstered magnum pistol and a .38 revolver out of the bedroom. "Keep it where you can reach it," he said to Maggie, giving her the smaller gun, then buckling the magnum around his waist. "I promise, I won't be gone long."

Jesse strode quickly past Crow, who almost had to run to catch up. Outside, the sheriff paused. "You got a gun? The way things have been going lately it might not hurt to carry one."

"In the truck, if you'll wait a minute."

Crow went to his pickup and fetched his puny weapon from the glove compartment. A few years ago he'd lost the ability to accurately shoot anything heavier than a .22. The pistol was loaded with magnum bullets, a bit more powerful than the standard long-rifle variety, but it was still just a .22.

Climbing into the sheriff's cruiser, he slid the embarrassing little gun out of sight, under the seat. As they pulled out of the driveway, he glanced at the house. Maggie was watching their departure through a lit window. Crow wondered how long it would take the sheriff to realize there was a kind of ghost living in his own house.

He stopped thinking about Maggie Surratt and concentrated on enjoying the ride in a patrol car. A touch of adrenalin tickled Crow's brain, a form of intoxication with which he was familiar decades before talk of "natural highs" filled magazines and newspapers. He and the sheriff were on a murder investigation, after all.

Crow could tell Jesse felt the excitement too. Making a left onto U.S. 60, toward town, he turned on the blue lights on top of the car and launched the cruiser into curves a little faster than necessary. Crow kept his voice level as he asked, "You thinking over what we talked about, before Maggie came outside?"

"What was that?"

Crow knew Jesse Surratt hadn't forgotten their discussion. More likely he just didn't want to talk about it. "Whether you're going to run for sheriff again in the fall. Or let a little piece of a man like Blaine Ingraham ruin everything you've done."

"I don't know if I've done so much." Their headlights showed a low shadow on the right, a lost hound on the highway shoulder. The sheriff eased the car to the left until they were past the dog. "And I'm not sure I want to spend four more years on it."

"Shit." Crow shook his head impatiently, wondering if Jesse Surratt was modest or merely ignorant of how the community had begun to think of its sheriff's department. "Talk to a few people. They'll tell you how many things you've turned around, things you've made better."

"I don't like having to leave a pistol for Margaret when I go out."

"Maggie don't mind that," Crow said. "Guns ain't what worries her."

"What *is* it then?" The sheriff's words cracked like a whip in the closed car.

"Why don't you ask her yourself?" Crow let his own voice rise in pitch and volume. "She'll tell you if you really want to know," he nearly shouted. And realized maybe Sheriff Jesse Surratt didn't want to know some things his wife was thinking, might even be afraid to ask the obvious questions.

Crow reached for his tobacco, then realized he'd have no place to spit. "Go ahead, quit being sheriff. Stay in that house all day with Maggie, not talking to her. Get you a nice domestic war started and run her off."

"You got all kinds of answers, don't you, old timer?" the sheriff snapped. He steered around a pickup that had slowed for the cruiser's lights. The road's shoulder was too narrow for the pickup to pull over. "You might see things a little differently if you'd ever been married."

"Might," Crow agreed. "Or might not."

The old man didn't mind sitting in the tense silence that followed. When he was younger, an angry quiet would have bothered him, the way it bothered the sheriff. Crow figured all he had to do was wait and the sheriff would say something honest.

He waited about three minutes before Jesse said, "I don't know what to do, Crow. I want to keep my wife. But I'm not sure I can. I know she's bored to death sitting in the house, doing nothing."

Then they were pulling into the driveway of Martha Compton's trim little house, and they couldn't talk about the election or the sheriff's marriage. Jesse dropped his gun belt on the driver's seat and locked the cruiser before leading the way to the door under the carport. When he tapped his knuckles lightly on the frame, Martha opened the door, told them to come in.

"I don't know if this means anything or not, Sheriff," she said in the kitchen, pouring coffee without asking if they wanted it. "Roy's in the front room. He'll tell you about it."

Crow and Jesse wandered into Martha's living room. On the floor Roy Compton stared intently at the television image of a pretty blonde girl dancing through a church. Or maybe it was a jail, Crow couldn't tell which. Then she wasn't in church or jail either one, she was in a bed, half-dressed, rolling around on wrinkled sheets.

The woman in the first "dirty picture" Crow Markwell ever saw, in a Midland barber shop the year he turned thirteen, had worn more clothes than the blonde. He sat on the sofa and watched intently. He'd seen the face before but couldn't recall the girl's name. Seemed to have a decent singing voice though.

The television screen faded to a commercial and Roy looked first at Jesse, then at Crow. "That's Madonna. That video's real old though. She looks different now." The boy got off the floor and sat in a chair opposite them.

The sheriff leaned forward on the couch. "Martha says something's going on at the Brent graveyard. She tells me kids are spooked over it."

The boy raised his eyebrows and shrugged his shoulders. He gazed steadily at Jesse, as though expecting the sheriff to prod him for details. "It's supposed to be a woman's ghost," he admitted, fidgeting in his chair when neither the sheriff nor Crow said anything. "She sits up there and cries every night."

Martha Compton carried a tray into the living room and put it on her coffee table. "You told *me* she don't just cry, she leaves things." Martha gestured at the tray. "You all have some cake."

Crow accepted one of the plates but took only a couple of bites before putting it down again. "You seen her yourself, Roy?"

132

The youngster shook his head. "A lot of other kids have, though. They're afraid to go around there anymore."

Martha settled heavily into a chair. "Young people got no business around a graveyard at night," she sniffed. "Can't be up to nothing but meanness, drinking and I don't know what all."

Crow winked at Martha Compton and watched her blush. She might be a grandmother now, but he remembered her as a sixteen year old vixen pursued by every boy in Hawkes County. One year when her daddy Charlie Rodburn was sheriff—and Crow's boss—there'd been hell to pay when Charlie found Martha in a country cemetery with a boy and a six pack of beer.

"How many times have people seen this woman?" Jesse asked Roy.

"For a while it was almost every night," Roy took a plate from the tray on the coffee table and made a thick slab of Martha's cake disappear quickly. "But like I said, nobody's going there anymore."

Jesse Surratt stared thoughtfully at the boy. "Would you give us names of the kids who saw her, if we asked you to?"

"'Course he will," Martha insisted. "You'll do that won't you, Roy?"

The boy winced. "They'd know I told."

Crow cleared his throat. "Maybe we don't need no names. You believe in ghosts, Roy?"

The boy shook his head, but the gesture was tentative. "I don't think so."

"Me neither," Crow admitted. "There ain't much to ghost stories, near as I can tell. But if this turned out to be important, and we *needed* them names, you'd have to give 'em to us."

"Could you fix it so nobody knew I told?"

"Roy!" Martha stared at her grandson for a moment, then looked apologetically at the sheriff.

"It's okay, Martha," Crow said. He turned back to the boy.

Roy nodded a concession. "If I had to, I'd tell you who's been up there and seen her."

"You probably won't have to," Jesse said, and Crow was relieved. There was no need to push on this youngster. Not yet. Crow wondered if Jesse Surratt realized how differently this scene would play if a bully like Blaine Ingraham wanted something from a sixteen-year-old.

Crow stood up when the sheriff did. "I thank you for the cake, Martha," he said. Turning back to Roy he asked, "That Madonna, is she as bad as everybody claims she is?"

The boy smiled. "I don't know. But she's sure rich." His smile turned into a broad grin. "And sexy."

"Roy!" The boy's grandmother blushed.

"Well, hell, Martha, she *is*." Crow winked at Roy Compton before following Jesse to the back door.

CHAPTER TWENTY-TWO

Backing the police cruiser down Martha's steep driveway into the street, Jesse waved at Martha, watching from the back door. She was speaking rapidly, glancing over her shoulder every few seconds. Her words couldn't be heard inside the patrol car, but it seemed a safe bet she was giving her grandson a verbal blasting.

"Martha's madder'n a wet cat over Roy not wanting to give you them names," Crow Markwell observed from the passenger seat. "I bet that's a young man who wishes he'd never told Granny about no ghost stories."

Jesse laughed. "Did you see her face when you told Roy he was right, about Madonna being sexy?"

"That good-looking singer on the television?" Crow stretched his legs, slouching lower in the seat. "She reminds me of women Rufus Kidwell kept when he ran a cathouse, out around Dry Fork."

Holding a police interceptor engine to a twenty-mile-an-hour idle through a residential area required all of Jesse's attention. It was like requiring a thoroughbred horse to drag a milk wagon. "Was Rufus any kin to Tracy Kidwell?" Jesse asked when the houses were more widely spaced and he could give the cruiser a little more gas. The hour and a half he'd spent mediating a property line feud between Tracy and Ted Jarnigan still rankled.

Crow thought for a moment. "Tracy's a first cousin to him, I believe. Rufus drank himself to death after his boy got killed in Korea, but before that he run a fancy whorehouse where the VanLandinghams live now."

The cruiser's engine responded smoothly to pressure from Jesse's right foot, carrying them away from town, into farmland and forest. Where the streetlights ended, the road was a pale concrete ribbon winding through a black tunnel precisely as wide as the headlight high beams.

"You'd of thought there was a factory turning them women out, they looked so much alike," Crow mused. "That girl on the TV could be a granddaughter to Rufus's whores." After a thoughtful silence the old man wondered out loud, "That singer ain't from Cincinnati is she? That's where he found most of them girls."

"I don't think so." Jesse was glad the old man felt like telling stories. Crow's voice gave him something to think about, other than how much he wanted to know why Dave Brent chose prison over speaking some woman's name. And any story was better than a recitation of what he was doing wrong with Margaret.

Crow reminisced a long time about Rufus Kidwell's women, recalled their perfume and provocative dresses, the brazen seductive behavior that on a few Saturday nights had some of Hawkes County's most respectable citizens engaged in jealous fistfights. He didn't fall silent until Jesse turned onto the unpaved hill road leading to the cemetery.

"Did it bother you, that Roy Compton wouldn't give us any names?" Jesse asked, hoping to spark another monologue from the old man.

Crow took the bait. "Didn't surprise me a'tall. But Martha like to have died over it."

While the car lurched over the rutted incline, Crow voiced surprise Martha expected Roy to tell on other kids just because he was a sheriff's great-grandson. Before long his train of thought derailed on Blaine Ingraham's name.

The old deputy speculated at length how the stubborn and foolish Ingraham would resort to pushing kids like Roy Compton around. "Be damn if I see how you can think about letting a piss-ant like that one take over at the courthouse." Crow spat the words angrily.

Cresting the hill, still a fair distance from the cemetery, Jesse parked the cruiser among some high old oaks. In the dark it would be almost invisible unless someone knew exactly where to look for the car. He got out of the vehicle, opened the back door and reached inside for a six-cell flashlight and his pistol.

Crow drew his smaller revolver from under the seat as well. "Don't know why I even brung this thing," he muttered, shuffling off into the night. "Little old twenty-two ain't good for a ghost nor much of nothing else."

At the forest's edge Jesse and Crow stopped to study the scattered tombstones from the cover of long shadows. Full dark had fallen while they were inside Martha's, but a canopy of stars above a sliver of moon cast light enough to show the graveyard was empty and still.

Jesse allowed the old man to lead as they crossed the cemetery. The clearing seemed larger than the day of the funeral, when cars lined dirt lanes and mourners crowded the resting place of half a dozen generations of Brents. Approaching his former deputy's grave, Jesse thumbed his flashlight and the beam eroded darkness around the plot of bare earth.

"Will you look at that?" Crow breathed. Jesse's light revealed an arrangement of wilted petals and faded greenery at the head of the grave. The old man prodded the dead flowers with a boot. "Roy Compton and them other kids wasn't just telling tales."

Jesse knelt and frowned down at the dead blossoms. "You know what kind of flowers these are?" At first the odd scent was like roses, but with each inhalation the difference was more pronounced, spicier, more exotic than any flower Jesse could recognize. And the air was cool, almost cold. In summer heat such blossoms would produce a riot of scent.

Crow shook his head. "Look like lilies, kind of. Smell a lot stronger though."

Not being able to put a name to the blossoms irritated Jesse Surratt, one more unanswered question to ponder. Reaching to touch a smooth, thornless stem, snapping the bloom free, Jesse's finger brushed something solid. He pushed dead leaves away from white candle stubs. "Wonder if we could get fingerprints off these things?"

"Before they melted you could of got prints good as a picture," Crow said. "But they wouldn't be worth fooling with after burning down so far."

Jesse wished he'd brought an evidence bag from the car, to protect a blossom while he carried it back to town. As he carefully tucked the flower into his shirt pocket, shifting light in the trees across the cemetery caught his eye.

"Somebody's here." Thumbing the flashlight's switch Jesse heard the satisfaction in his own voice. "Maybe whoever left these things is coming back."

The old man straightened and raised his head. "Where?"

"Car headlights." Jesse pointed the direction, a second before the glimmer winked out. "Only I don't remember a road past those trees."

"Ben Wilkins and his boys cut timber off that ridge, five, six years ago. They may've left a logging road when they was done." The ex-deputy stared in the direction Jesse had pointed. "Might just be some of them kids coming back though."

Jesse shook his head. "I don't think so. Roy said kids have stopped coming here since they decided the place is haunted." The sheriff needed to believe *she* was there, not a troop of ghost-hunting adolescents. "Let's get into some cover."

The nearest trees were twenty yards away. Jesse could have reached them in a few seconds, but held himself to a fast walk so Crow could keep up. Leaving the clearing they pushed into waist high weeds and circled to the left, into a thicket of blackberry vines. The tangled growth offered concealment from which the whole of the graveyard could be seen.

"If I live maybe I'll come here next year and pick a mess of berries," Crow whispered. "See if I can get Maggie to make us a cobbler."

Jesse lowered himself to his knees as Crow muttered, "Listen. I believe I hear . . . "

The old man's words were cut off by whispered swearing as a stout blackberry thorn buried itself in Jesse Surratt's knee. He couldn't stop muttering a series of stage-whispered curses before he pulled the wretched briar free.

"If you're through cussing you might hush and listen a while," Crow hissed. "Somebody's coming, over yonder."

Jesse stopped swearing, stopped moving, stopped breathing as his face flushed hotly. He wasn't a real law enforcement officer, not like Crow Markwell. Embarrassed, he felt as though he belonged in "Abbott and Costello Play 'Cops and Robbers.'"

Autumn wind rattled dry leaves, and somewhere close a night bird fluttered into flight, but Jesse neither saw nor heard anything that suggested a human being was approaching. "You sure you heard something?"

"Somebody's out there, not making no more noise than a deer." The old man looked at Jesse. "Can't you hear it?"

After a while Jesse *did* hear something, or perhaps only pushed his imagination hard enough to create a rustling out of sync with subtle night sounds from the forest. It was hard to watch and wait when he wanted so badly to know who was in the darkness.

Closing his eyes, Jesse forced his breathing to slow, and when he felt in control again, looked over the graveyard in time to see a black shadow separate itself from the treeline and move across the grass. "Did you see that?"

"Seen *something*," Crow replied. "I was sure I heard it, but my eyes ain't worth a damn." He pointed toward the trees. "Seemed like something come out of the dark over yonder."

The shadow moved steadily, and when it reached the tombstones seemed to meld with the dark shapes and disappear. "It came from the same direction I saw those lights," Jesse whispered. The shadow was visible again, became a human form, a silhouette without detail. "Can you tell who it is?"

"In this light I wouldn't recognize *you* if we bumped together." Crow sighed. "If we was just a little bit closer . . . "

"She's wearing black," Jesse told the old man. "Or maybe blue jeans and a dark coat. Hard to see anything for sure."

"You sure it's a woman?"

"Gotta be," Jesse said. There was something too innately feminine about the way the figure moved for it to be a man. "Damn. Why doesn't she sit up straight and get in the light?"

After a moment light flared at the grave site, and the slim body bent over a burning match, face and features still hidden. "Ease over half a foot," Jesse pleaded with the woman. "Just six inches, give me one good look at your face." Inch high flames capped the woman's candles, but she kept her back turned as she knelt at the foot of Dave Brent's grave.

Then Jesse and Crow heard the crying.

It began as a low moaning, and ended on the same note. The middle, though, was an angry shriek that seemed to plead with and curse God at the same time.

"Lord have mercy." Crow Markwell shook his head as he whispered, "That woman don't think there's any hope left in all the wide world."

The old man sounded sympathetic, and Jesse understood. He felt an urge to comfort the woman himself. There was too much pain in her cries not to feel sorry for her. Still mesmerized by what he'd heard, Jesse watched as the figure straightened and took a few steps away from the grave.

"This is the sheriff!" he shouted, stepping around the briars into the clearing. "Stop!"

Pointing his long flashlight at the grave, Jesse saw her turn and lope away with feline grace and speed. To his amazement she stopped and came back for her flowers, and was gone again into darkness.

"Shit," Jesse muttered, and began running after her.

CHAPTER TWENTY-THREE

What Lorena did in the cemetery felt familiar. It reminded her of being the little girl whom Dr. Hannan encouraged to have imaginary conversations and pretend fights with the people who hurt her.

Curled into a broad leather chair in Lois Hannan's office, Lorena had talked to her tormenter Ezra Stillwell, though it was a certainty *he* could never bother her again. Lorena damned Ezra to the worst horrors her young mind could conjure, while Lois nodded encouragement.

She was always encouraging, no matter what awful things Lorena imagined. For her first seven or eight months at St. Catherine's, Lorena was mute, said not a word to anyone. When she began speaking again, the psychiatrist was pleased with *anything* the child said.

There had been pretend talks with Irene, Lorena's mother. With Lois Hannan's help, Lorena raged and howled condemnation at her mother. Months went by before Dr. Hannan was able to teach Lorena how to forgive Irene for dying, for leaving her alone and helpless with Ezra.

Lorena smiled, wondering what her gray-haired lady psychiatrist would think if she could see her former patient speaking to a dead man, over his fresh grave.

David hadn't been cruel like Irene and Ezra. But he was *gone*, and Lorena was abandoned all over again. Her bereavement seemed painful and disabling as losing a hand or foot without anesthesia. She came to the cemetery to bleed hard shrieking grief, in a place where, like Lois Hannan's office, self-control was never necessary.

It was more than just anger. If she stood beside the grave, and listened hard enough (figuratively, of course; Lorena wasn't so maddened by grief to believe she actually heard David's voice), answers to difficult questions came to her.

She'd gotten past the crying and was speaking out loud her plans to leave, to build another home someplace else, when a shout interrupted her musings. Someone charged out of the trees toward her, yelling words she didn't quite understand. Too stunned for anything but flight, after half a dozen steps Lorena turned back and retrieved the fresh flowers and candles from David's grave. She wasn't about to leave them for someone to paw over or ridicule.

White light swept across the grave as Lorena reached for the floral arrangement, and she was careful to keep her back turned to it. When she turned to flee she ran into total darkness. Someone was shouting, but she couldn't understand the words over the sound of her own breath. Damned high school boys, she thought, come to capture the ghost in the graveyard.

Tales of a haunting were circulating around the high school. Lorena heard the rumors from her elderly neighbor, who collected and repeated whatever gossip came her way. That the youngsters made Lorena into a ghost was amusing, but boys curious enough to talk about her would come back again, if only to be frightened into new stories. She'd been expecting them.

An ice pick was tucked in the pocket of her denim jacket, its sharp point safely wrapped with plastic tape. It wasn't a weapon. Lorena had survived too much real horror in her life to think a group of superstitious schoolboys might hurt her.

If they followed, though, the boys wouldn't know the woods half so well as she did. Leaving them to flail around in brush and high briars, she'd double back to their car. A pair of flat tires would make them think twice before trespassing on her grief again.

As she ran, Lorena wondered if she was turning into the kind of crazy woman Gothic novels were written about. In a few years she'd be a gray eccentric whose best hours were spent standing over a moonlit grave. She ought to leave, and very soon. The depressing vision of herself if she stayed was reason enough to abandon the place.

At the far edge of the graveyard Lorena stopped to look back from the shelter of the treeline. As soon as she recognized her pursuer, the fever of panicked flight eased, the frenzied heartbeat in her chest began to quiet. The sheriff, Jesse Surratt, ran behind her, not a pack of dreadful boys.

Well ahead in their race, Lorena could afford a brief rest. The sheriff lumbered along like an old bear. She was tempted to step outside the shelter of the trees and let him close on her by a few yards. Not enough to catch her, just enough to further frustrate the sheriff.

During a prison visit Lorena had heard David say the worst part of standing trial was not explaining to Jesse Surratt what really happened, their last night at the motel, why David didn't save himself at the trial. If there was only herself to consider, she would have exposed her hiding place to the sheriff, told him what David refused to.

She envisioned how it would be, walking out of the woods to meet the sheriff halfway across the shadowy cemetery. She'd smile at him (he was David's *friend,* after all) and answer all the questions he asked. The sheriff would probably smile back, leading her off to jail.

The image of her son, sleeping peacefully at home, intruded on the fantasy. She'd die before she gave up the boy, something David understood. Talking to the sheriff would separate Lorena from her son for a long, long time. She was ashamed to even fantasize sacrificing his small future.

Jesse Surratt lost momentum, slowed and stopped. His chest heaved with the effort of pursuit, and ragged breath was audible across fifty yards of open ground separating him from Lorena. She was stunned to see him reach for the pistol at his side and fire into the air, twice. Flinching at the unexpected noise, Lorena stepped backward as an orange muzzle flash lit a small circle of the world.

"Jesse!"

The shout from behind the sheriff sounded flat and faint after the pistol roar, but it was loud enough to echo off the flint ridge behind Lorena.

"Was that you a'shooting?" someone called.

Lorena hadn't realized anyone else was in the cemetery. Looking past the sheriff she saw the other man, far behind Jesse Surratt. "That was *your* gun wasn't it? Are you all right?"

The sheriff took a deep breath before bellowing a weary reply. "I'm okay, Crow." Another deep breath. "Everything's okay."

Lorena laughed softly as he put the gun away and began a laborious jog toward the treeline. After a while she had to clap one hand over her mouth to keep uncontrollable giggles from giving away her hiding place.

She wished *she* had a pistol to aim at the stars. What would slow, clumsy Jesse Surratt do if another shot cracked the graveyard silence? Fall to the ground like an acrobat? Turn and run the other way? It would be funny, watching from the shadows.

Lorena thought about staying to watch him hunt for her. He was moving too far to the right to pose a serious threat. If he changed direction and came closer, the path behind her was nearly as familiar as her front yard. The sheriff didn't worry her at all. The man coming along behind Jesse Surratt could pose a problem though.

He was headed straight for Lorena without even looking up to see where he was going. The man's pace was slow and labored, and Lorena figured he was an old man. He kept his eyes on the ground, head bent over the glow of a flashlight. He was *tracking* her. Lorena realized she must have left faint footprints in wet grass as she ran from the sheriff's light. Jesse Surratt missed them, but his companion was coming for her.

The older man's purposeful march across the cemetery was as frightening as the sheriff's pursuit was comic. Lorena took a reassuring look at Jesse Surratt, still moving away from her, before turning to push deeper into the woods.

She held her pace to a brisk walk, rather than breaking into the run that was her natural urge. Her progress would be faster if she was able to take frequent bearings from the moon and familiar old trees towering overhead.

Low on the hill, sputtered curses broke the silence, and Lorena guessed the sheriff had blundered into the stand of locust trees on the east side of the cemetery. Inch-long spikes on the limbs would make retreating difficult. He might not know it, but Jesse Surratt had just lost their race.

There were no sounds from the other man though. Lorena turned around and stared into the night. That one had moved so slowly she didn't think he could have caught up yet. Still, he frightened her. She shook herself, clearing the image of his stubborn pursuit.

Her feet found a path she and David had used, shortcutting through a grove of evergreens, the thick carpet of pine needles comforting. Jesse Surratt could thrash around the woods all he wanted; he'd never see her, sheltered by the trees' thick limbs, or hear light steps across the soft ground below them.

At the logging road where she'd left her car—the road David had shown her, so no one would see them enter or leave the woods together—Lorena watched for a while before leaving the shelter of the forest. She was afraid the second man, the tracker, might have reached the vehicle ahead of her.

No one appeared near the car. Lorena couldn't hear footsteps other than her own when she approached it, and there were no shouted orders at her to stop. She got in her vehicle and steered it to a wide curve where she could turn around, driving off the hill a little faster than usual.

It was time for her to go away, Lorena thought, not slowing the car until she reached the edge of town. The notion of leaving was troubling. She'd made a home where her son was safe, she had her greenhouse, even a few friends who were important, even if they knew almost nothing about her. David was gone, forever gone, and he was the only thing that had anchored her in Hawkes County. Leaving was just part of a new reality.

At the Jerry's on the east end of town Lorena stopped, parked her car and went inside. She ordered a cup of hot chocolate and sat at a window, gazing into the night. She was finishing the chocolate as the sheriff's car drove past, headed for his farm.

Lorena drank another cup of sweet comfort. Then she went to her car, and carried David's flowers back to the cemetery, where they belonged.

CHAPTER TWENTY-FOUR

For over an hour Margaret looked toward the door at every small noise, listening for Jesse's return. She sighed as the county cruiser pulled into the driveway.

Across the living room, in contrast to her nervousness, Mark Turner exhibited an icy calm, providing three-or four-word answers to a few of her questions, ignoring most of them. The boy was far more attentive to the shepherd Casey, whose head rested on his lap.

Margaret left her chair and stepped toward the back door. Jesse would need a *lot* of preparation for Mark. When the sofa springs creaked beneath the boy she turned to look at him. "I hope you aren't thinking about leaving."

His only response was more of his silent pouting.

"Don't even think about going anywhere until you've talked to the sheriff," she said, then walked to the back door.

Margaret waited a long time. When Jesse didn't come inside she stepped onto the porch, where the air smelled clean and fresh after the reek of anger and fear in her house. Jesse and Crow Markwell slouched against the old man's pickup truck. Margaret couldn't hear words, just the rhythm of their sentences.

When she walked through damp grass to stand with them, the men hushed. "Is something wrong?" she asked.

Jesse lifted his left arm and Margaret slipped under it. "Crow and I were just talking about how your husband acted like a damn fool tonight."

She leaned into the heat of Jesse's body. "Did you see who Martha's grandson was talking about?"

"We seen her," Crow acknowledged. "That's all we done though, just seen her."

"She showed up like Roy said." Jesse sighed, shamefaced as a child explaining a bad report card. "I wish you could have heard how she stood over that grave and cried. Patsy was hard to watch at the funeral, but this was worse."

"It *was* a woman then?"

Jesse nodded. "Then she ran when I came galloping out of the woods like a lawman from a bad cowboy movie. I pulled my gun and shot in the air a couple of times, trying to scare her. But she still got away."

Crow laughed. "Like to scared water out of me when that pistol went off. I was coming along behind with a good-for-nothing .22 pop gun and when I heard them shots all I could think of was who might be dead."

Margaret shuddered, wondered how Crow could find something to laugh about in such a thought, wondered how Jesse could enjoy reliving such an experience. Their excitement was as tangible as the sweat of a long distance runner, though her husband still looked embarrassed.

"I don't know it was a bad idea to fire into the air," Crow continued. "I'd stop, if somebody shot at me."

"The gun was pointed straight up," Jesse objected, raising his free hand to demonstrate. "Like that. I wasn't shooting *at* anybody."

"Did you arrest her?" Neither of them had mentioned a name. "Did you find out who it was?"

The security light over the garage illuminated Jesse's blush. "All I know is it was a woman," he said. "And she can run like a damn deer."

Margaret couldn't help smiling. The men didn't have an awful story to tell, just wanted to brag about how close it had all been.

"I sure as hell wasn't going to outrun her." Jesse frowned at his feet, as though an explanation for what happened was written in the gravel of the driveway. "So I used the gun, trying to make her stop."

"Before it was over with we found where she'd parked her car," Crow said. "And the path she walked to get to it."

"Only because *you* had sense enough to look down and follow her footprints." Jesse managed a shamefaced grin. "This old man knew what he was doing. I was the one who screwed up."

Crow shrugged. "If I'd had a gun that would make serious noise maybe I'd've shot too."

Jesse reached in his shirt pocket and took out a wrinkled, dying flower, held the blossom toward Margaret. "Smell this."

"Roses?" Margaret guessed, after a breath from her husband's hand. "No, not roses, something else."

"Do you know what kind of flower it is?"

"It's familiar," Margaret told him. "But I can't place it."

"We found a pile of them on Dave Brent's grave," Crow explained. "Wilted, but that woman was bringing a fresh batch."

"They look a little bit like lilies." Jesse turned the flower in his hand, studied it from another angle. "The stems didn't have thorns, and you could smell them a long way off."

As Jesse put the flower back in his shirt pocket Crow opened the door to his truck. "I'm a'going home. This has been a big night for a old man."

"How about a cup of coffee?" Jesse offered. "Or a beer?"

Margaret was relieved when Crow declined the invitation. Mark Turner was waiting for a meeting that would stretch Jesse's patience to its limit. Rolling the window down, Crow told Jesse, "I'll get back up to that graveyard tomorrow evening."

Margaret waited until Crow's truck left the driveway to ask, "Crow's going back up there by himself?"

Jesse shook his head. "He's taking Glenda, his hound."

"Aren't you going?"

"The woman'll be watching for us now. Crow will go onto that hill before dark, stay all night if he has to. She won't outrun Glenda."

As Jesse turned toward the house Margaret laid a hand on her husband's shoulder. "Somebody's waiting for you."

"Who?"

Margaret took a deep breath. "Mark Turner. Darlene brought him about an hour ago."

"So? What does he want?"

Tears Margaret had contained since Darlene left spilled down her cheeks. "God, Jesse."

Sobs racked her body and she fell against her husband's broad chest, inhaling the fragrance from the broken blossom in his pocket. Arms wrapped around her, Jesse held her wordlessly. It was all so sad and scary, so silly and pointless. Wiping her eyes with one hand, for a moment Margaret would have given anything to have never come to Hawkes County, Kentucky.

"Tell me why Mark Turner's here," Jesse murmured in her ear. "And why you're so upset."

Trying to find words to explain brought more tears. Margaret fought them back before speaking. "After I tell you about it, we've got to talk. You've got to listen to me before you do anything else." Margaret was pleased her voice didn't shake.

Jesse nodded.

"Mark was the one who shot at us, coming back from the funeral." she began.

The change in Jesse's face was instantaneous, cold anger suffusing his features. He turned toward the house but Margaret held onto his shoulders, made him look at her. "We have to talk *before* you go in there."

Jesse pulled away, got as far as the porch before Margaret voiced the threat she hoped would stop him. "I'll leave you." Her husband turned and glared across the yard. "Go through that door without talking to me and I'll leave." Swallowing hard, Margaret willed Jesse to believe what she wasn't sure was real. "I swear to God I won't spend another night in this house."

"The little bastard *shot* at me!" Jesse roared. "What is there to talk about?"

Margaret came to the edge of the porch and took Jesse's hand. "Mark didn't shoot at *you*. He shot at the *car*, because *I* was in it. You had nothing to do with it, Jesse."

Jesse was about to say something harsh, and she watched him chew his lower lips, biting the words off.

"If someone did to you what we've done to Mark Turner, you might look for a gun too. Especially if you were sixteen." Margaret pulled at Jesse until they were close to the porch swing. "Sit down," she insisted, and settled next to him.

"God in heaven, I've never even talked to the kid," Jesse said. "Sometimes he gives me the finger when I drive by. That's the sum and goddamn total of our contact. What does he think I did to him?"

"You put his father in prison."

Jesse looked at her, exasperation in his eyes. "Len Turner moved marijuana for Bradley Smallwood."

"All that boy knows is his father was trying to meet payments on their farm," Margaret countered. Waving her free hand toward the hills Jesse loved, Margaret demanded, "Tell me you wouldn't do the same thing to hold onto this place."

"That's different," The objection was so weak Margaret decided it didn't really count. Jesse took a deep breath, let it out slowly. "What do you want me to do?"

"I don't know," Margaret admitted. "But I wish you'd been here when Mark and his mother came. It was awful."

She'd been in the living room, trying to lose herself in a novel when Darlene Turner knocked on the front door. Flinching, she'd reached for Jesse's revolver, even though Casey the shepherd wagged her tail instead of growling. "Who is it?" she'd demanded.

"It's me, Mrs. Surratt," Darlene called from the porch. "Me and my boy." Margaret opened the door after she turned on the porch light. There was no car in the driveway; Darlene and her son had walked the mile from their farm.

Certain the woman's haggard eyes signaled some awful wrong in the house down the road Margaret invited them inside. As they crossed the threshold Margaret realized she was still holding the pistol, and put it behind her back, while Darlene explained why they'd come.

"My boy told me he was the one shot at you the other evening." Darlene Turner took a deep, quavery breath. "I whipped him for it already, but I know that ain't going to be enough. Your husband will want to see him."

Margaret had stared dumbly. "Jesse's not here," she said when she found her voice. "But he'll be home soon."

"You set down," Darlene told her son, who lowered his lanky frame onto the sofa. "And don't you move until the sheriff comes home."

Mark nodded, his eyes frightened and wet.

Darlene Turner turned to go, but looked back at Margaret from the door. "Ask the sheriff to call me before he takes my boy to jail. He'll need some money in there, and some clothes. I'll have go to town and cash a check."

The woman was gone before Margaret could tell Darlene to take her son home, that Jesse would talk to him in the morning. Margaret wished she'd said Mark wasn't going to jail, that everything was going to turn out all right.

She was left alone with a boy trying hard to appear tough, looking at her with a bleak, wounded expression, eyes hopeless as his mother's. She tried to talk to him, but when Mark wouldn't speak, they began a silent wait for Jesse's return.

On the glider Margaret buried her face in Jesse's shoulder. "That family's beaten, Jesse. You took their father. I took the land where Len said Mark could live someday. Houses are sprouting there like mushrooms but none of them are for Mark."

"What if he'd flinched with that rifle?" Jesse said. "Someone could have died."

"I don't care," Margaret replied. "Take that woman's son and you'll the same as kill her. Him too, probably. And if that's what you're going to do, I won't stay and watch." She was back to the threat, the one she wasn't certain she could keep.

Inside the house, the telephone was ringing. Margaret got up to answer it. "Talk to him, Jesse. Threaten him, scare him, do whatever you have to. But don't you dare take that boy to jail."

Margaret walked into the house and heard Jesse's heavy steps behind her. She smiled at Rita Bailey's voice at the other end of the line and began telling how silly Crow and Jesse had been at the graveyard.

She wouldn't talk long.

She needed to know what happened between Jesse and Mark Turner.

CHAPTER TWENTY-FIVE

As he slipped past Margaret at the hall phone, Jesse thought the serenity of his house seemed out-of-place as a dog in church. The presence in *his* house of the assailant who turned an automobile into a shell of shattered glass and cold fear was serious business, even if it was only a sixteen year old boy. Margaret's laughing with her friend about his misadventures in the cemetery, his dog's calm tail-wagging greeting at the door seemed completely out of place.

He found Mark Turner in the living room. Some small portion of the anger carried in from the porch was defused by the youngster's appearance. Thin to the point of near emaciation, stringy shoulder-length hair framed a frightened face, above a t-shirt advertising a rock band Jesse'd never heard of.

Jesse jerked his thumb in the direction of the kitchen. "We can talk in there."

Mark Turner looked past him wordlessly, watching Margaret at the phone, and didn't move. He stayed on the couch, didn't follow Jesse to the kitchen until Margaret discreetly nodded. Casey trailed after them and when Mark sat in the chair Jesse pointed to, shoved her head in the youngster's lap.

Jesse closed the door, and recognized the boy's trick of not really looking at someone. It was something he remembered from his own adolescence, the subterfuge of aiming eyes at a threatening person while focusing on the wall behind them. It was an effective way to hide fear or shame, a subtle deception Jesse Surratt used well into adulthood.

Measuring grounds into the coffee maker Jesse heard the music of Margaret's laughter in the hall beyond the kitchen door. Not even the realization she was giggling—with Rita Bailey, from the sound of it— about his slapstick chase through the Brent graveyard detracted from his appreciation of her laughter. She didn't sound like someone who'd just threatened to leave her husband again.

While water ran through the coffee maker Jesse stood with his back to Mark Turner, studying the boy's reflection in the windows over the sink. He watched Mark Turner while remembering his wife's words on the porch, when she insisted he go easy with Mark: "I swear to God I won't spend another night in this house."

The threat could be avoided easily enough, cutting some kind of break for the kid. Looking at the boy, Jesse didn't even feel bad about doing it. Mark Turner was terrified, not terrifying.

"Know what I think about your story, your telling Darlene you shot at my car?" Jesse poured two cups of coffee and carried them to the table. "I think maybe it was only a story, something to tell your mama, make her think her boy had become some kind of king-hell bad ass. I think you were only trying to impress her, maybe scare her a little bit."

Mark Turner wrapped slim fingers around his cup and shook his head. "Mama figured out what I did. When she asked about it I told her."

So much for offering an easy alibi, Jesse thought. "Why'd you do that? You could have lied," he said. "We searched that hill for two days and didn't find anything to make you a suspect."

Mark frowned as though the idea of lying to his mother never occurred to him. "Mama *knew*." The boy carefully set the cup down, crossed thin arms over his chest and glared at Jesse. "She couldn't of *made* me tell, though."

"I can believe that." In the Navy Jesse had seen youngsters like Mark Turner endure more than a mother's anger without whimpering. "I don't suppose she could have *made* you say anything,"

"I never told her I done it till she started in crying again." Mark broke off his angry scrutiny and looked down at the table, his defiance fading. "Mama cries a lot."

Jesse sighed. "You must have had a reason for taking a rifle up on that hill. Did you know Dave Brent? Or Ray Bailey?"

Mark lifted his shoulders in a weak shrug, then shook his head. "People say you're out to clear that deputy's name. How come nobody's doing that for my dad?"

Jesse mashed his cigarette into the ashtray, lighting another while the first still smoldered. "Your father pleaded guilty. I heard it myself."

153

"That Brent guy got convicted of killing somebody," Mark argued. "That's worse than anything my dad did."

"I'm pretty sure Dave Brent was covering up for someone else." Jesse wondered why it felt necessary to defend himself to a sixteen-year-old, especially one who had big troubles of his own. "If I'm right, that means there's a killer walking around Midland. Shouldn't I find out who it is?"

The boy didn't answer.

"I'm not sure what to do here," Jesse said when the silence seemed unbearably heavy.

Mark Turner stared at the floor, whipped-puppy frightened. He raised his eyes for a moment, then dropped them after one brief look at Jesse's face. He didn't answer, just lifted his shoulders again, a gesture that was beginning to irritate hell out of Jesse Surratt.

"What would Len Turner do?" Jesse asked, almost whispering, voice so low the youngster opposite his seat had to lean toward him to hear. "If someone shot at a car Darlene was riding in, what would he do?"

"Dad would make them real sorry."

Lifting both hands, Jesse slapped his palms flat onto the table, coffee splashing from their cups, a set of salt and pepper shakers falling to the floor. The noise was sudden and unexpected as a gunshot after a funeral. Mark flinched and looked ready to dive under the table, Casey lunged for the kitchen door, and in the hallway, Margaret fell silent.

"Do you think I care less about my wife than your father cares about his?" Jesse roared at the boy.

When he was assigned to train recruits at the naval base in San Diego, Jesse Surratt had become an expert at getting the attention of surly teenagers. This boy would talk to him before either of them left the room. When Mark Turner's breathing slowed, Jesse spoke again, his voice so low the youngster had to lean forward again, more wary this time.

"The only reason I'm not breaking your ass is my wife thinks you deserve a break." His cigarette had burned down to the filter, and Jesse hadn't taken more than two puffs off it. He stabbed the butt into the ashtray. "You can put this in the bank, son: if it wasn't for Margaret I'd lock your sorry ass up and forget where I put you."

Mark Turner's ears flushed the color of ripe plums, and his eyes narrowed to slits. "So do it. I don't care."

"You pointed a gun at me," Jesse taunted. "Seems like you ought to have guts enough to tell me why you did it."

"God *damn* it." The boy's body was taut as a guitar string, and the hand he lifted to brush long hair away from his eyes trembled. "We couldn't get ahead *no* way till my dad got involved with that marijuana business. And just when we was getting so we lived like everybody else they sent him off to prison."

"What 'they?'" Jesse demanded. "Who do figure 'they' are?"

"People like you. People who don't know what it is to have problems."

Jesse couldn't help laughing at the boy's perception of his life, didn't stop laughing until the color in Mark Turner's face deepened. "The main difference between you and me is twenty-five years of experience," he said at last. "I grew up poor as dirt on this farm, and my dad scrambled for a living just as hard as yours did."

If he told the truth, Jesse didn't have any problems picturing his own father in a marijuana field, tending plants worth their weight in gold, with a pistol on his hip. Joe Surratt would have done that and more to keep his farm. He would have raised thistles for the devil to keep his farm and family together.

"Daddy wasn't doing nothing so bad," Mark said, his voice shaky. "He didn't kill nobody."

"You're right," Jesse admitted. "Growing pot's not as bad as killing someone." He got up from the table to refill his cup, watching the boy in the windows again. "It's not as bad as climbing a hill with a rifle either. So one more time: why'd you do it?"

In the room's reflection the boy looked at Jesse for only the second time since sitting at the table, not at the wall behind him. "I watched Carl Edwards' bulldozers all day, and got madder and madder." The youngster hugged himself, as if the chill wind blowing off the ridges touched his bones. "I got so mad that after a while I didn't care about nothing. That's when I went home and got the rifle."

"Then what?"

"I just meant to scare your wife, for selling Carl Edwards that land. I didn't mean to hurt nobody." The boy reached for his coffee cup, sipped at it and blurted, "There's an old mine ventilation shave, runs from one side of that hill to the other. That's how I got away."

Jesse came back to the table. "I'm glad you didn't hurt Margaret." He sat down, feeling very tired. "Then I'd have to hurt you back, and maybe your mom or your dad would have tried to hurt *me*. It could have been hard to end, like those old-time feuds they used to have in these mountains."

They were both quiet until Mark muttered, "I'm sorry."

"I hope to God you're *real* sorry." Jesse wondered what words would move them away from the table, wondered where he would find them. "Did you think of maybe talking to someone about being mad enough to pick up a gun? Talk to them before you did it?"

Mark's face wrinkled in a dismissive sneer. "Talk to who?" Tears beaded in the boy's eyes but he wiped them away before they spilled. "There *ain't* nobody to talk to, Sheriff. Mama got a preacher to come out to the house once to try and get me to talk about what happened to Dad, but that old man only wanted to tell me about Jesus."

"What about a teacher at school?"

Mark shrugged again. "If you don't play basketball or work on their dumb-ass yearbook, something like that, they don't care neither."

Jesse thought about the dark secret he'd carried when he was about Mark's age, a brutal assault by a sick man who seared his soul with shame. There hadn't been anyone for Jesse to talk with either.

"Am I going to jail?" the youngster asked when they'd sat in silence a full minute.

Jesse shook his head.

Mark was quiet for another half a dozen heartbeats. "What're you going to do then?"

"I don't know," Jesse admitted. He didn't have a clue about anything useful he could do to, or for, the boy. "But if I decide the best thing for you is to climb onto a bridge and jump into Three Doves Creek, I expect to see you in a swimming suit."

Mark Turner managed a small grin. "I can't swim a lick, Sheriff."

"Maybe I won't say swim. Maybe I'll just say jump." Jesse stood up. "Margaret's off the phone. I reckon we can call your mother, tell her she can come and get you."

"Our car's broke." Mark flushed his embarrassment. "I'll walk."

Jesse shook his head. "I'll take you. I ought to talk to Darlene anyway. Go on to my car. I'll catch up." As Mark left the kitchen Jesse carried the coffee cups to the sink and rinsed them. He watched outside as the interior of the police cruiser lit up when the boy got inside, then there was only darkness beyond the windows.

"I thought you handled that very well, Sheriff Surratt."

"I figured you were listening." Jesse turned to find his wife smiling at him. "I also heard you talking to Rita Bailey about men who ought to have better things to do than go goofy in a graveyard."

Margaret came close enough her breasts pressed against him, and Jesse put his arms around her. "Lord, I thought she'd never hush so I could eavesdrop on you and Mark." Margaret increased the pressure of her middle against his.

"Damn." Jesse let his hands drop below Margaret's waist, until they cupped the swell of her bottom. "If I knew I was going to get propositioned I'd've let that kid walk home."

"Go on," Margaret said. "I'll be in bed, waiting." She backed away, glancing down and grinning. "From the looks of things you better hurry."

Jesse laughed and squeezed Margaret's rear end one more time before heading for the back door.

Mark Turner sat quietly while Jesse started the car, didn't speak until the county cruiser turned left at the end of the drive, toward the Turner farm. Then he blurted, "Does my Dad have to know about this?"

"That's up to you and your mama," Jesse told him. "Offhand I'd say the fewer know about it, the better. Tell Darlene I said that."

When Jesse braked the car in the Turner driveway Mark seemed to fly out of the vehicle. The front door opened as his feet hit the wooden porch, and Darlene stepped into the glare of the cruiser's headlights. She hugged her son, her eyes red-rimmed and teary.

She pushed Mark through the door and came down the steps, before Jesse could put the car in gear and go away. "You brought him home," Darlene said after Jesse rolled down his window. "Will he have to go see a judge?"

Jesse shook his head. "I'm not going to tell anyone about this, Darlene," he told her. "But I *am* going to find someone Mark can talk to." He shrugged his shoulders. "Trouble's easy to find when a boy feels like he does."

"It's been hard on him since. . ." Darlene's voice faltered. "Since Len went to prison."

Jesse nodded. "Mark told me a little about it."

"I thank you for bringing him home, sheriff," the woman said. "Mark's not a bad boy, not really."

"I don't reckon he is," Jesse agreed. "When Len comes home, Margaret and I would be pleased if you all would come and see us, have dinner with us some night."

Darlene Turner smiled wearily and nodded. One hand lifted in a small wave as Jesse backed away from her house.

At the end of the Turner driveway, Jesse decided the letters he'd meant to write about an early release for Dave Brent could be written for Len Turner instead. County sheriffs in Kentucky had political clout. It would be foolish not to use it for a good cause.

He mashed the accelerator, and gravel spewed behind the car as it sped away from the troubled Turner home.

CHAPTER TWENTY SIX

Harvey Gartland put the receiver of his expensive office telephone gently back into in its cradle, leaned back in his chair and lit a cigar. As a rule he seldom smoked so late at night. His wife Frieda loathed the dark tobacco to which Harvey was addicted, and he seldom lit up at home. In his office, though, an hour before midnight, there was no one to resent his indulgence.

Or for that, matter, to complain about two inches of raw whiskey in a paper cup by his elbow.

As LaGrange warden, Harvey took home an almost embarrassing salary. Frieda had learned to recognize and expect quality, but Harvey's preferences leaned toward the cheap smokes and rough liquor of his youth. The box of expensive Honduran cigars on the desk was for visitors. The forty-cent stogies Harvey smoked when he was alone reminded him how far he'd come, from a family which had survived largely on charity.

He felt slightly sick to his stomach, though whether that was due to bourbon with no dinner or to the message he'd just received was debatable. The message had been a simple one, delivered by a voice so matter of fact it might have belonged to the "time and temperature" operator. Anyone tapping Harvey's phone would have learned nothing from the curt, "It's done."

The warden stared at his high-tech telephone and tried to decide whether a call to the sheriff down in Hawkes County was warranted. On the one hand Jesse Surratt deserved to know what Harvey Gartland had just learned. On the other, unless he'd wildly misjudged Surratt, it was knowledge which could make finding sleep again difficult, should the sheriff be in bed when Harvey called.

Harvey tapped the rural sheriff's number into his fancy phone, but returned the receiver to its chrome hook before the connection

159

was complete. Gartland had risen to the top job at LaGrange by being careful about whom he trusted. All he really knew about Jesse Surratt came from one meeting and a couple of brief conversations on this same telephone. He reminded himself his caution about saying anything of substance on a public wire was, after all, based on experience.

Harvey drank the rest of his whiskey in two swallows, tossed the wadded cup in a trash can and stood up. The cigar had gone out, but he didn't relight it, though he kept it clenched in his teeth. Strolling through the maze of security between his desk and the parking lot, Gartland made sure every guard on duty saw him. It didn't hurt to let them know sometimes the Old Man stayed late.

Not that they needed a reminder. Even in the last hour of the day no one was sleeping, or reading a pornographic magazine confiscated from some inmate. No one was tying up a line with personal calls or otherwise risking Harvey's wrath.

Once outside the LaGrange gates, Gartland pointed his state-provided Oldsmobile toward home, and for ten minutes lost himself in twangy guitars from a country radio station. A hundred yards from the road where he lived, he stopped at a gas station where the pay phone was conveniently outside, an old fashioned booth with a folding door. He'd used it before.

A doughy-faced adolescent slouched against the glass. Harvey wondered briefly why an apparently healthy youngster would so assiduously avoid sunlight. Though the warden stared openly, the boy didn't seem to notice someone else was waiting to use the public instrument.

Harvey got out of his car after three minutes, taking with him the leather pouch of quarters he kept for such occasions. He approached the booth and tapped on the glass. When the boy looked up, he flashed the silver badge issued to LaGrange staff, and drew a finger over his neck. "Cut it short, son," he directed.

As the boy left the booth, Harvey pressed a two quarters into his too-soft hand. "Won't be but a minute, son. Then you can ring her up again."

Something—the badge, or Harvey's hard stare—made the kid nervous. He pocketed the quarters and drove off in a rusty pickup truck, presumably on his way to a phone where he wouldn't be interrupted by an old guy with a badge.

Harvey stepped into the booth and relit his cigar before dialing Surratt's home number. When a robotic voice asked for money, he deposited the required amount. The sheriff answered on the fourth ring. "Sorry to call this late," the warden said. "But I thought you'd want to hear this from me instead of third- or fourth-hand." Gartland paused. "Or maybe you wouldn't want to hear about it at all."

The sheriff was silent long enough Harvey wondered if he'd lost the connection. "Hear what?" Surratt's voice was wary.

"I know how your buddy Dave Brent got fingered as a snitch." Harvey took a deep breath. Sharing what he knew with Surratt might not be wise. Harvey Gartland was about to tell a hick sheriff something that could cause years of trouble, if the wrong person ever proved the LaGrange warden spoke the words.

It would be a hard proof to make though, and part of Harvey Gartland's personality was a reluctance to rethink decisions he'd already worried over. He seldom backed off potential consequences. "And I can tell you what somebody did about it."

The sound of a lighter scratched across the phone lines as a cigarette was lit in Hawkes County. "I'm listening."

"Turns out we had us a little prison romance," Harvey said. "One of those social workers the state says we got to have managed to fall in love with a resident robber." Less than twenty four hours earlier, a guard walked into mousy Charlene Puckett's office without knocking. Charlene was on her knees in front of Osgood Lewis.

Three hours later, after they'd been interrogated separately, Osgood grinned when three state troopers led a handcuffed Charlene past the office where he was being questioned. In truth, most of the interrogation time was for the convict. It took less than half an hour to wring the truth from poor little Charlene.

"So?" the sheriff asked from his end of the line.

"Don't you find it interesting, who people decide to fall in love with?"

Harvey knocked an inch of ash off his cigar and wondered at how foolish poor homely Charlene could be. "In court three eye-witnesses swore this man shot a 7-Eleven clerk who didn't move fast enough to suit him. But our social worker decided he'd been framed. Thought he deserved to look through whatever files she could get for him. She gave him everything in Brent's folder, even the confidential stuff."

The warden hushed, relit his cigar and waited. Surratt could ask for the rest, if he wanted it.

"What else?" Surratt muttered.

"Charlene made bail this afternoon. Poor little thing might be in love, but she'll moon over her robber boyfriend from a hospital bed for a while. Somebody broke both her legs an hour after she got out of jail." Harvey opened the folding door on the phone booth to let some fresh air inside. "She won't be back in her office for a long time."

"What'd you do that for, Gartland?" the sheriff demanded, disgust thick in his voice. "Did hurting that woman help anybody? Couldn't you have done something other than sending your thugs to do something like that to her?"

The warden sighed. "You're assuming I had it done, Sheriff. Maybe I'm thinking the same thing about you."

Harvey didn't say anything else, just held onto the telephone receiver until he heard the click of a broken connection. Then he put the instrument back in its cradle and walked to his car.

Driving home, Harvey Gartland wondered if the Hawkes County sheriff understood there were things you couldn't stop, even if you wanted to. The warden wondered if he'd ever have a chance to explain that to Jesse Surratt.

He hoped he might.

CHAPTER TWENTY SEVEN

Shadows danced in the wavering light of the single candle illuminating the Surratt's bedroom. One part of Margaret's mind wondered why, with the air so still even her breath seemed loud, the flame shivered so. Another listened to Jesse at the telephone and wanted to know who had interrupted their lovemaking.

Someone was saying things that disturbed her husband, judging from his angry, clipped responses. If it was truly bad, Margaret doubted Jesse would tell her what it was. And that was fine: she wasn't sure she wanted to know anything more about the world outside their bedroom for a while.

When Jesse came back from taking Mark Turner home, Margaret had been naked, already waiting in their bed. She hadn't wanted to make gentle love, she needed something raw and more powerful, wanted her husband to create a stretch of intense minutes in which she could stop thinking about all the kids who were lost as Mark.

Jesse had dropped his clothes where he stood while Margaret told him explicitly and graphically what she needed him to do. Then he obliged her so forcefully Margaret felt a slight discomfort between her legs, a lovely ache that made her wonder if her husband could repeat what he'd done.

After their initial explosive release, by candlelight their bedroom felt like it was their sanctuary, the one place which nothing from the world outside could touch. Then the telephone's discordant ringing pulled Jesse away from her. Listening to his voice, Margaret stretched lazily.

She smiled, remembering how poor Owen Vinson desperately pretended to accept her sexual energy, though in truth it frightened him. Jesse Surratt was the only man she'd ever found who valued passion others found off-putting, even peculiar, who gloried in making her body respond on a primal level beyond sweet words or overly soft caresses.

She heard her husband put the phone down, and listened as he moved around the living room. Margaret wondered what he was doing until she recognized the sweet strains of Joan Baez singing to them from the sixties. That Jesse wanted to hear old music meant the call was very upsetting indeed. When he lay down beside her Margaret rolled over so her head rested on his shoulder. "You don't have to go out, do you?"

"No." Jesse sighed an exhalation expressive as a scream.

"Want to tell me about the call?"

Jesse's acquiescence surprised her. "It was Harvey Gartland."

"Who?"

"The warden at LaGrange."

"So late? What did he want?" Margaret reached for the cigarette between Jesse's lips, took a drag and put it back with a promise to herself someday she'd actually quit.

"He wanted to tell me it was a social worker who set Dave Brent up to be killed." Jesse was silent a long time. "She probably didn't mean to, didn't know what she was doing, but tonight somebody broke both her legs."

"My God." Margaret slipped closer to Jesse's warmth. "That's awful."

Margaret lost herself in the old music, waiting to see if Jesse wanted to say anything else. When he didn't speak she asked, "What are you going to do about Mark Turner?"

"Beats me what *anybody* can do about that kid," Jesse muttered. "He's one seriously pissed off young man."

"Do you blame him?" Margaret thought about the hurt living in Mark's eyes, the look of a wounded creature whose pain was permanent. "When his father went to prison he lost everything he cared about."

Jesse's hand came up to stroke her hair. "As soon as I asked if he ever talked to anybody about how mad he is, I saw what a stupid question it was. There's nobody for kids like Mark to go to. No place in Hawkes County."

In the living room Joan Baez lyrics from a generation back faded, another record rattled onto the dated turntable Jesse wouldn't give up, and Carolyn Hester's voice drifted into the bedroom. Margaret wondered if anyone else in Hawkes County still remembered the woman, or played her music when they felt bad.

"Kids like Mark oughta have someone on their side," Jesse said. "Not a probation officer or a teacher, somebody outside the system." He sighed another long breath. "That kid doesn't need to go to jail. I wish I knew what he *does* need."

When her husband was quiet a while, Margaret put her hand on his middle, fingers straying through coarse pubic hair to tease the flesh swelling in her hand. Turning her head so it rested on his chest, she listened to Jesse's breathing.

Then Jesse's hands were on her, and Margaret obligingly rolled onto her belly, arranging her body to suit her husband's mood and inclination. She felt probing tumescence between her legs, rose up on hands and knees to make it easier for him. Lowering her head to the pillow, she shoved back at him, hard.

Jesse's groaning response pleased her, and Margaret made noises of her own as one of his hands came around her body to find and pinch a swollen nipple until she cried out raw satisfaction.

They rushed quickly toward the end. Jesse's breathing was ragged and rapid, and his hands moved to her shoulders, urging her further, lower. Something very close to a growl, the roar of a triumphant beast broke from her husband's throat as the first tremor of orgasm shuddered and twisted, deep inside Margaret's body.

When neither of them could move any more, Jesse wrapped his arms around her, and Margaret felt enveloped and hidden by his bulk. She was always surprised she didn't feel smothered when Jesse squeezed her so close, so tightly. "Pretty good for middle age," she teased.

Jesse pulled her closer as he rolled over and collapsed onto the mattress.

The candle on the dresser sputtered out, leaving the room in darkness, and Margaret turned so her bottom pressed against her husband's middle. It was how they went to sleep every night. Morning usually found them still nestled together.

The Carolyn Hester album played itself out, and Margaret was almost asleep when Jesse said, "I was sure whoever shot at the car was involved with Dave Brent's getting killed. I'm making everything connect with Dave lately."

"He was your friend." Margaret remembered how Elmer Brent insisted Jesse could clear his son's name. "Too many people expect you to figure everything out for them."

"I ought to be paying more attention to you instead of trying to figure out an old killing. I ought to give up the sheriff's office and stay home."

"But you're a good sheriff." Margaret wrapped one hand around Jesse's and pulled it to her breast. "You're good for Hawkes County."

She dozed off wondering if further remodeling of the house would make her feel better. Her drift toward sleep was interrupted by the telephone ringing again. "Want me to get it?" she murmured sleepily, but Jesse was already out of bed.

When he came back Margaret listened drowsily as Jesse told her about a conversation with a drunken Sid Varney, Midland's tombstone dealer. "Sid says a woman is trying to buy a headstone for Dave Brent's grave, keeps calling him at home, late at night. Sid checked the order out with Patsy, and she doesn't know anything about it."

Before they slept, Jesse added. "Sid wants me to run for re-election. Says a lot of other people do too."

CHAPTER TWENTY-EIGHT

Jesse didn't wake until Margaret's alarm sounded at 8:30, the first time he'd stayed so late in bed in weeks. He slapped at the clock and swung his legs over the side of the bed, reaching for a first cigarette.

And remembered his decision. Sometime in the hours before dawn he'd come wide awake, his mind made up about being sheriff for another term. He was going to run for re-election. Crow was right, Blaine Ingraham was an arrogant bully against whom kids like Mark Turner or any other helpless citizen wouldn't stand a chance.

The people of Hawkes County deserved better than Blaine.

There was a lot to do if he meant to stay in office, even though the election was more than a year away. He'd have to form a committee of support, raise money from those who wanted him to be sheriff. An effective campaign might cost the whole of a county sheriff's annual salary. He'd have to make sure people knew he'd be on the primary ballot in six months. Jesse was certain Blaine Ingraham was already courting endorsements, would have been doing so for months.

Lurching off the bed, Jesse snagged his bathrobe from a hook on the back of the door, wrapping it around himself before padding off to the kitchen. The house was chill, and after pouring a cup of coffee, he went to drop three chunks of wood into the stove. Then, despite the cold, he stepped onto the back porch.

Casey came with him, wandering into the grass to examine scents left behind by skunks and possums who crossed the yard at night. Jesse sat on a step, sipped coffee, and liked what he saw in the fresh light of a new autumn morning.

His garden was ready for winter, and would be in good shape for replanting in the spring. Weeks ago, after some erosion from late summer rains, he'd graded the tractor road winding onto the ridges from the wood lot. Jesse wouldn't have the road to fret about while worrying about the election. A good supply of winter wood was stacked and split. Politics didn't leave time for things like cutting firewood.

Before he was elected sheriff and before Margaret came back to him, Jesse Surratt's life had been a steady cycle of rising early to work on an endless series of projects. He kept all the fencing around his hundred and sixty acres in good repair, patched the tin roof on the barn whenever it leaked, and every summer grew three times the food he could eat.

For a long time it had seemed enough.

In those days his isolation from the rest of the world was a steady ache, a pain from which he tried to escape with hard work. The fight with the crooked Bradley and Noah Smallwood forced him to react to the world beyond his farm, made him part of the community of Hawkes County. It hadn't been a planned conflict, it just happened, and if he could have avoided taking on the Smallwoods Jesse would have done so.

Change had been forced on him, but it had been for the best. He liked being part and parcel of life in Hawkes County. He couldn't live as a hermit again.

A chill breeze whispered off the ridges and down the hollow, and Jesse Surratt shivered. He felt foolish, sitting in the cold when his house was warm, and he called Casey inside as he opened the back door. Fetching another cup of coffee he heard Margaret getting up, and poured her a cup as well.

He went to sit with her in the living room and blurted, "Here's the truth: I want to run for re-election." He kept his eyes on the credits from a news program scrolling over the television screen. "I *want* to run. I don't *have* to."

He felt Margaret studying him over the rim of her coffee cup. "When did you decide?"

"Last night, I guess," he told her. "When I woke up this morning I knew I didn't want to walk away from being sheriff."

Margaret reached for the remote control and shut off the television set. Jesse wished she'd left it alone. His wife hated having it in the background of conversation, but the moving images were a safe place to direct his eyes. "I'm a better sheriff than Blaine Ingraham would be."

Margaret smiled at him. "I knew all along you'd run again."

Jesse lit a cigarette, inhaled deeply, and shoved words out with the smoke. "If you're going to leave me over it though I'll give it up." He stole a look at his wife but wasn't able to read the expression on her face.

"I'm not going to leave you, Jesse." Reaching for his cigarette, Margaret took two quick puffs and gave it back.

"I was worried about what you'd say if I ran again." Jesse wished they could have conversations like this one on paper instead of talking them out. Passing notes back and forth like school kids would be easier. "Or what you'd do."

"Why would I do anything?" Margaret put her cup down and sighed. "Whenever I'm in town people come up to me to say they appreciate what you're doing. I can't go to the grocery store without hearing things like that."

"They'll *say* things like that." Jesse couldn't help smiling. "And then vote for their third cousin by marriage if he happens to run against me."

"You know what *you're* good at," she said. "I used to know I was good at selling land and houses, only after what happened with the Turner place I don't think I can do that anymore." She stood up. "Come on. For once I'll fix breakfast before you go to work."

Jesse followed her to the kitchen. "If you hadn't sold that land, somebody else would have." He leaned against the door frame and took a drink of coffee. "There's no way Darlene Turner could hold onto to all of that farm. And she's got another sixty acres."

Margaret dropped bacon strips into a skillet and opened the refrigerator for eggs. "I don't want to put myself in a situation like that one again. But I wish I was doing more than sitting around reading novels."

"What you did with Mark was good." Jesse lit a cigarette and pulled an ashtray closer. "If it'd been just me when Darlene brought him here, that kid would be in jail right now."

Margaret's gaze was piercing, like a light from which Jesse Surratt couldn't hope to hide. "I kept thinking of you at that age, when you had nobody to tell about Tom Johnson."

He nodded. "I didn't get a rifle and climb a hill though." An idea was forming in his mind, not quite clear enough to define, yet close enough Jesse knew the things to say that would help him recognize it.

"Doing something doesn't necessarily mean working for other people does it?" Jesse got forks and a butter knife from a drawer and put them on the table, then sat down.

Margaret put food on two plates and brought them to the table. "I don't know what you mean."

The half-formed idea was clearer. "What if I found some space in the court house, gave you a desk and a phone? What if you were the person kids could talk to besides a school counselor or a preacher?"

Margaret frowned across the table. "You think that's wise when you're running for re-election? Putting your wife in the courthouse? Doing something that might make those teachers and preachers mad?"

Jesse shrugged.

"Besides, I'm not trained to do anything like that."

"It doesn't take training to get kids to talk." Jesse broke his egg's yolk and soaked a piece of toast in it. "If they need a counselor or some kind of special help, you could make sure they find it. You'd be there to help them decide what they *do* need."

For a long while both of them ate without speaking. When her plate was cleared Margaret stared off toward the kitchen windows. Jesse wished he could read her mind.

"At least think about what I said," he urged. "And when you've got some ideas sorted out, we can talk about it some more." He pushed away from the table and stood up. "I've got to get going. Martha'll be wondering where I am."

"Are you serious about this thing?" Margaret put her hands on his shoulders and looked into his eyes. "That I could try to help kids like Mark Turner?"

Jesse nodded. "Sure."

"I *will* think about it then, maybe write some ideas down. Maybe I'll get Rita to help. She's smart."

When Jesse came out of the shower Margaret had a legal pad at the table, making notes. She didn't look up from whatever she was writing. In the bedroom, on top of the bureau he found the piece of flower, all he had to show for his midnight chase through the Brent cemetery.

It still carried the odd scent, though not so strong as when he'd picked it up. He put it in his shirt pocket again. Maybe somebody in town could tell him about the fading blossom, at least put a name on it. Maybe they were ordered from a florist.

Back in the kitchen he put a hand on Margaret's shoulder. "If Martha calls, tell her I'm on my way."

Margaret raised her eyes from her writing only briefly. "You and Crow chasing ghosts again tonight?"

Jesse shook his head and moved his hand high enough to ruffle his wife's hair. "I don't have time to chase ghosts. I'm going to give up this whole thing, tell Elmer Brent it's too late to do anything with it."

"Really?" Margaret put down her pen and peered at him curiously. "What if the killer's still here, Jess? Can you live with that?"

"It could have been someone from out of town. Ray was a bootlegger. Plenty of people might've had reasons to come looking for him, shoot him and then go back to where they came from."

"Still, the man would be walking around loose, right?"

"I suppose." Jesse tried telling himself it didn't matter. He didn't believe it, and knew he couldn't make Margaret accept it either. He looked at her until she lowered her eyes back to her notes.

"See you later," he said.

CHAPTER TWENTY-NINE

Lorena worked with her flowers and tried to make herself believe that leaving Midland would be easy. She'd made up her mind about it. Still, three or four times a day she'd realize she'd spent minutes staring mindlessly into space, wishing she didn't feel compelled to go.

It was funny, how complicated her life was, had always been. Lorena could remember laughing about it with Lois Hannan, when she attended the doctor's retirement party as an adult, one of the psychiatrist's success stories.

Lorena had friends in Midland. There were people who looked forward to seeing her, who liked her. They made Lorena laugh and sometimes they wept with her. And she had her greenhouse. Just going into the humid space, knowing she was about to lose it, was enough to make her cry.

"You have a *home*, not just a house," Lois Hannan told her. "It's wonderful what you made for yourself after all you've been through. You have a home and you have your son and I'm so proud of you."

Lorena *had* made a home for herself and her son, but now it was like living in a haunted place. David especially haunted the greenhouse, what had always been Lorena's private and most personal retreat, where she felt his presence even more strongly than at his grave.

She'd begun decorating the grave in mid-day, rather than by night. In the afternoon she could park on the logging road and watch the cemetery until she was certain she wouldn't be disturbed. If another car came, she'd hear it long before anyone could see her, and she didn't have to worry about being bothered by nosy high school kids or chased by a bumbling sheriff.

She picked a set of fresh freesias and arranged the new blooms around a set of pristine candles. Lorena lingered in the greenhouse until she heard her son calling from the back yard. This once she wasn't going to leave him or call the neighbor who didn't mind baby sitting.

"Not much longer," Lorena called loudly. "I'm almost ready." She could leave Midland with at least one thing to look forward to, the joy of watching her son begin to talk.

Lorena backed her vehicle up to the greenhouse and loaded David's new flowers into it, hurrying from the door to the vehicle. They were delicate things, and the cold air outside would begin killing them almost immediately. Then she positioned her son in his special seat, made certain all the buckles and straps were in place, and started the car.

At the last moment Lorena steered the van toward town. She had dry cleaning to pick up before going to the graveyard.

CHAPTER THIRTY

Jesse took a cup of Martha Compton's strong coffee to his desk, along with a couple of telephone messages. Teddy Sparks, the newspaper editor, had called, but that could wait a bit. Another message was from a county councilman who'd probably support Blaine Ingraham in the election. Jesse decided he might wait a *long* time before returning that call.

Martha's radio fell silent and Jesse called to her, "If Buddy Upchurch is in the building, would you ask him to come in for a minute?"

When the tall deputy appeared in the doorway Jesse gestured toward the sofa along one wall of his office and eyed the stack of official forms and other paperwork in the deputy's hand. "About to get caught up?"

Disgust wrinkled Buddy's face. "Filling all this out almost makes arresting somebody more trouble than it's worth. Unless maybe you're talking capital murder."

Jesse nodded. "I saw in the log you were out to the Martin house again last night."

The deputy nodded. "Tony Ray got a belly full of whiskey and Connie called again."

Connie and Tony Ray Martin regularly required the attention of the Hawkes County Sheriff's Department, each frequently demanding the other be arrested for some real or imagined offense. The three times Jesse had gone to resolve one of their disputes, both had been staggering drunk.

"Connie had her a big ol' black eye." The deputy grimaced. "I fetched Tony Ray to jail for the night. How much you want to bet Connie don't bail him out before I get all these reports filled out?"

Jesse was quiet for a moment, letting the Martins' ongoing feud fade from the conversation. "I need a favor, Buddy, and I want you to see if you can get the other boys to go along with it too."

Curiosity narrowed the deputy's eyes. "What are you talking about?"

"I want you to go easy on finding out who shot at my car."

"You serious, Jess?" Upchurch stared across the desk. Any Hawkes County deputy would happily work hours of unpaid overtime to find someone foolish enough to aim a gun at another law officer. Buddy lit a cigarette and squinted through his exhalation. "Shooting at a squad car's a hard thing to ignore."

Jesse nodded. He was going to have to offer more than a simple request. Buddy Upchurch was the strongest personality on the county's police force. If he was persuaded, and told the other deputies to terminate the investigation, they'd do it.

"I know who did it." Jesse leaned toward the deputy as he recounted the story of his meeting with Mark Turner. "Before Len Turner went to prison, I must have heard him brag a dozen times what a great shot his boy was. It wasn't an accident Mark Turner didn't hit anybody."

Buddy stubbed his cigarette out, looked at the sheriff a moment, then nodded. "You're the boss. You don't want to arrest Mark Turner, I'll let it go too."

"And get the other guys to let it alone, too?"

"Won't be easy." Upchurch sprawled on the sofa. "But I'll see what I can do."

"One other thing." Jesse stood up to refill his coffee cup. "I'm going to run for re-election."

"Hell, that's great news, Jess."

"Blaine Ingraham wouldn't agree with you."

Buddy Upchurch grinned. "Who gives a shit what *he* thinks?"

Jesse laughed. "Let the guys know about the election. And Buddy? If anybody wants a leave of absence to work for Blaine's campaign, it's okay by me."

"I don't believe that'll happen, Sheriff," the deputy said. "Martha know you're gonna run again?"

"I'm going to talk to her right now."

Upchurch scooped his stack of forms off the couch and stood up. "I'll tell the guys to go easy on that shooter business, Jess." In the doorway the deputy paused. "I don't believe I'll tell them who it was though. That boy would live hard for a while, if they knew he was the one that done it."

Jesse nodded. "Thanks, Buddy."

The deputy lifted one hand in a wave and was gone.

Jesse stood up from behind his desk and strolled into Martha's office. "Did you hear what Buddy and I were talking about?"

The old woman waved toward the radio. "Too busy with this thing to listen. Otherwise I would have."

Jesse let his dispatcher's white lie alone. The only time Martha Compton didn't hear what happened in his office was if Jesse closed his door. He cleared his throat. "I was telling Buddy I've decided to run for re-election."

Martha nodded. "I figured you would. Especially when that fool on the state police started talking about wanting to be sheriff."

"One other thing. Margaret might be calling later on, asking about finding some empty space for an office. Would you help her out?"

Martha Compton peered over her desk curiously. "What's Margaret want with an office?"

Jesse explained his plan to use his wife as an unpaid advocate for teenagers in Hawkes County. "She'll tell you more about it when she calls. Maybe you can help her with some ideas."

Martha nodded. "You talk to Teddy Sparks yet?"

Jesse shook his head.

"He told me Blaine's going to have an ad in the next issue of the paper, announcing he's a candidate." Martha grinned. "I told him to save you a space too."

Jesse smiled back at the old woman. "I'll swear, Martha, keeping a secret from you is hard as smuggling daylight past a rooster." He stepped back into his office long enough to retrieve his hat and a hand-held radio that could be hung off his belt. "I'm gonna be out and about for a while."

"In the car?"

Jesse shook his head. "Just taking a walk. I'll stop and see Teddy on my way back."

Martha nodded. "If you was to go by Ed Tomalin's he could take your picture and have it ready for the announcement in the paper."

"Good idea," Jesse agreed. "Want to give Ed a call, let him know I'm coming?"

He walked out of the office whistling. The election might turn out to be a squeaker, but at that moment Jesse felt confident he might kick Blaine Ingraham's ass in every single Hawkes County precinct.

And enjoy doing it.

Bright sunshine outside the courthouse elevated Jesse's mood a few more degrees. Joe and Bert Fraley, retired storekeepers whose tiny grocery once operated near Jesse's farm, exited Collins Drugs as he passed.

"Mornin' Jesse *Lee*-roy," Joe said as Jesse stepped aside for the elderly couple.

Jesse grinned. Anyone using his middle name in everyday speech had known him since he was too small to tie his own shoelaces. He wouldn't want to be called "*Lee*-roy" every day, but there was a comfort in knowing people still lived who'd been part of his life so many years.

Ardmore Florists was on his way to Ed Tomalin's studio, and Jesse paused at the doorway, remembering the withered bloom in his shirt pocket. The young girl behind the counter looked at it only briefly and shook her head. "That one's new to me, Sheriff."

"What you got, Jesse?" Julian Ardmore strolled out of the back room, his hands grimy with damp topsoil.

"Just a flower nobody seems to recognize." Jesse held the blossom higher off the counter.

Julian came closer, fishing in his pocket for reading glasses. "That there's a freesia," he announced after a cursory glance. "Haven't seen one in years."

"I never heard of them," Jesse said.

The florist nodded. "Don't surprise me. Used to be real popular, something a man would send to a woman." Ardmore turned to his clerk. "Dorsey, notice how strong that smell is? Even from a wilted bloom?"

The old man's apprentice nodded and leaned closer to the bloom, looking at it more closely.

Ardmore lifted his gaze from the flower. "Hard to keep freesias looking nice, you know. They wilt even faster than roses. That's why nobody orders them anymore."

"You could order them if you wanted to though, couldn't you?"

Julian Ardmore stowed his spectacles back in his shirt pocket. "Oh, you *could*," he admitted. "But nobody does. I doubt I've filled a request for freesias in twenty years."

"Think Branham's might've ordered some?" Midland's other florist had moved from downtown into the mini-mall near the interstate.

"I doubt it." Julian shook his head. "Anything like that's got to be flown in. If Liz Branham's going to that kind of trouble she'll ask if I want some as well." Julian nodded toward the telephone. "We could call her but I'd bet anything she won't know where it come from either."

"That's okay." Pocketing the blossom, Jesse turned to go.

"Come back and see us," Julian said.

Jesse nodded and stepped into sunshine again.

It was frustrating, that he learned so little from the odd flower. But within a block his good humor returned, and Jesse was smiling when he almost bumped into Rita Bailey, outside Hobson's Cleaner's. She was trying to ease Bobby's wheelchair through a doorway barely wide enough, at the same time nearly losing her grip on some plastic-wrapped dry cleaning.

"Let me help you, Rita," Jesse said, taking over the task of maneuvering Bobby. "You going to your van or someplace else?"

"The van," Rita said. "What's Margaret's big secret anyhow?"

"Secret?" Jesse slid the van's side door open and reached for the switch to Bobby's ramp.

Rita shrugged. "She called and asked me to stop by this morning. Said she'd tell me about it when I got there. Whatever it is, it's making her happy."

Jesse lifted Bobby into the seat and fit a shoulder harness around him. Rita hung her dry cleaning from a hook behind the door and climbed in the driver's seat, lifting her hand in a wave.

Jesse didn't wave back.

Rita's van reeked of freesias. As she drove away he looked in the back. Just below window level there was an enormous bouquet of the rare flowers.

He walked slowly back toward the courthouse, had the hand-held radio raised when he realized anyone with a scanner would hear what he had to say. He put the radio away and stopped in Nathan Rule's barber shop to use the phone. He asked Martha to cancel the appointment for a campaign photograph, and told her to call Crow Markwell, tell him Jesse was on his way to pick him up.

"Tell Crow I know who she is," Jesse said. "He'll know what I mean."

Then he hung up the telephone. Jesse Surratt didn't smile as he walked back to the courthouse to get his squad car, and his pace was much faster than when he'd strolled away earlier.

CHAPTER THIRTY-ONE

Margaret filled half a dozen pages of her legal pad in no time at all. There was so *much* to say about troubled kids in Hawkes County. Jesse's idea of having an advocate for youngsters was wonderful. She'd never thought of herself as a counselor or "do-gooder," but she liked kids. That was more than could be said for lots of people who claimed to be on their side.

And she wasn't going to waste time with tired old ideas like a "teen center." Every military base where she'd lived with Jesse had one of those, a badly lit room equipped with a worn out ping pong table, usually used by the chaperones who waited in vain for kids who wouldn't be caught dead there.

Margaret wondered how many of Hawkes County's "problem" kids had untreated learning disabilities because the proper diagnostic tests had never been arranged. How many stayed away from school activities—the way Mark Turner was contemptuous of yearbooks and athletics—because they weren't interested in the things adults assumed they'd want to do?

She asked herself what *would* kids want to do nowadays?

What if someone found the funding to set up a mini-television studio at the high school? Would the kids who didn't care about yearbooks tell stories their own way if they had access to modern equipment?

What if the high school had a shooting team as well as the standard football, basketball and track squads?

Margaret laughed out loud, thinking about the uproar such a proposal would create in her politically correct home state. Hawkes County wasn't California though. Kids like Mark Turner hunted as soon as they were old enough to walk into the woods alone. And

Margaret Surratt knew better than most how well Mark could control a rifle.

She didn't look up from her notes until she was distracted by the hollow pinging of tires on gravel. Peering through the window she saw Rita's van brake to a stop near the house. By the time Rita maneuvered Bobby's wheelchair into the kitchen Margaret had poured orange juice for the boy and coffee for Rita, anxious to tell what she was going to be doing.

"Sit down, I want you to hear about the idea Jesse had." Margaret slipped a long straw into Bobby's juice and fastened it to the arm of his chair. "It started when he found out who shot at his car, a kid from right down the road. It was only a high school boy. and he wasn't trying to hurt anyone, he's just mad, the way kids get when they think their world's fallen apart."

Without pausing for breath, Margaret explained Jesse's notion she could stay busy as someone Hawkes County kids could talk to. She faltered, describing the ideas she'd written down. Some didn't sound so good as they looked on her yellow pad.

Margaret laughed nervously. "All right, so I haven't designed a brilliant program for kids in my first hour and a half of thinking about it. But it'd be worthwhile to try *something*, don't you think?"

Rita nodded. "Of course it would. It's a wonderful idea."

"I'm glad you said that." Margaret sipped coffee that had gotten cold while she'd talked. "Because I need you to help me."

Rita smiled, but her eyes were sad when she said, "I wish *I'd* had someone like you to talk to, before . . . "

"Before what?"

"Before everything happened to me."

Rita had told Margaret what no one else in Hawkes County knew, about the hell that had been her childhood. Her years at St. Catherine's Home with Dr. Hannan had been the first time she felt as though she belonged anywhere.

"That's why I want your help." Margaret reached across the table, took her friend's hand and squeezed it hard. "I don't mean just listen to my half-baked ideas. I need you to make this thing happen."

Rita smiled again, her expression more regretful than happy, and pulled her hand away. "I don't see how I can do that."

"Why not?"

Rita's mouth tightened. "Because I'm moving."

"You're what? *Why?*"

"Why not?" Rita glanced at Bobby. "Maybe I want to go where Bobby can see better doctors than in Midland. Maybe I want to live where I don't have to drive for two hours before I get to a mall. Someplace other than this little town." Rita's voice trailed off into a whisper.

Margaret went to the drawer where Jesse kept his cigarettes and opened a new pack. After hearing her only close friend in Hawkes County was about to leave, she couldn't *not* smoke. Clumsily clawing at cellophane she shook a cigarette loose and rummaged in the drawer for a match, tears blurring her vision. "You need to think about this, Rita."

"I've *been* thinking about it," Rita said. "I want you to help me sell the house. If you'd do that I could leave a lot quicker."

Margaret turned and faced the kitchen windows, fixing her eyes on the distant barn. What would she do if the only person she knew other than characters in the pile of novels beside her bed went away? The excitement built by thinking about wonderful things waiting to be done for kids like Mark Turner evaporated.

There was the sound of another vehicle in the driveway, and Margaret was surprised to see Jesse's patrol car pulling in. Waving his hands excitedly, Bobby made it obvious he'd spotted Jesse as well. Margaret was wondering why Jesse would be taking something from Rita's van when she was startled by angry shouts from the table.

"That son of a bitch!" Rita erupted from her chair and ran to the back door. "What does he think he's . . . "

The last words were lost as the door slammed shut. Puzzled, Margaret moved to stand near Bobby's wheelchair. "It's okay," she crooned. The boy's smile had disappeared with Rita's loud departure, and he looked uncertainly up at Margaret.

Outside Rita and Jesse were face to face, glaring at one another, reminding Margaret of boxers in a ring. Instead of a referee Crow Markwell stood behind Jesse, thin arms supporting the flower arrangement Jesse had given him.

Jesse and Rita were both talking but Margaret couldn't understand a word they were saying. She went to the storm window, opened the lock and yanked on the aluminum frame. It slid upward as Rita shrieked, "Put them back it's none of your goddamned business they don't belong to you put them back where you got them!"

Jesse was no calmer than Rita. "You talk to me first, goddamnit. You have to talk to *me*!"

Bobby Stillwell whimpered bewilderment at the angry voices in the yard. Margaret closed the window and hurried outside. She was barefoot and nearly fell, running to stand between two people she cared about. Raising both hands she shouted, "Stop it! Both of you!"

Jesse and Rita hushed. Crow Markwell moved to stand at her elbow, a tiny smile creasing his face even further. "I don't believe I ever heard a woman yell like that before, Maggie."

Panting as though she'd run a hundred yards instead of only thirty or so feet from her back porch Margaret turned to Rita. "Bobby's crying. He's scared." When Rita didn't move she added, "Go take care of him."

Facing her husband after Rita had gone in the house Margaret tried to read his eyes. "Why are you so mad at *her*?"

Jesse shook his head. "She's got to talk to me . . . " he said again.

Crow Markwell shot a puzzled glance at Margaret and muttered, "See can you calm this man down before you bring him inside." The old man put the flowers on the porch swing and stood with his hand on the door latch. "I'll see Rita Bailey don't go no place. But that man needs to catch his breath before he charges off blind the way he done at the cemetery."

Jesse tried stalking off after Crow, but turned when Margaret put a hand on his arm. "What?" he asked. "I don't care what Crow Markwell thinks. I'm tired of not knowing."

Margaret nodded. "What do you expect Rita to give you?"

"Oh, that woman's got a whole bunch of answers for me." Jesse tried to pull away but Margaret wouldn't let go. "I'm sick of riddles everyone expected me to solve when nobody'd tell me anything. That woman knows a whole lot of what I've been trying to find out."

"Rita has a lot of secrets," Margaret acknowledged. "Maybe some of them are answers for you. But I want you to listen, just for a minute before you go after her."

"Listen about what?"

Margaret took a deep breath. Jesse wasn't trying to pull away anymore, and instead of clutching his arm she stroked it. "Remember what it was like, when you first came back to Hawkes County?"

"What's that got to do with . . . "

Margaret cut him off. "You were the kid who got raped by a crazy man, Jesse. Remember what that was like?"

"Jesus Christ, Margaret, are you ever going to let that go?"

"Can you remember what it was like, Jesse?"

"It'd be a lot easier to forget if my wife didn't throw it at me whenever she wanted to make a psychological point."

Margaret ground her teeth together. Getting angry at Jesse, fighting with him, wouldn't do anyone any good. "I want you to know, before you go raging into the house, Rita knows what it was like for you in those days."

Jesse laughed, a bitter ugly sound. "I doubt that."

"It's true. She has the same bruises as you. Don't make them hurt any more than they already do." Margaret sighed. "Does the name Lorena Stillwell mean anything to you?"

He thought a moment, then shook his head. "Should it?"

"Rita thinks everyone remembers her real name."

"'Rita Bailey' is an alias?"

Margaret took a cigarette from Jesse's pocket, let him light it for her. "Rita is her middle name. Her birth name was Lorena Stillwell. She started using Rita when her first name was all over the papers."

"Is she wanted for something?"

"No." Margaret studied her husband's face while she took a long drag off the cigarette. He wasn't quite so angry as before. She allowed herself to relax the tiniest bit. "She's not wanted for anything."

CHAPTER THIRTY-TWO

Once he saw Rita Bailey was too focused on taking care of Bobby to think of running away, Crow drifted to the back door, basking in heat from the wood stove while watching what happened between Maggie and the sheriff. Young Jesse didn't know what a smart woman he had in Maggie, smart enough it was never a mistake to listen to her.

"This is your second 'Don't be mean to some poor soul' lecture in two days, Margaret," Crow heard the sheriff snap at his wife. "Maybe Mark Turner only needs somebody to talk to, but Rita's different. She knows a world of facts about the night one man was murdered and another one was framed."

"You mean the night Dave Brent threw his own life away," Maggie retorted. "What if he *did* it?" Maggie glanced toward the door, and Crow felt his face grow hot with embarrassment. She'd known he was listening. "What if Dave Brent shot Ray Bailey after all?"

Crow reluctantly stepped outside, away from the stove. "'What if' don't make much difference, not right here, right now."

Jesse pulled free of Maggie but she moved close enough to take his arm again. "Do whatever you've got to," she said, "just don't make things worse than they already are."

The sheriff allowed himself to be led into the house, and Crow followed, pausing in the back room to stretch his hands toward the stove. Something was about to happen, something important, but he had no idea at all what it was. He wished it would happen nearer the fire.

After Martha called, Crow Markwell had put on his jacket and waited patiently for Jesse on his back porch. When the Hawkes County car made it up the hill, the sheriff was livid with anger. He swore they'd find the mystery woman from the cemetery at his house.

Crow was puzzled when there was only Rita Bailey's van to be seen in Jesse's driveway. As soon as they were parked, the sheriff snatched a big bouquet of the same flowers they'd seen at the graveyard out of the vehicle, handing them off to Crow like he was presenting a trophy.

Now it was twenty minutes later and Crow Markwell was no closer to knowing what was going on than when he slipped to the door to eavesdrop. Jesse Surratt was a good sheriff, but on this thing with the Bailey killing he was a blind frog, jumping without caring where he might land.

In the kitchen they found Rita bent over Bobby's wheelchair, paper towels wadded in her hand. Kneeling, the woman swabbed apologetically at the carpet. "Bobby got that plastic bottle loose somehow and sent it flying."

"Don't worry about it." Maggie's voice was a soothing croon. Crow kept his eyes fixed on Rita, wondering what she was about to tell them. "Who wants coffee?"

"I'll take some," Crow said. Coffee was a poor substitute for standing close to a wood stove, but it would do. He took a step toward the table, where the chairs looked awfully inviting. "Can an old man make himself comfortable here?" he asked. "Or are we going someplace else to talk?"

"You all can talk wherever you want to." Rita tossed paper towels at the waste basket beside Maggie's electric range. "Bobby and I are leaving." She shoved the wheelchair toward the door.

Jesse stepped in her path, filled the doorway with his body. "No. Not yet." He put a hand on the wheelchair's frame.

A rough guttural protest erupted from Bobby Stillwell's throat, arms flailing as he tried to push the sheriff's hand off the chrome rail. Crow wondered if Jesse realized how threatening he looked, standing over Bobby and Rita in his khaki uniform.

Rita Bailey moved ahead with the chair until it bumped Jesse's ankle. "You're scaring Bobby, and you can't make us stay here." She pushed the chair again, more forcefully.

It must have hurt where the chair slammed against him, and Crow was impressed by the passivity of Jesse's face. "Margaret told me you're real name is Lorena Stillwell," he said. "And there's a prison warden who'd like to talk to Linda Carroll. That's you too, isn't it?"

Rita made a half turn toward Maggie. "You swore you'd never tell."

186

"I'm sorry." Maggie took a step toward Rita, and suddenly the two women were hugging and Rita was crying. "You've got to tell Jesse about it. Some of it anyway."

The name Lorena Stillwell put a sick feeling in Crow's belly, and he wished the sheriff hadn't come to get him. It would have been better to have stayed home and taken a long walk with his dogs. Anything would have been better than thinking about what the name Lorena Stillwell meant.

"Is this Stillwell name an alias?" Jesse demanded, ignoring Bobby's angry protests. "What about Rita Bailey? Or Linda Carroll? Why do you need more than one name?"

Crow stepped around Jesse and rested a hand gently on Rita-Lorena's back. "Me and Jesse are going outside for a little bit," he told her. "He needs to know some things, and I imagine I can tell them easier than you can." Crow massaged the woman's shaking shoulders, the way he caressed Glenda when thunder rolled across the ridges and threw his favorite dog into a panic.

He lifted his hand and pointed a finger at Jesse Surratt. "Come on, Sheriff. I'm going to hold school on some things that happened while you was off in the Navy."

Jesse resisted the tug on his arm, but Crow wasn't about to let anyone go at Lorena Stillwell like an angry bull. He'd let the child down once, a long time ago. It wasn't going to happen again. He pulled at Jesse's arm until he followed, through the wonderfully warm stove room to the back door.

In the cool air outside Crow stepped to the porch swing, wondering where to begin the sad, sick story. "Where was you in nineteen and eighty seven?

The sheriff didn't sit down in the swing until Crow settled in the chair opposite. "Right about then I guess I was stationed in the Brewer, a destroyer out of San Diego."

Crow nodded. "Was a long time ago. In Hawkes County that year all anybody talked about was Lorena Stillwell, a child found wandering a road in Forrest County, the Tuesday before Thanksgiving. She didn't have on nothing but sandals and a little old cotton slip. There was an early snow on the ground that year too."

The retired deputy reached in his pocket for his tobacco plug, shaved a piece off and let it soften in his jaw before he spoke again.

"She'd had a dress and a coat on, but took it off to wrap up the baby she was toting."

"I think maybe my mother wrote me something about this in a letter," Jesse admitted.

"Prob'ly so," Crow agreed. "Anyway, she was a mystery 'cause she wouldn't tell which one of them hollers over there she come from. And nobody reported a missing girl or baby. Near as anyone could tell she'd never been out of it, not for school, not for going to movies in town, not for nothing."

Jesse sighed his impatience. "I assume this story has a point. I wish you'd tell me what it is."

Crow shook his head. "Sometimes a story gets better for a slower telling. But there ain't going to be nothing good about this one." The old man rubbed his hands together. "Damn but it's cold out here."

"What's the rest of it then?"

"All right. I'll just give it to you straight, Jesse." Crow Markwell took a deep breath, remembering, and let the tale tell itself.

He had a personal connection of sorts with Lorena Stillwell. The world found out about her dark life as he began thinking about retiring from the sheriff's department. Maybe what happened to her had something to do with the fact he quit when he did.

Two or three times, he'd arrested her uncle, Ezra Stillwell, when the man came to Midland to get drunk instead of staying in Forrest County. For months after the girl and the baby were found on the road, well after the snow melted and trees bloomed again, Crow considered how close he might have been to ending the girl's ordeal, if he'd only looked harder, asked a few more questions.

When they found Lorena on that wind-swept two-lane country blacktop in the cold of a moonless winter night she couldn't read or write, wouldn't say where she lived, wouldn't say much of anything. She wouldn't tell the names of her people or explain how she came to be wandering that road, half dressed.

Abner Riley was sheriff of Forrest County, and he asked lawmen from other jurisdictions to look at pictures of the little girl and the baby she'd carried, but no one recognized either one. Then someone noticed Ezra Stillwell hadn't been seen for a few days.

Everybody knew Ezra was crazy, and mean as a boil. He'd used his hard fists on more than one person and no one cared if they saw him again ever. But by and by some overly curious soul stopped at his cabin, perhaps to see if it held anything worth taking.

Ezra was in a chair in his cold house, dead. There was a shotgun at his feet, and a story got out that Ezra killed himself after the little girl got loose. Until he was found, no one had connected the lost child with him, but a few clothes and other things made it clear that was where the little girl and the infant had come from. Abner Riley let it be known Ezra Stillwell faced the barrel of that twelve gauge out of shame.

The day Abner assured Lorena that Ezra Stillwell was dead, she told him her name. No one else ought to have known it, outside of law enforcement and the courts, but in those days the papers were sloppy with such things.

As nearly as anyone ever pieced together the chronology of the child's life, her mother was Ezra's sister Irene. Nobody was certain who her father was, though some believed it was Ezra himself. It was certain he fathered the baby found with Lorena.

The baby's name was Bobby. Crow nodded toward the windows. "That's the same Bobby Stillwell sitting in your kitchen, Jesse, locked in a wheelchair."

Jesse sighed. "So Lorena, or Rita, whatever she calls herself, was a victim. It happens, Crow."

"Not like this. Not often."

Irene Stillwell died when her daughter was seven. Ezra brought the child home from the funeral and put a story out some distant kin in Oregon had adopted Lorena. Not a soul laid eyes on her till she showed up on a two-lane blacktop six years later. Once she believed no one was going to send her back to her uncle, Lorena explained she'd run away because Ezra was threatening to hurt the baby, because it was a cripple.

The chains holding the porch swing creaked as Jesse shifted his weight. "Did you know Rita Bailey was this famous Lorena Stillwell?"

Crow shook his head. "In eighty seven I went to Forrest County and seen Lorena myself. That little girl didn't look a thing like the woman in your kitchen."

"Is that all you wanted to tell me?"

"Not quite."

Crow Markwell measured his next words carefully, weighed his perceived failure to the young Lorena against his friendship with the sheriff of Hawkes County. He didn't speak until he was certain he meant what he said. "If you do a solitary thing, Jesse Surratt, to let the rest of the world know where Lorena Stillwell is, I'll make you sorry."

"Jesus, Crow!" There was shock in Jesse Surratt's voice. More than that, there were hurt feelings too. "Why would you threaten *me?*"

"Lorena Stillwell's suffered enough. She ought to be left alone."

"Even if she killed Ray Bailey and let Dave Brent take the blame?"

Crow took a deep breath and spat his cud of tobacco into the yard. "Seems to me everybody but you and Elmer Brent has figured out Dave done exactly what he wanted to." The old man stood up slowly, careful not to ask too much of his knees. "Now let's go see what that girl wants to tell you."

Following Jesse to the door, Crow wondered what the Hawkes County sheriff would say if he knew what Abner Riley told, one evening he and Crow emptied a bottle of Wild Turkey bourbon, out on a ridge, listening to the fox hounds run. Abner was confident when Ezra Stillwell faced a twelve gauge shotgun in his last moments of life, Lorena Stillwell was holding it.

Ezra didn't kill himself. Lorena shot him.

Crow hoped Lorena, or Rita, whatever she wanted to be called, hadn't killed Ray Bailey. If she had, he hoped she had sense enough to keep quiet about it.

CHAPTER THIRTY-THREE

Crow Markwell's unexpected threat leeched the heat from the rage simmering inside Jesse Surratt. If a man old enough to have been his hero when Jesse was a kid felt compelled to issue a threat, something was wrong. Jesse let himself cool down enough to take a closer look at his anger.

The rage had begun building with a random glance into Rita Bailey's van, spotting a dozen or so familiar flowers. Jesse's memory faltered as he tried to recall what Julian Ardmore called them. Freesias, that was it. When he'd seen the freesias he knew the woman in the cemetery had been Rita Bailey.

As he drove to fetch Crow Markwell Jesse's anger grew. He felt like a clown, wearing the sheriff's uniform as though it was a Bozo suit. All the time he'd been puzzling out the identity of the wailing lady in the graveyard, he talked about the mystery to Margaret, who discussed the particulars with her good friend Rita Bailey.

Who no doubt found Jesse Surratt's awkward bumbling after how and why his friend Dave Brent came to die in prison to be hilarious.

In the house, Jesse paused by the wood stove with Crow. Rita and Margaret were talking in the kitchen, but he couldn't understand their words. Rita was speaking through tears, from the sound of it, and Margaret's responses were more lullaby than conversation.

It occurred to him he might simply leave the house until Rita was gone. He and Crow could get in the cruiser and drive to the old man's farm. If they stopped to buy a bottle of bourbon from a bootlegger they could sit on Crow Markwell's hilltop till dawn, get drunk and forget the kinds of hurt and sadness capable of making women's voices mourn like the ones in his kitchen.

The old man's hand fell gently onto Jesse Surratt's shoulder, urging him forward. In a moment the sheriff gave in to the pressure and went to the women. Margaret looked up at his entrance, but Rita Bailey kept her eyes fixed on the hills beyond the windows when she said, "What do you want to ask me, Jesse?" Her voice seemed terribly weary.

"I just want you to tell me things you know about."

"Like what?"

Rita Bailey wasn't offering anything. Jesse thought about the thing he wanted to know most of all. "Who killed Ray?"

"I don't know," Rita Bailey said softly.

Jesse wondered briefly about the relief that eased across Crow Markwell's face. "But you were there in the motel with Dave, weren't you?"

Rita nodded.

"You knew *he* didn't kill Ray?"

Another nod.

"Were you the woman who visited him at the prison, gave him money?" She nodded again. Where did the money come from?"

Rita shrugged. "Ray was a big believer in life insurance, Jesse. He left me almost rich."

Jesse shook his head. "How could you let Dave . . . "

Rita didn't let him finish. "Because that's what David *wanted* me to do. All of it was what *he* wanted. At the motel he had one of those portable police radios. We knew Ray was shot before you did, Jesse. David made me go home. He said this town wouldn't let me alone if people found out where I'd been while my husband was murdered. David said I'd lose Bobby."

At the sound of his name Bobby Stillwell turned toward Rita and grinned a senseless pleasure grimace. Reaching to stroke his hand, Rita looked up at the sheriff again. "No one's ever going to take Bobby away from me."

"Did Ray know about you and David?"

Rita shook her head. "I would have left Ray in a heartbeat, Jesse. But you know what?" Tears ran in small rivulets down her cheeks, but Rita Bailey's voice didn't break. "David wouldn't leave that little mouse he was married to. He *wouldn't.*"

Jesse looked away. There was no reason to hurt this woman further.

"Find a judge who'll promise no one will take Bobby away from me, and I'll swear under oath Dave was with me that night. He couldn't have shot Ray." Rita wiped at her eyes with a shredded tissue. "But you get that promise first or I won't say a thing."

She looked as though she was losing control again, and Jesse found himself both admiring and pitying the sheer force of will keeping the tears beading in Rita's eyes from slipping down her cheeks. "We'll be going now," she said, her voice firm.

She turned Bobby's chair so it faced the door. "You know where I am if you want anything else," Rita told Jesse, and was gone.

"*Somebody* killed Ray," he muttered.

There was silence at the table until Crow broke the quiet with a brusque, "Let it go, Jess. Turn loose and let it pass."

Jesse had believed hearing what truth Rita knew would make things simpler, but he was as confused as ever. "Maybe I will, Crow. If I can." He stood up. "I got to get back to town. You want to go?"

Margaret stood up with Jesse. "Why don't you stay for dinner, Crow?"

"I'd be pleased to eat with y'all again, Maggie." The retired deputy looked at Jesse. " 'Less there's something you wanted me to do in town?"

Jesse shook his head. "Not a thing, Crow," he told the old man, and turned to go. Margaret came to the car with him. "Is Rita leaving town right away?"

Margaret shrugged her shoulders. "Who knows? I'm still going to try and talk her out of it, but she seems determined to go."

"I've got a couple of people to see this afternoon," he told his wife. "I'll be home early as I can."

Margaret nodded and kissed his cheek. "I'm going to talk to Crow about your idea of setting something up for kids," she told him. "That's a smart old man. It'll be interesting to see what he says about it."

When Jesse was behind the wheel Margaret tapped on the glass. "I was proud of you in there," she said when he rolled the window down.

Jesse nodded and started the car. He thought he was going directly to town until he was on the highway. Then he steered toward the narrow road leading to Patsy Brent's house.

Elmer Brent grew an enormous garden behind the small frame dwelling, and Jesse found the old man at the edge of his field, leaning on an aluminum walker. Marnie Brent was astride a Ford tractor, mowing weeds and high grass that had taken the plot since Elmer harvested his vegetables. She had to stretch to reach the pedals, but the girl handled the machine confidently.

Jesse allowed the tractor to reach the other end of the field before he spoke. "Looks like you taught her pretty good."

Elmer nodded. "Marnie's been riding that thing since she was old enough to set up straight in my lap. This is only the third time she's drove it all by herself."

Jesse lit a cigarette and sighed smoke into the air. "I got some news." He told Elmer only the basics and left Rita Bailey's name out of his accounting. As he finished, Jesse assured Elmer he'd meet Tom Carruthers later in the day to see about officially establishing that David Brent hadn't been a killer.

"I knowed you'd figure out a way to prove it," Elmer said. "Patsy and Paul, they been telling me to let it go, that it was enough everybody in the family knew Davey wasn't no killer. But it wasn't enough for me. Nor you either, I reckon."

"I reckon not," Jesse agreed, and turned to go.

Elmer reached out to touch his shoulder. "Do me one more favor, Jesse?"

"What's that?"

"I don't guess I need to know exactly who that woman was. Nor Patsy neither."

Jesse shook his head. "I don't think so, Elmer."

"You know who she is though," the old farmer continued. "Tell her something for me." Elmer lowered his voice, though there was no way Marnie, atop a laboring tractor, could have overheard. "Davey done his share of tom catting. But he'd of never left his family for any of the women he took to motels. You tell her I said so."

Jesse left Elmer beside his field, admiring his granddaughter's skill with the tractor. The old man would not need to know Rita Bailey's name. And he didn't have to know Jesse Surratt would never deliver that message.

Driving back to town Jesse reminded himself to mention Dave Brent's children to Margaret. Most of the young men who drew the attention of his deputies had grown up without fathers. In a few years Dave's kids would be at that age where it was easy to slide into trouble. He picked up the radio and told Martha he needed to speak to the county attorney.

Tom Carruthers was waiting when Jesse reached his office. He listened to what Jesse said about Rita Bailey's providing the alibi that would exonerate Dave Brent, but when all the facts had been spoken, the lawyer was curiously quiet.

"You know what?" he said after a time. "I don't have the faintest idea how to fix this. I suppose there'll be a hearing. We'll need a judge who'll cooperate, keep this quiet if Rita Bailey doesn't want to become a celebrity again."

"Ron Davidson is who I'd talk to," Jesse offered.

"That's what I was thinking." Nodding to himself, the young attorney took one of his nasty cigars from a jacket pocket. He noticed Jesse's glare and instead of lighting it stood up to leave. "I'll let you know how we'll do it."

"Thanks Tom. I owe you one."

When the county attorney was gone Jesse called Martha Compton into the office. "Would you call Ed Tomalin for me? See if he can still fit me in for that campaign photograph for the paper?"

"Already done it," Martha said. "He wants you there soon as you can make it."

"I'm on my way then." Jesse stood up and walked around his desk.

CHAPTER THIRTY-FOUR

Rita didn't bother picking up the flower arrangement Jesse Surratt had taken from her van and then abandoned on the porch swing. In the few minutes she'd been in his house, cold had begun to destroy the fragile blossoms. But neither was she going to stop remembering David in the way that made her feel closest to him.

Her house was only fifteen minutes away, and it wouldn't take long to cut fresh ones.

Wheeling Bobby up the ramp to her back door Rita was seized by a pang of regret. This had been her first real home, and for a time Rita had believed she'd live in it until she died. Before buying the place and making a friend in Margaret Surratt, she always lived with other people. After Ezra Stillwell, the places she stayed were safe enough, but none ever felt like a real home.

Bobby was sleepy, and she tucked him into bed. Then she went to her kitchen, sat at the table to drink a cup of strong tea. She wondered if she'd ever find another place that was just *hers*.

She'd lived with Ezra in his house until he . . . Until he died, and for a few days she and Bobby stayed with Sheriff Abner Riley and his wife. The middle aged couple did everything they could to make Rita and Bobby comfortable. They even took her baby to his first doctor, who explained the permanence of his problems.

It was Victoria Riley who found St. Catherine's Home near Cincinnati and explained to Rita the kind of care Bobby could get there. The Rileys only briefly resisted when Rita demanded to go wherever Bobby went. They were the first people to realize Rita was never going to give up her baby, no matter who wanted her to.

After a few attempts at separating them, the German nuns who ran St. Catherine's allowed Rita to be a mother of sorts. The boy wouldn't eat unless Rita fed him, wouldn't cooperate with rehabilitative exercises unless Rita stood near the physical therapist. When he began to talk only Rita understood Bobby's garbled sounds. St. Catherine's had its own school on the grounds of the home, and Rita was the first and last student to attend classes while balancing a baby on her hip.

By the time she was nineteen Rita had a high school diploma. The nuns sent her on to a two-year vocational school, where she learned secretarial and basic accounting skills. Afterward she found a job in an attorney's office, in Lexington. That was where she met Ray Bailey.

She married Ray because he wanted her, because he seemed to take charge of things. And after learning about Bobby, Ray promised if she lived with him in Hawkes County Rita wouldn't have to work, could spend every day taking care of her son.

So one more time, she and Bobby moved into someone else's place, the house Ray Bailey owned. Life with a hard, taciturn man who bootlegged alcohol in dry Hawkes County wasn't always easy, but Ray's house was a far gentler place than the shack she'd shared with Ezra Stillwell.

Ray didn't start drinking heavily until she'd been with him four or five years, and even then he mostly ignored her. He did hit her a couple of times, but never raised an angry hand to Bobby.

It seemed enough until one weekend Ray was in Cincinnati. He spent two or three days a month there, doing things somehow related to his business. Rita didn't care enough to ask why or what. But one evening she thought she heard a prowler outside the house, and soon after she called the sheriff's office David Brent showed up at her door.

Within two weeks they were lovers, and after that nothing but having David seemed enough. The only pieces of her life that mattered were minutes spent touching him, talking to him, having him and being his. When that part of her life ended like a sad song, everything was gone with no way to bring any of it back.

Ray was dead.

David was in prison.

Bobby deteriorated.

Rita waited.

While she waited she bought her own house, had it renovated to fit Bobby's disabilities and her love of soil and flowers. She and Bobby made a real home for themselves, made the world beyond their front door a distant place visited on their own terms.

And she was going to leave it all.

The phone rang before she could start crying. "Maggie had to run to the grocery store. And before she gets back here I want to tell you something." Crow Markwell's voice was a mere whisper. "I gave Jesse Surratt everything I knew except what Albert Riley told me. About who was holding the shotgun when Ezra died."

Rita closed her eyes and wished when she opened them the phone would still be ringing, and she could let it ring, wouldn't hear this voice. "Why didn't you tell him the rest then?"

"Because if he knew the rest, Jesse Surratt might decide the same person who shot Ezra Stillwell killed Ray Bailey." For a moment there was only an old man's breathing at the other end of the connection. "I've known some men in my life who needed killing," Crow said at last. "Maybe Ray was one of them."

"I didn't kill Ray," Rita said. "That's the truth."

"I don't care if you did or didn't." Crow's voice wasn't a whisper any more. He spoke quickly, as though he needed to say the words without thinking. "I always felt like I could have helped. I arrested Ezra more than once in those days. But I never asked the right questions, never looked close enough to help *you*."

Rita didn't have any words that seemed to fit. A lot of people could have helped, and didn't. "It was a long time ago," she said at last.

"Yes it was," Crow agreed. "But I was always sorry I didn't do more. I'm still sorry."

"I don't care what Jesse Surratt knows," Rita lied. Then she told the truth again. "I didn't kill Ray."

"I reckon that would matter to Jesse," the old man said. "But not to me."

The connection was broken, and Rita could put the telephone down.

It was nearly time to wake Bobby from his nap, and she needed to make another flower arrangement for David. Peeking into Bobby's room to satisfy herself he was still asleep, Rita went on to the greenhouse.

Selecting and picking a second batch of flowers she vaguely recalled a face like Crow Markwell's among those who came to stare, in the days Albert Riley was still trying to figure out who she was. She hoped the deputy had been one who looked at her with something more than naked curiosity glittering in his eyes.

In her last days of answering to the name Lorena, Rita had feared three things.

She was afraid someone might take Bobby away from her. Something was obviously wrong with the baby. His eyes didn't quite focus, and his cooing laugh carried an odd, lost note. The last time Ezra came to her, drunk, he'd mumbled something about "getting rid of that little idiot."

Secondly, she was afraid of being sent back to Ezra. When she dropped the shotgun and ran from her uncle's house, before the door slammed shut behind her she heard ragged, choking breath wheezing from his lungs. Ezra Stillwell alive might be able to claim her.

Some of the curious men who drifted through Abner Riley's office had eyes like Ezra's. Rita's third fear was being sent to live with one of them.

Albert Riley took care of all her fear one evening when he took her into his office, closed the door and settled into the big chair behind his desk. Abner was good about keeping space and furniture between them. That first night they brought her to him, Rita flinched at Abner's purely chaste caress of her head, meant to be comforting. After that he maintained a distance.

"You can sit down," the sheriff told her.

Lorena did so, cradling Bobby in her arms. Abner was good about Bobby too, only taking him away when doctors wanted to examine him.

"Are you Ezra Stillwell's niece?" Abner asked.

Rita said nothing.

"If you are, I need to tell you he's dead." Abner Riley looked straight into Lorena's eyes. "He shot himself, with a shotgun."

And so Abner defused Lorena's second fear. Then he took care of the third by keeping her with himself and Victoria Riley until she could be placed as a permanent resident at St. Catherine's Home.

St. Catherine's was part school and part jail, part orphanage and part asylum. But it was safe; the nuns found a pediatrician for Bobby, and they found Dr. Lois T. Hannan for Lorena.

When the new arrangement of fresh flowers was done she woke Bobby, fed him his favorite lunch of peanut butter on toast, and it was time to leave for the cemetery. When she'd strapped Bobby into the back seat Rita straightened and glanced regretfully back at her house, across the roof of her vehicle.

And vowed to move them away from Midland soon, no matter how painful an uprooting it might prove to be. Anything would be preferable to Jesse Surratt's learning the rest of what she knew.

Anything.

CHAPTER THIRTY-FIVE

Ed Tomalin's studio was a single room above the Ben Franklin Store, Midland's last "five and dime." Jesse arrived as Carly Wilson's newborn son was falling asleep under the photographer's warm lights. Carly wanted pictures that would show the boy's green eyes. "Can you come back in about thirty minutes?" Ed pleaded.

"Take all the time you need to get it right," Jesse told him, and walked back down the creaky wooden stairs outside the studio.

As a kid, Jesse had loved a solitary rummage through the Ben Franklin. Passing between the old building's double doors he inhaled the familiar old mix of odors—dust and new fabric, perfume for elderly ladies, pipe tobacco from near the front—and decided to start coming in more often.

He strolled the aisles slowly. He felt as though he ought to buy something, show belated support for a small town merchant, and was standing in the toiletries section when he met Phil Evans turning the corner of the aisle.

Phil was a doctor at the hospital and a member of the county council as well. He and Jesse had campaigned together as part of a reform slate. Others who'd run with them stopped being reformers and turned into politicians, but Jesse had never sensed any such change in Phil Evans.

"Ever use one of these, Doc?" Jesse held up a shaving mug and brush. He remembered his father making his own lather every morning, and was surprised the requisite utensils were still sold.

"Can't say I have, Jess," Phil admitted.

The soap that came with the mug smelled nicer than the aerosol stuff, and Jesse decided to try it. "Looking for something in particular, Phil? I've been walking every aisle in the place, waiting to get my picture taken upstairs. I bet I can tell you where to find half the store's inventory."

Evans shook his head. "The wife's across the street, getting her hair worked on. I mostly came in here to wait for her. Buy you a cup of coffee?"

Jesse looked at his watch. He had ten more minutes to kill. "Sure."

They still served lunch at the Ben Franklin, but when they settled in one of the booths, an elderly woman behind the counter told them she only had deserts and coffee after two o'clock. Jesse let her talk him into a piece of coconut pie.

"I heard you've decided to run again," Phil said as the waitress went to fetch their order.

Jesse nodded. "Finally made up my mind." He lit a cigarette.

Evans scowled. "One of these days you need to quit those things."

"I suppose. But the only thing I hate worse than smoking is *not* smoking." Jesse grinned as the waitress slid a slab of pie in front of him. "Besides, the best way to make your food show up is to light up." He stubbed the smoke out in a glass ashtray.

"You talk to Steve Logan lately?" Phil asked. Logan was another reform candidate who'd won election to the county council when Jesse ran for sheriff.

"He's going to run again, isn't he?" Logan was a valuable presence on the council. Like the doctor, he tended to vote his conscience.

Evans nodded. "He's gonna run. But he's got a weird idea all of us should run as independents,"

"I thought we wanted to win this election." Since the Civil War anyone serious about politics in Hawkes County ran as a Democrat.

"Steve thinks it'd be better if people didn't connect us with what he calls 'real politicians.'"

Jesse frowned. "I'll talk to Steve. Our margin last time was people who vote Democratic the way I smoke." He lit another cigarette and carefully exhaled away from Phil Evans. "They don't think about it, they just do it."

"I heard you're going to start something for kids too. And wonder of wonders, you're not going to spend government money doing it."

"Word's out on that already?" News traveled fast in Hawkes County, but it seemed a record of sorts, if the county council knew about an idle conversation between Jesse and Margaret Surratt that was only a few hours old.

Phil Evans laughed. "Martha told me about it. She wanted me to approve clearing one of the offices they use for storage now."

"You think it's a good idea then?"

"Sure I do." The doctor lifted his hand in a signal to the waitress. "Right now we send kids to preachers or state detention facilities. There ought to be something in between." When the older woman brought the coffee pot, Phil shoved his cup out for a refill. "How're you coming with that Dave Brent thing?"

"I gave up on it." Jesse looked away from Phil. "Too much time gone by, too many people moved on. The only witnesses were those college kids. God knows where they are by now."

"I saw you earlier, talking to Rita Bailey, outside the dry cleaner's. She won't mind if you drop it?"

Jesse shrugged. He didn't like telling lies, no matter how necessary. "Rita wasn't too crazy about my looking into it again in the first place."

Phil Evans lowered his voice. "I'll tell you a secret, Jess. One of the first kids Margaret could help might be Rita's brother."

"Bobby? What could Margaret do for *him*?"

"This is the sort of confidential thing a doctor's not supposed to talk about." Evans put his elbows on the table and leaned closer. "But for the past few years Rita's had some quack over-medicating her brother."

"Really?"

Phil Evans' face knitted into a frown. "It's a crying shame too. She takes him to Lexington, I guess. No doctor in Midland has seen Bobby for years."

A vague awareness, a piece of knowledge he couldn't quite bring into focus buzzed at the edge of Jesse's mind, like an annoying summer insect. "It's bad enough you think Margaret ought to say something?"

"Bad enough somebody ought to *do* something." Evans emptied his cup for the second time, shook his head when the waitress approached them again. "Bobby doesn't even need that wheelchair. He's just drugged to the point he can't walk."

"You're sure about that? Rita thinks the sun rises and the moon sets on that boy."

"Maybe so, but she's turning him into a vegetable. You notice she doesn't go anywhere without him? Three, four years ago she had him enrolled in a rehab thing at social services. She took him out of that right after Ray was killed."

Jesse glanced at his watch. He was two minutes away from Ed Tomalin taking his picture, but leaving what Phil was telling him might divert that bug of a burgeoning idea to a place where he'd be months finding it again. "You said right after Ray was killed?"

Phil nodded. "She had an appointment with Qualkenbush, the neurologist at the hospital the same week. She canceled, and that was reasonable, I guess. I mean, it was a rough time for her and all that. But she never rescheduled."

Raising his eyes, Jesse saw Carly Wilson outside the big front windows of the Ben Franklin store. Ed must have managed to make her baby smile. Carly looked proud and pleased.

"Rudy Qualkenbush doesn't have to chase patients," Evans continued. "Too good at what he does for that. But he tried for a year to get Bobby back to his office, especially when he noticed the wheelchair."

After another reminder about the promise to talk some sense into Steve Logan, Phil Evans went to collect his wife. Jesse sat in the booth, staring at his empty cup another five minutes. What he almost knew was coming clearer.

When he saw it, the knowledge burst full blown into his consciousness. Feeling foolish for not catching it earlier, Jesse left the Ben Franklin and walked quickly to his squad car at the courthouse. As he pulled into traffic, he got Martha Compton on the radio, asked her to call Ed Tomalin and reschedule the photograph.

"How many times are you going to have me make this appointment and then not keep it?" Martha complained.

"This is the last time, I promise." The hell with it, Jesse thought, reaching for the dashboard switch that made blue lights on top of the car whirl and strobe. "Tell Ed if he can see me tomorrow sometime I'll be there."

Traffic moved off the road in response to flashers on the sheriff's vehicle, and Jesse kept the lights on after entering Hill View Estates, the upscale housing development where Rita Bailey lived. Hill View was mostly a community of college professors and doctors, nearly all of them from out of state. Locals called it "Snob Knob."

Jesse cruised the quiet streets until he spotted a house he knew had to be Rita's, though he'd never been there before. A long ramp led to the front door, and to the rear an enormous greenhouse filled most of the back yard. Jesse parked in the driveway, and when he got out he recognized Wilma Frasier, peering at him from the house next door.

He'd left the emergency flashers on. Reaching back inside the car to tap the switch that shut them off, he waved casually to Rita's neighbor. Tempted to hurry, he held himself to a relaxed amble. If Wilma thought something funny was going on next door she'd be on the telephone to half the county before the sheriff left.

Jesse rang the bell twice, and hadn't had time to drop his hand when the wide oak door swung ajar. Rita stared from the other side of a storm door.

"I came to hear the rest of it." Jesse kept his voice low.

Rita shook her head. "There is no rest of it."

Half turning, Jesse nodded toward Wilma Frasier's frank curiosity. "We're going to talk," he said. "Inside your house, or out here where that old lady might hear every word."

Rita took a deep breath, then stepped onto the porch. "Come on then."

Jesse stepped aside and followed her to the greenhouse. Rita opened a glass door for him, stood aside as he entered a dank humidity that had him stripping off his jacket before he sat down on a worn sofa. "Where's Bobby?"

Rita nodded in the direction of the house. "Sleeping. I was about to wake him."

Jesse settled deeper into the well-used furniture and wondered where to start. "I figured out some more of what happened, the night Ray got killed."

Perched on the edge of an old rocking chair, Rita dug her fingernails into the wooden arm rest. Jesse thought of a deer, surprised in someone's field, ready to bolt at any second.

"What do you think you know, Jesse?" She caught him looking at her fingers, and pressed them between her knees.

Jesse Surratt said out loud for the first time what he'd known since Phil Evans left him at the Ben Franklin. "Bobby killed Ray, didn't he?."

Fingers extended like talons, lips curled as though she might bite, Rita launched herself out of the rocking chair in a blind attack. Jesse caught her wrists and held on tightly, narrowly avoided being raked by neatly manicured nails. Rita shrieked a stream of threats as Jesse shifted his weight and rolled on top of her.

She didn't stop struggling until Jesse began chanting assurances no one would take Bobby away, repeating them over and over like a mantra. As she began to relax Jesse eased his grip on her wrists, and warily stood away from the sofa, not sure if his next move would be to defend himself or stop Rita Bailey from running away.

Hitching childlike sobs racked the woman's body, and when they receded Rita didn't speak. Jesse moved to the rocking chair and sat down, exhausted. "I know you're over-medicating Bobby. Is that true?"

Rita's voice was a soft monotone. "Thorazine."

She stood up and walked to a shelf of plants, stroking the long leaves of something Jesse couldn't name. When she looked in his direction, the sheriff wasn't sure Rita really saw him. "Bobby used to talk. You didn't know him then, but once upon a time he loved to talk."

She dropped her hands to her side, shaking her head slowly from side to side as if denying the reality of what Jesse had figured out. "He couldn't keep a secret, you know. And never lied, if anyone asked questions."

Jesse's arms ached from restraining Rita, and he wondered if her body hurt where he'd held her. "Did Dave know what Bobby did?"

Rita nodded. "We left Bobby at the movies. I didn't imagine he'd follow us." A glow of maternal pride passed briefly across her wan face. "Bobby's smarter than I thought. He figured out where David and I were going."

When she didn't speak Jesse lit a cigarette and held it out until she moved three steps closer to accept it. "So why did he shoot Ray?"

Rita took a long drag from the cigarette. "Bobby was walking down the street. That was another thing he liked to do before, take

206

long walks, by himself sometimes. Ray saw him and asked Bobby where I was. Bobby told him I was at the Trailview Motel with David."

"I see what you mean about not keeping secrets." Jesse lit a cigarette and relaxed a bit, fairly certain Rita wasn't going to run. "What happened next?"

"I guess Ray said something about what he was going to do to me when I came home." Rita shrugged. "Bobby went where we'd parked our cars and got Dave's gun. Then he went to that filling station where Ray sold liquor. I think what happened was Bobby had the gun and meant to scare Ray with it. And Ray tried to take the gun away."

Jesse tried to picture helpless Bobby Stillwell wrestling with anyone over anything, and couldn't. Phil Evans was right. Margaret *would* need to talk to Rita about her son.

Rita lifted one hand to wipe at the tears beading on her cheek. "When it was over, whatever happened, Bobby ran to me. To David. Bobby *loved* David."

"And then what did you do?"

Rita swiped at her eyes with one hand. "David told me when he went to work the next day, if anyone connected Bobby with what happened he'd call. We never thought anyone would decide David killed Ray. We forgot Bobby was wearing his sweatshirt." Rita shook her head and sighed. "And until the next morning we didn't know Bobby had taken the gun out of David's car."

When Jesse stood up the scent of freesias washed over him, lovely and delicate. There was a bouquet of cut flowers on one of Rita's shelves. He understood what Dave Brent had done, if he thought about it. Given the man's track record, in another six or seven months the affair with Rita would have burnt itself out.

But what was it Patsy Brent said the day of the funeral? "Dave can't stand to see a child hurt. Any child." That included nineteen year old Bobby Stillwell. If anyone knew who held the pistol that killed Ray Bailey, the best Bobby Stillwell could hope for would be a long-term stay in a state institution. He'd lose his mother.

Jesse decided that soon he'd go up in the woods again, alone. He'd spend some time thinking about everything he'd learned since the last time he'd carried his pistol into the forest for target practice. Maybe it would begin to make sense.

Maybe it would, but he didn't think so.

"What are you going to do, Jesse?" Rita had stood up with him, and was watching his eyes.

He shook his head. "Me? I'm gonna run for re-election."

"What about Bobby?"

"Talk to Margaret," Jesse urged. "She'll help."

He left Rita in the greenhouse.

If he hurried, maybe he could still get that damn campaign photo taken.

Printed in the United States
52622LVS00008B/64-99